Right: Reynaldo Hahn,
Hamburg, c. 1898

(Family photograph)

Above: Marie with her bicycle:
'The only thing I had in
common with Albertine was
that I rode a bicycle!'

Right: Illustration for *Les
Plaisirs et les jours*; short story
'Le Diner en ville'. Madeleine
Lemaire draws portraits of
Proust and her daughter

Left: Title page for Proust's
Les Plaisirs et les jours by
Madeleine Lemaire

L
ES PLAISIRS
ET
LES JOURS

Marcel Proust, 1896

Left: Marie Nordlinger;
portrait in oils done by a
fellow student, signed Nils.
Shown at the Paris Salon of
1898

The Translation of Memories

P. F. Prestwich

The Translation of Memories

Recollections of the Young Proust

PETER OWEN
London and Chester Springs

PETER OWEN PUBLISHERS
73 Kenway Road, London SW5 0RE
Peter Owen books are distributed in the USA by
Dufour Editions Inc., Chester Springs, PA 19425-0007

First published in Great Britain 1999
©1999 P.F. Prestwich

A catalogue record for this book is available from the British Library

ISBN 0 7206 1056 7

Printed and bound in Great Britain by Hillman Printers (Frome) Ltd

Contents

Illustrations

Unless otherwise indicated next to illustration, all photographs are from P.F. Prestwich Collection

Introduction

This is the story of the friendship between three remarkable young people, an English girl who left Manchester
College of Art in 1896 to continue her studies in Paris
and two Frenchmen, her mother's cousin, Reynaldo
Hahn, and his friend, Marcel Proust. Marie Nordlinger
was twenty when she joined the life class at the Courtois
studio in Neuilly; Hahn was twenty-two; he had left the
Conservatoire de Musique and was already making his
name as a composer and performer. His first opera was
awaiting production. Proust, three years older, with
degrees in law and philosophy, had just published his
first book, a collection of short stories, poems and occasional pieces.

Marie was one of the first of Proust's circle of close
friends to publish some of the letters he sent her; forty-
one of them were included in *Lettres à une amie*
(Editions du Calame, Manchester, 1942), with an introduction in French by Marie giving a brief account of her
collaboration with Marcel on the translation of two
books by Ruskin, *The Bible of Amiens* and *Sesame and
Lilies*. Of the letters which she kept and published, over
half date from 1904, the year when they were correcting
the proofs of *La Bible d'Amiens* and translating the lecture on reading from *Sesame and Lilies*. She was the only
woman, apart from his mother, to be actively concerned
with his work, and she published his letters in the hope
that they would bring more English readers to his novel
and also to show how the discipline and dedication at
this stage of his career was carried over to the writing of

A la recherche du temps perdu. There are only a few casual references to Ruskin in the novel, but his influence on Proust's development as an artist was profound.

Their shared enthusiasm for the fine arts, cathedrals, the countryside and Ruskin drew Marie and Marcel together, but the mainspring of their friendship was their tacit devotion to Reynaldo Hahn – they were both in love with him. His good looks, elegant manners, his charisma as performer and speaker exerted a strong attraction over both women and men. Although he had been born in Caracas, and is still often referred to as 'Venezuelan', he was a Parisian through and through – the family made Paris their home when he was three. He had a French verve and wit combined with Spanish pride and melancholy. He soon came to appreciate his Manchester cousin's character and capabilities, treating her as a younger sister to be encouraged, teased, educated and advised. With Marcel he shared a passion for reading, an eager curiosity and a love of music (in Reynaldo's case particularly a love of singing); he was as talented a writer as he was a composer. He learnt as much about literature from Marcel as Marcel learnt from him about music, which plays an important role in *A la recherche du temps perdu*. The letters he received from Marcel are quite different from those to any of Proust's other correspondents and show how close their relationship was for nearly thirty years, ending only with Marcel's death. So, too, the friendship between Reynaldo and Marie, though interrupted by two world wars, lasted until Reynaldo died in 1947.

During the exhibition of Proust manuscripts and memorabilia held at the Wildenstein Gallery in Bond Street in the autumn of 1955, there was an essay by Marie on 'Proust and Ruskin' in the catalogue. The following year, when she was eighty, she organized an exhibition of her own at the Whitworth Art Gallery, Manchester, with the support of Professor Eugène Vinaver, then head of the French Department at the university and French cultural delegate in the north of England. He asked me to help her with the catalogue and we became friends in spite of the difference in age. To please her daughter and other friends she began, reluctantly, to draft her memoirs, but it was apparent that she felt she had said all she had to say about Marcel and it was now Reynaldo she wished to commemorate. When she died in 1961, the memoirs ended in 1905 after her first visit to America.

During the years we worked together transcribing her letters from Reynaldo and those he wrote to his sister, Maria de Madrazo, she often told me about her family; her conversation was not all reminiscence, fascinating as her memories were. Certainly she was a woman of her era, an Edwardian; her views were well in advance of many of her contemporaries, but by upbringing and temperament she did not care to talk about herself. Not one of us among the family and close friends had the least suspicion about the depth of her feelings for Reynaldo. There were questions I did not think to ask, or did not care to press. And she never gave me a satisfactory answer to one question I asked more than once: 'What made Marcel so enthusiastic about Ruskin?'

She had always hoped to publish an English edition of her letters from Proust, but never did so. Both she and Reynaldo planned to make a selection of the letters Marcel wrote to him, which Reynaldo described as 'high-spirited nonsense, full of jokes which amused us but were incomprehensible to anyone else'. They are quite different to the letters he wrote to his numerous correspondents, they sparkle with humour (sometimes malicious), affection, gossip and inventive play with words. Reynaldo hoped that a selection might show Proust's admirers something of his true nature. All Proust's available letters have now been published in French.[1] With this shorter memoir, *The Translation of Memories*, we hope to add a new dimension to the friendship between these three young people in the early years of the twentieth century and especially Proust's debt to Ruskin and the part played by Reynaldo in the development of *A la recherche du temps perdu*.

Many potential readers of Proust's novel are deterred by its length. The three volumes of the revised translation by Terence Kilmartin and D.J. Enright contain over 3,000 pages (there is a more convenient paperback version in six volumes). Some readers never get further than *Swann's Way*, the first of its seven sections, discouraged by the absence of paragraphs and the long, involved sentences. Marie always maintained that no one should try to read all the volumes straight through but should dip into them and return to them at leisure.

A few days before the publication of *Swann's Way* in 1913, an interview with the author appeared in *Le Temps*. Proust described his work as a multi-volume novel in which he tried to isolate what he called 'the invisible substance of time', something which could only be done at length because he wanted to show each character from different angles at different periods and as they appeared to different observers. He made a distinction between voluntary memory, which is a matter for the intellect, and involuntary memory, which belongs to the senses – a smell, a taste or sound can unexpectedly bring back the forgotten past. Such memories, according to Proust, fill the gap between the present and eternity; as they are outside time, only they are authentic and universal in their essence.

The character who recounts the story, as Proust explained to his interviewer, the 'I who is not I', is a child at the beginning of *Swann's Way* and grows up during the course of the novel. He is a shadowy figure, articulate, over-sensitive and intelligent. The reader never learns his name, though twice, perhaps by an oversight, he is called 'Marcel'. For this reason, to avoid confusion, we will refer to him as 'M'. 'M' seems to exist on at least three different levels: he is the child who loves reading and hopes to become a writer; he is a man recounting the history of his search for identity as an artist; and he is the author himself who observes, comments and philosophizes.

Roughly a third of the novel is concerned with love – M's for his mother and grandmother, his infatuation with Gilberte Swann and the Duchess of Guermantes, his tortuous affair with Albertine. In addition to these, there is Swann's passion for Odette, Robert de Saint-Loup's for the actress Rachel, the involvement of the Baron de Charlus with the young violinist Charlie Morel, the long liaison of the elderly diplomat M. de Norpois and the former beauty Mme de Villeparisis. Scenes in high society make up another third of the story – the eight or nine parties and social gatherings begin with a concert at Mme de Saint-Euverte's in *Swann's Way* and end with a musical evening at the Princesse de Guermantes' in *Time Regained*. And the last third consists of the author's reflections on sleep, dreams, time, memory, love, growing old, art, mortality – all woven into the fabric of the novel with irony, humour and detachment. For Proust, style was a matter not of technique but quality of vision, 'the revelation of the particular universe which each one of us sees and that no one else sees'. He was fond of quoting a line of Victor Hugo's: 'How little time it takes for everything to change' – people, places, fashions, ideas, beliefs and feelings; only art, perhaps, endures.

In a letter to C.K. Scott Moncrieff, written a few months before his death in 1922, Proust criticized the title in English, *Remembrance of Things Past*, which Scott Moncrieff borrowed from a sonnet by Shakespeare (No. XXX). He complained that it did not in any way reflect the ambiguity of his own title, *A la recherche du temps perdu*: 'Remembrance' implies a looking back on former joys and sorrows by a middle-aged author, while '*In Search of Lost [or Wasted] Time*' indicates a more dynamic philosophical process and has, in addition, a hint of two well-known novels by Balzac, an author greatly admired by Proust. Balzac's titles, *Illusions perdues* (*Lost Illusions*) and *La Recherche de l'absolu* (*The Search for the Absolute*), could apply just as appositely to Proust's work. For this reason we refer to the novel as *In Search of Lost Time* or *The Search*.

1
A Youthful Prodigy

In the final pages of *In Search of Lost Time*, when his narrator was just beginning to write the novel we have been reading, Proust described the construction of his work as like that of an architect building a great cathedral, or, at a different level of craftsmanship, he compared it with the specially tasty dish, spiced beef with carrots and aspic, prepared by his old cook from many carefully chosen ingredients. Of all the themes which Proust used in the orchestration of his novel, as Wagner used the various leitmotifs in his operas, one of the most obvious is music.

Proust's close friendship with a professional musician affected the way in which he wrote about and listened to music – although he always said he had no technical knowledge, he could play the piano, compose a ditty and read a score. When he met Reynaldo Hahn for the first time at the end of May 1894, Reynaldo was nineteen, still a student at the Conservatoire, hoping for a production of his first opera. They both had a great love of books, a sense of humour and a keen interest in the social scene – the Paris salons where music was taken seriously were as important to Reynaldo's career as the radio, television and recording studios are to the young artists of today.

The Hahn family background was rather different from that of Proust. Marcel's paternal grandfather was a shopkeeper in a small provincial town not far from Chartres; his father, an only son, became a highly respected doctor and diplomat, an expert on cholera, professor at the university of Paris and widely travelled.

Dr Proust married Jeanne Weil, the only daughter of a prosperous Jewish stockbroker. Both Reynaldo and Marcel were brought up as Roman Catholics though neither was a church-goer. Reuban Hahn, Reynaldo's paternal grandfather, was one of the first Jews in Hamburg to secede from the synagogue; he was the eldest of a large family, and he and his wife, Caroline Delavie from Paris, had ten children. Their eldest son, Carlos Hahn, left Germany at the age of twenty-two in 1845 to seek his fortune in Venezuela, where his business affairs prospered. In partnership with a friend, Guzman Blanco, he introduced railways, gas lighting, the telegraph and other innovations to the country, and when Señor Blanco became President of the Venezuelan Republic, Carlos Hahn was his financial adviser. Her married a beautiful and talented Spanish girl, becoming a Roman Catholic in order to do so – Elena de Echenagucia's father was Spanish, her mother partly Dutch, partly English (her maiden name was Ellis); she shared her husband's love of music, the theatre and botany. The family had a large town house and a villa in the country with a superb garden. Reynaldo, born on 9 August 1874, was the youngest of five sons and five daughters.[1]

When the government in Caracas changed, Carlos Hahn decided in 1877 to return with his family to Europe and find treatment for his failing eyesight. He had relations and well-connected friends in Paris where they found a large, hospitable home at 5, rue de Cirque near the Elysée Palace. A daughter of Guzman Blanco's was married to the son of the Duc de Morny, illegitimate half-brother of the Emperor Napoleon III; another family friend was Comtesse Mélanie de Pourtalès who had been a lady-in-waiting to the Empress Eugénie. Princess Mathilde, niece of Napoleon I, was also a family friend.

Reynaldo made his first public appearance at the piano in her drawing room when he was six, and at an even earlier age had sung popular songs to her on the beach at Trouville. He began lessons in composition with an Italian lady teacher when he was eight.

Carlos Hahn was a keen theatre- and concert-goer and had many friends among artists and actors. Federico de Madrazo, known as Coco, was Reynaldo's close friend from childhood; he was the son of the painter Raimondo de Madrazo, and nephew of the Director of the Prado. When Carlos Hahn went to the theatre he had a habit of reserving two stalls, for himself and his hat and coat, because he disliked queuing at the cloakroom. One evening he decided to take his small son with him, and this became a regular practice. A chance meeting with the actor Coquelin *aîné* led to an introduction to Massenet and a place for Reynaldo at the Conservatoire to study piano and harmony. He began there in 1885, knowing nothing, as he said, but eager to learn, and was horrified to discover that he was expected to practise the piano for three or four hours a day. An avid reader, he made these hours bearable by propping his book, a novel by Dumas *père* or Jules Verne, on the music stand while he rehearsed his scales. His favourite author, Alphonse Daudet, was kept for later reading on the hearth rug. He played the piano well, but he enjoyed composition even more. When he joined Massenet's composition class he found an inspiring teacher. Massenet, a man of great energy and charm, was the most popular professor on the staff. In his journal, and later when he became a music critic, Reynaldo often referred to Massenet's excellent teaching, his original ideas for the production of opera, his lectures on eighteenth-century composers; he became 'le Maître', adviser and friend, who did everything he could to promote his favourite pupil. A photograph of Massenet dated 1890 is inscribed, 'To my dear pupil, Reynaldo Hahn, in whom I believe'.

Reynaldo loved to write small-scale vocal works, *mélodies*,[2] a genre he thought little appreciated in France, unlike Germany where, as he told his sister Maria, '*Das Lied* sends the public into raptures.' He was fifteen when his first two songs were published by Heugel. 'Rêverie' was a setting of a poem by Victor Hugo, and the ever-popular 'Si mes vers avaient des ailes', also by Hugo, was dedicated to Maria – both songs were written the previous year, before his fourteenth birthday. He was soon in demand to play and sing his compositions, at first for family and friends in Paris and Hamburg, then in wider social circles in the drawing-rooms of London, Rome and Venice.

In the middle years of the nineteenth century the Opéra and the Opéra-Comique were dominated by Rossini, Meyerbeer and Halévy, while Offenbach ruled the boulevards. The only way for an ambitious young composer to earn a living was to write for the theatre. The teaching at the Conservatoire reflected this tendency in its emphasis on orchestration and dramatic cantatas. It was Edouard Risler, Reynaldo's best friend in the piano class, who was indirectly responsible for starting him on a theatrical career. At Risler's home, where he was a frequent visitor, he met a cousin of Alphonse Daudet, an artist, Louis Montégut, who recommended him to the novelist and playwright as a rising young composer. Reynaldo was thrilled to meet his favourite author, and they took to each other at once. He was asked to write two short pieces for Daudet's new play, *L'Obstacle*, which was performed at the Gymnase Theatre in December 1890.

The sixteen-year-old composer attended rehearsals with the author and soon became a friend of the family in the rue de Bellechasse, playing the piano to Daudet who was ill and often in great pain. On Thursday evenings it was open house – not a salon, Reynaldo explained to Maria, but a meeting place for everyone who was interested in politics and the arts. Here he met many well-known writers – Emile Zola and his wife ('an excellent woman, but frightening'); Edmond de Goncourt, who did not care for music and usually left the room when the piano was opened; Jules Lemaître; and especially Stéphane Mallarmé, the leading Symbolist poet.

Maria, his only unmarried sister, nearly ten years older than Reynaldo, was his favourite correspondent. The many letters she kept are fluent and lively, showing an acute eye and ear for the social scene and a keen interest in everything to do with music and the theatre. From his father he inherited a love of theatre in all its forms, opera, drama, ballet, music hall, café concert, musical comedy or circus. During the summer of 1891 Maria Hahn spent some weeks in London with their cousin, Carl Meyer and his wife Adèle, to learn English and enjoy what Reynaldo called 'the ardent pleasures of the city of fogs!' On his annual visits to London, Reynaldo usually stayed with the Meyers at 35, Hill Street, Mayfair, or at their country home at Balcombe in Sussex, and they were frequent visitors to Dieppe and Paris. Like his uncle, Carlos Hahn, Carl Meyer was a dedicated theatre-goer. It was probably through the Meyers that Reynaldo became friendly with such patrons of the arts as Lady de Grey and Lady Sassoon.[3]

In the examination for harmony at the Conservatoire at the end of June, Reynaldo came top out of twenty-eight in the class – greatly to his own surprise and even more that of his father. Massenet advised him to go and see his own publisher, Hartmann, for a subject to work on during the summer vacation; it was to be a three-act opera, with a libretto taken from a novel, *Le Mariage de Loti*, 'a Polynesian idyll, quite modern and charming', Reynaldo explained to his sister. The novel was written by a naval officer, Julien Viaud, who took from this early work his pseudonym, Pierre Loti. His books with their exotic settings were much in vogue at the time and Delibes had already based his opera *Lakmé* on themes from Loti.

In a letter to his sister (written in English) from Hamburg at the end of October, Reynaldo listed the operas he had heard at the Stadttheater. *Lohengrin* had just been revived in Paris and was badly received. 'As soon as I arrive to Paris, I will go to hear it. *Tannhäuser* is *kolossal*, as they say here . . . as for *Meistersinger*, it is beautiful from beginning to end and always interesting.' But he had reservations about Wagner: genius he might be yet he could also be 'long-winded, boring, exaggerated and unnecessarily eccentric'. The following summer, 1892, he joined Risler in Bayreuth and heard *Die Meistersinger* again as well as *Tristan und Isolde* and *Parsifal*; these three operas, or parts of them, were always his favourites and he wrote many pages about them.

His *mélodies* were selling well; he had come to a satisfactory arrangement with the publisher Heugel: '100 francs now, and 200 francs after the sale of the first 500 for each song.' Before the advent of gramophone and radio, sales of sheet music were an important source of income for a composer – by 1914 Reynaldo's songs were sung in drawing-rooms all over Europe, boosted by his performances and popular lecture recitals. In 1891, probably at Daudet's suggestion, he set to music a poem by Verlaine, to which he gave the title 'Offrande', as the same poem had been set by Fauré and Debussy together with other lyrics by Verlaine. The title of his first collection of Verlaine poems, seven of them, was taken from another work by the poet, 'L'Art poétique': 'Rien de plus cher que la chanson grise, Où l'Indécis au Précis se joint.'[4] *Les Chansons grises* launched him on a successful career as performer and composer.

In August 1893 Reynaldo celebrated his nineteenth birthday in London with the Meyers. He sent the third act of his opera to Risler (the title had been changed from *L'Ile des rêves* to *L'Ile du rêve*): 'Massenet sets great store on my *Ile du rêve* being staged. Funnily enough, I'm not so keen as he is . . . One thing only interests and obsesses me and has all my enthusiasm, *the reconciliation of literature and music*.' By the end of the year the opera was finished, but he had to wait four years before it was produced. Writing to Coco de Madrazo shortly after its production in 1898, he remembered that when he was composing it he had been 'in a state of amorous exaltation such as I hope never to experience again. There are things in this score that I could never write again because they have a naïve tenderness, a youth, a poetry, that my spirit has lost.' The role of Mahénu, the heroine of the opera, was based on the voice and movements of Cléo de Mérode, a ballet dancer at the Opéra. They met during rehearsals for one of Massenet's operas when he was sixteen or seventeen and she two years older. He adored her grace and dark beauty and soon became a frequent visitor to the apartment where she lived with her mother; a lasting friendship grew up between them, all the more enduring for being chaste.

Both Reynaldo's parents were devoted admirers of Sarah Bernhardt and first took him to see her act when he was six or seven. He and his sister, Clarita, had been to see the great actress in one of her favourite roles, the courtesan Marguerite in *La Dame aux camélias* by Alexandre Dumas *fils*. At the end of January 1894 they went to see her again, this time in a new play by Armand Silvestre, *Isëyl*, set in India six centuries BC. She was, Reynaldo told Maria; 'astonishingly young in the first two acts, sublime in the last two . . . it is clear that she is now completely mistress of her art.' Massenet's new opera *Thaïs* was produced in March at the Opéra, and at the end of the month Reynaldo went to Spain with Carl and Adèle Meyer, where he enjoyed speaking Spanish. On 22 May he was invited to a musical evening in the garden studio of Mme Madeleine Lemaire to hear Léon Delafosse, who was a fellow-student at the Conservatoire, play his own settings of some poems by Count Robert de Montesquiou. Among the guests was the man who was to become his greatest friend.

2

Patrons and Friends

A portrait in oils of Marcel Proust, often reproduced, shows a well-groomed young man-about-town with an orchid in the lapel of his frock coat. It was painted by a family friend, Jacques-Emile Blanche, and exhibited at the Paris Salon in 1893 when Proust was twenty-one. This is Proust the socialite who, since the age of seventeen, had been a seasoned diner-out, welcomed by the mothers of his school friends at the Lycée Condorcet for his charming manners and lively conversation. There is another version of this portrait, a quick pencil sketch by the same artist done when they were both on holiday at Trouville in October 1891; in this study Proust's large, dark eyes stare through and beyond the spectator, absorbed, dispassionate – Proust the omnivorous reader, scholar, artist.[1]

He was well aware that the portrait in oils was a flattering one and made fun of it in a draft for his early novel, *Jean Santeuil*. Jean's portrait was painted by a fashionable artist, La Gandara, but the sleek young dandy it depicted would certainly not have been recognized by his classmates at the lycée who thought of him as untidy, with uncombed hair and dark circles round his eyes due to worry, insomnia and ill health.[2] In a letter to one of his friends, Marcel gave a frank description of himself: 'I must confess I don't like him much, with his perpetual over-enthusiasms, his fussy ways, his tremendous passions and his adjectives.'[3] The ill health from which he suffered began with a frightening attack of asthma at the age of nine, and also hay fever, which meant he could no longer enjoy the countryside he loved so much and caused him to miss classes at school. In spite of this he did well, especially in his last year when he came first in philosophy, thanks to a much admired teacher, M. Darlu. Besides the usual school subjects he studied Latin, Greek, German, perhaps a little English as a second language, though he never learnt to speak it. His mother, whom he adored, encouraged him to read widely. Before he left Paris to do a voluntary year's service in the army as a private at Orléans, he spent evenings in the literary salon of Mme Arman de Caillavet, an erudite and rather domineering lady with whom Anatole France, the leading novelist of the day, had a close liaison and whose writing she actively encouraged. He became friendly with her son, Gaston, and greatly admired the latter's fiancée, Jeanne Pouquet.

His greatest admiration, however, was reserved for the mother of his school friend Jacques Bizet, son of the composer of *Carmen*. After Bizet's early death his widow married a wealthy Jewish lawyer, Emile Straus. Geneviève Straus was the daughter of Fromental Halévy, professor at the Conservatoire de Musique and composer of many operas, notably one which had been a popular success in 1835, *La Juive* (*The Jewess*). Marcel adored her elegance and caustic wit and soon became a favourite visitor to her salon in the Boulevard Haussmann. He sent her extravagant bouquets of chrysanthemums, then newly fashionable, and long letters – their correspondence began when he was still at school and continued for over thirty years when they were both invalids. He sent her copies of everything he wrote and discussed his work with her.[4]

Another hostess who played an important part in

Marcel's life was Mme Madeleine Lemaire, who lived with her daughter Suzette in a small house with a large studio in the garden, 31, rue Monceau, at the top of the Boulevard Malesherbes. She had been a pupil of a painter known as 'the French Tiepolo', an Englishman called Charles Chaplin who had taken French nationality. The Salon of French Artists was an exhibition held annually in Paris similar to the Summer Exhibition at the Royal Academy in London. After her successful début at the Salon of 1866, she was soon able to sell every picture she painted, many of them flower studies and portraits. In May and June after her paintings had been sent in to the Salon, she held musical evenings every Tuesday in her studio, attracting increasing numbers of socialites and celebrities. She had a flair for discovering promising young artists, and the evening's entertainment would be given by a composer playing a new work, a foreign artist, a well-known actor or actress, or a young unknown whom she would encourage and introduce to sponsors. She insisted always on complete silence during the performance.

After leaving school and completing his year in the army, Proust took a degree in law and political science at the Sorbonne which his parents hoped would qualify him for a career in the Diplomatic Service or the Ministry of Finance. He, however, had other ideas, as he told his father anything other than literature or philosophy would be, for him, simply a waste of time (*'du temps perdu'*[5]) and the choice of a career was postponed so that he could read for a further degree in philosophy and enjoy private lessons with M. Darlu. He had already written several short stories, essays and reviews for small magazines produced by his friends at Condorcet, and at university he contributed to each of the eight numbers of *Le Banquet* (named after Plato's *Symposium*) edited by three fellow-students in 1892–3, and to the avant-garde *Revue blanche*, which succeeded *Le Banquet*. He hoped to publish a selection of these articles, with new stories and prose poems, in a book for which Mme Lemaire had promised to provide illustrations.

He was a regular visitor to Mme Lemaire's soirées. At one of them, in the spring of 1893, he was introduced to Comte Robert de Montesquiou, whose eccentric character and leading role in Paris society caused him to pursue the acquaintance eagerly. The Count was a bachelor of thirty-seven, the same generation as his friend Oscar Wilde, and like him a dandy, literary man and poet. He was related to members of the aristocracy, and was the friend and patron of contemporary artists – Verlaine, Mallarmé, Moreau, Helleu, Gallé, James McNeill Whistler. If Marcel returned Montesquiou's insults with excessive politeness it was because, as Robert de Flers remarked, Proust had decided that Montesquiou was indispensable to his researches into high society and knowing the Count's need for admiration 'flattered his mania like an alienist treating a case of delusions of grandeur!'

During the autumn Marcel met a nineteen-year-old pianist who was just beginning a career on the concert platform; he introduced Léon Delafosse to Montesquiou who became his patron and was persuaded to allow some of his verses to be set to music by his new protégé. These pieces were played by Delafosse at Mme Lemaire's soirée in May 1894, where Marcel was surprised to meet a musician who could talk about literature, someone younger than himself who was already successful in his chosen career and whose first opera was based on a novel he had read and enjoyed when he was still at Condorcet.

Madeleine Lemaire had a country house, the Château de Réveillon, in the Champagne region a hundred kilometres east of Paris. In mid-August 1894 she invited Reynaldo, Marcel and Léon Delafosse to spend a week or so there with her and her daughter Suzette, together with an elderly aunt and an old friend of hers and of the Hahn family, Mme Ernesta Stern, a novelist who wrote under the pen-name Maria Star. Mme Lemaire had already promised to illustrate Marcel's book (its provisional title was *Le Château de Réveillon*) and intended to begin work during the holiday.

'Lovely weather, interesting and artistic old house, exquisite company,' Reynaldo wrote to his sister on 20 August, 'Mme Lemaire smiling, Mlle Suzette good-natured, Ernesta pompous, Delafosse svelte, Proust ecstatic and dreamy, me brilliant, the aged aunt amiable . . . Everything is rustic and unpretentious but comfortable, the WC's mediocre, the cooking absolutely succulent, abundant and choice!' He was working a little and dreaming a lot, he told Maria. 'Dreaming is the only true pleasure in life. To combine, in gentle, cerebral musings, a profound knowledge of the human heart, a love of art and a thorough knowledge of music, this is real happiness.' These were thoughts he could share with Marcel.

An incident occurred at Réveillon which Reynaldo recounted in a posthumous tribute to Proust[6] – how, walking in the garden, Marcel became so absorbed in the contemplation of a bed of roses as to be oblivious of everything else. Reynaldo walked on and returned later, and they resumed their stroll without question or comment. On another occasion, during a walk in the park at Versailles, he remembered that Marcel, looking at some trees, a sunlit pool or a flower-bed, had 'moments of innocent joy and tenderness, like a child with its first toy'.[7] Why should Reynaldo choose to record, from nearly thirty years of memories, such early and apparently trivial ones? Probably because he felt them to be typical of Marcel's need for contemplation and solitude – he experienced the same pleasure in front of a rosebush as he did before a painting by Van Dyck or listening to a piece of music. As for 'knowledge of the human heart', in two short stories which had already been published Marcel had written about the power of the imagination, and the deadening effect of habit and laziness on once-fresh perceptions. Françoise, in 'The Melancholy Holiday of Mme de Breyves',[8] was irrationally obsessed with longing for an undistinguished young man she hardly knew – she had no control over her imagination. Violante in the story 'Violante or Worldliness', written in 1892, was also a prey to unsatisfied desire. She gave up her solitary life on her country estate for the corrupting pleasures of fashionable society, which became so much a habit that she could no longer enjoy her 'profound need to imagine, to create, to live alone with her thoughts'. She could not give herself up entirely to what she described as 'son perpetual roman intérieur' – 'the story running continually in her head'.

Proust did not yet have enough material to fill the book for which he had already written a foreword. This was dedicated to a young Englishman who had died in Paris the previous autumn. The young man's proud, melancholy elegance reminded Marcel of Van Dyck's portraits which he had seen in the Louvre, especially that of the Duke of Richmond described in his own poem on Van Dyck. He had reproductions made of this portrait and two others and gave them, in a handsome frame, to Reynaldo, with extra verses and a note inscribed on the mount. He wrote poems on three more painters, Cuyp, Paulus Potter and Watteau, and Reynaldo composed four piano pieces with the same titles to be played after recital of the poems. *Portraits de Peintres* were to form the centrepiece of the book; the four poems on musicians which follow them reflected Reynaldo's enthusiasm for Chopin, Gluck, Schumann and Mozart.

They were enthusiastic about writing a biography of Chopin together – it would be meticulously documented and reveal the musician's psychology in its smallest details. They also thought they might collaborate on an eighteenth-century opera based on a painting by Watteau, 'L'Embarquement pour Cythère' – Cythera, the island of Venus and Love, *L'Ile joyeuse*. Unfortunately, nothing came of either project. The last three lines of the extra verses on the mount of the Van Dyck portraits were:

> O bel! au bois dormant, qu'éveille Reynaldo
> Pour qu'il en soit béni, souris à l'enchanteur
> Reynaldo, cytharède, poète et chanteur.[9]

Reynaldo, cytherean, poet and singer – Marcel had really fallen in love! And Reynaldo? He was less forthcoming about his emotional life; in his journal there is a cryptic note written at the end of the year: 'The pleasure love gives is really not worth the happiness it destroys.'

During the next few months Proust wrote more pieces for his book, including a light-hearted sketch, 'The Melomania of Bouvard and Pécuchet', the two characters in Flaubert's last, unfinished novel whose conversation consisted entirely of platitudes; these light-hearted pages reveal a stylish, rather malicious humour apparent in his letters to Reynaldo. (In *Swann's Way* the conversation at the Verdurins' dinner parties was a sophisticated version of the same style.) He wrote about a family listening to a young pianist sing. Each listener was absorbed in his own thoughts: 'A thinker finds the whole of his moral life going through his mind . . . The hidden depths and riches of his memory quiver with the powerful murmur of the harmonies . . . I hear in the music the most universal beauty of life and death, of sea and sky, and in the playing of the beloved performer a particular, unique charm.' Thoughts on listening to music would be developed in several chapters of *The Search*.

Marcel was busy with a new story to be dedicated to his friend, 'La Mort de Baldassare Silvande, vicomte de Sylvanie'. He did not much care for the nickname Reynaldo had given him, 'Marcel le pony', but it stuck and became part of the private language they used.

At one of Mme Lemaire's evening parties Reynaldo met Saint-Saëns, the composer he admired most of all. Saint-Saëns was often away on tour, but when he was in Paris he lived at the corner of the rue du Cirque and the rue du Faubourg Saint-Honoré, quite near to the Hahns' home, so it was convenient for Reynaldo to call in and see him from time to time, to show him his work and have a chat – he was never one of Saint-Saëns' pupils, but it was certainly due to him that Reynaldo's scholarly interest in Mozart was roused. One evening he and Marcel heard a performance of the sonata for violin and piano in D minor by Saint-Saëns. An insignificant little tune in the first movement appealed so much to Marcel that Reynaldo had to play the piano arrangement for him over and over again.

In spite of Marcel's approaching examinations, the social round of concerts, theatre visits and dinner parties continued. Early in March he and Reynaldo attended a soirée at the home of the Prince and Princess de Polignac in the rue Cortambert. The Prince, a talented musician and composer, was forty years older than his wife. She, born in New York in 1865, was Winaretta Singer, heiress of the Detroit family which made sewing machines. Educated in England and Paris, she was an excellent musician and a painter; she played duets with Fauré and exhibited her pictures at the Salon. It was she who enabled Fauré to go to Venice in 1890, and his five Verlaine songs of that year were dedicated to her. Other young musicians enjoyed her patronage, Reynaldo among them. Falla, Stravinsky and Satie wrote works for her and she subsidized Diaghilev's Ballets Russes when they came to Paris. Reynaldo continued to play for her in London, Paris and Venice up to the outbreak of war in 1939 – she was always his much admired 'Princess Winnie', though he did not approve of some of the modern composers she supported.

Marcel got his degree in philosophy at the end of March and applied for a post, part-time, unpaid, in the Mazarine Library at the Institut de France (where Sainte-Beuve had once been librarian). The first public performance of *Portraits de Peintres* was given at Mme Lemaire's studio on 28 May 1895. Risler came specially from Chartres where he was completing his military service to play the piano pieces, and the verses were recited by M. le Bargy from the Comédie Française. The following month there was another evening performance at the studio, with Reynaldo at the piano, and prefaced by a poetic tribute to him from Stéphane Mallarmé, which Reynaldo found incomprehensible.

In the course of his philosophy studies Marcel discovered Emerson, the American poet and man of letters, a superb stylist and deep thinker, whose essays were a revelation – he read them 'with rapture', and five of the epigraphs for the stories in his book were chosen from Emerson's work. He had finished the story about Baldassare Silvande which he had promised Reynaldo; it is an interesting psychological study of a man destined, like the young men in Van Dyck's portraits, to die before his time. In the opening pages Baldassare, stricken with a fatal disease at the age of thirty-five, is seen through the eyes of his thirteen-year-old nephew to whom he has given a pony as a birthday present (hence Marcel's nickname), just as the adults in *Swann's Way* are seen from the viewpoint of the young M. The luxurious setting, unhappy love affairs, chinoiserie and peacocks have a fin-de-siècle feel about them; as Anatole France noted in his preface, the atmosphere is of 'a tropical greenhouse among rare orchids – the poet has delved deeply into the secret thought, the unconfessed desire. He is not innocent, but he is so sincere and without subterfuge that he becomes naïve and so gives pleasure.' The epigraph Marcel chose for this story came from Emerson's essay on History: 'Apollo kept the flocks of Admetus, the poets tell us; each man too is a god in disguise who acts the fool.'

Another short story, 'Un Dîner en ville', was submitted through Reynaldo to Mme Lemaire for approval. She illustrated it with a sketch of Suzette, Marcel and other guests at the dinner table. In this account of a Parisian hostess and her acquaintances, Proust showed how well he understood their social ambitions and snobbery.

In May there was a highly acclaimed revival of Wagner's opera *Tannhäuser* at the Opéra. As Marcel explained to Suzette Lemaire, he and Reynaldo had discussed the treatment of Christianity in *Parsifal*, comparing it with the redemption of Tannhäuser's soul by Elizabeth's death:

'I hide my Wagnerism even less from Reynaldo since he shares it. The point about which we disagreed is this: I believe that the essence of music is to rouse in us that mysterious depth of soul (something which is inexpressible in literature, and in general in all kinds of definite things or ideas, or definite objects like painting, sculpture) which begins where the finite and all the arts which have a finite objective leave off, where science leaves off, too, and which might be called because of this, a religious feeling. This doesn't make sense written so quickly and deserves more discussion . . . Reynaldo, on the other hand, in considering music as perpetually subordinate to the word, thinks of it as expressing particular feelings, even as a variant to conversation . . . I can see quite well how [his] way of thinking about music arises naturally from his literary musician's temperament . . . Finally, and above all, any discussion on music exhausts Reynaldo very quickly and is painful to him. If I have anything to say to him about theories, to satisfy my conscience, I say it to him when we're alone.'

There was one more story to write. 'La Fin de la jalousie' begins with an account of a happy love affair – unusual in Proust's work. Such happiness does not last; Honoré's tormented jealousy, his suspicion of imagined infidelities, led him to act as inquisitor to Françoise, just as Swann would do to Odette and M to Albertine. It all ended with another lingering death-bed scene when Honoré, fatally injured in an accident with a runaway horse, remembered, as Baldassare had done, his mother's tenderness to him at bedtime. His book, provisionally entitled *Le Château de Réveillon*, was now complete. Thanks to an introduction from Mme Stern, the firm of Calmann-Lévy had agreed to publish it at the author's expense, but Anatole France had not yet delivered the preface and Madeleine Lemaire was still working on the illustrations.

3

Dieppe and Beg-Meil

In August 1895 Mme Lemaire invited the two friends to join her and Suzette on holiday again, this time in Dieppe where she had rented a large house on the promenade. In letters to his sister Reynaldo described the quiet but pleasant time they were having. Mme Lemaire was 'quite astonishing' away from home. He and Marcel enjoyed her reminiscences and appreciated her disinterested generosity while making gentle fun of her behind her back, referring to her as 'La Veuve', the Widow, and Suzette as 'La Jeune Veuve'. Marcel too wrote to Maria, asking her to return the manuscript of the story he had written for Reynaldo about Baldassare Silvande, as he was anxious to know what she thought of it. In spite of asthma and insomnia he sent her a high-spirited letter of nautical and astronomical compliments; it was as safe to flirt with Maria as with Suzette, since they were both nearly thirty.

Maria declined Mme Lemaire's invitation to join them as she had already gone to Saint-Germain to stay with her sister Clarita. Marcel was much better, Mme Lemaire wrote, and Reynaldo the most delightful of companions. 'Ah! if they would only give up the idea of a journey to Brittany! I dare not talk to them on the subject for fear of making them think about it. I am sure they are resting better here than they would in a poor hotel. I make them eat at fixed times, but once they are left to themselves at whatever time will they get their meals? We are spending every day in the open air . . .'

A popular meeting place for visitors to Dieppe was the

chalet under the west cliffs where Jacques-Emile Blanche had his studio. His portrait of Suzette had been shown at the Paris Exhibition of 1889, the one in oils of Marcel at the Salon of 1893. Blanche's studio was full of callers, including Mme Lemaire and her guests; Pierre Loüys, Aubrey Beardsley and his sister and Arthur Symons all sat for their portraits by Blanche during the summer.

One of the main subjects for discussion at the studio was the trial of Oscar Wilde, who had been sentenced in May to two years' hard labour after the failure of his ill-advised libel action against the Marquis of Queensberry, father of Lord Alfred Douglas ('Bosie'). As a writer and as a conversationalist Wilde was well known in Paris, Dieppe and London. He and his wife, Constance, had spent their honeymoon in Dieppe; on a visit to Paris in 1886 he had twice been to tea with Blanche at Auteuil, and on another visit, this time in 1894 with his lover, Bosie, he was entertained by Mme Straus and Mme Arman de Caillavet, and by the Prousts in the Boulevard Malesherbes, when, to Marcel's dismay, he commented unfavourably on the flat's old-fashioned décor.

When the scandal broke, two comedies by Wilde were playing to large audiences in London. Material success had coarsened him physically and morally – he had become an egocentric, sensual exhibitionist. And yet, many of the people who knew him well wrote of his great charm, his irresistible well-spring of nonsense in conversation, about which Frank Harris said: 'His talk made me forget his repellent physical peculiarities . . . There was an extraordinary physical vivacity and geniality in the man. Every mental question interested him, especially if it had anything to do with literature or art.'

Released from the horror and isolation of Reading

Gaol in May 1897, Wilde went to Dieppe, causing some embarrassment to his former friends. He did not stay long in Normandy; after further disastrous meetings with Bosie he settled in Paris, where, in spite of his insistence on 'a high standard of destitution', absinthe and casual encounters ruined his health and he died, at the age of forty-six, in November 1900. What a subject for a novel! There is a parallel between Wilde's trial and degradation and the disgrace of the Baron de Charlus in *The Captive*. Pride and sensuality meet the same fate, brought about by the beauty and treachery of two much-loved young men, Lord Alfred Douglas and the fictional Charlie Morel. Whatever characteristics of Baron Doazan, Robert de Montesquiou or from his own experience Proust may have borrowed for his portrait of Charlus, Wilde's notoriety and downfall must have made a deep impression on the young writer. It was more than ten years before Wilde's plays were produced again in England. *Salomé* had its first production in Paris and was subsequently successful in Germany, France and Belgium, paving the way for the rehabilitation of its author's reputation, long before his work for the theatre was revived in England. Homosexuality was not a crime punishable by law in France. Reynaldo commented in his journal on a performance of *Lady Windermere's Fan* in London: 'Formerly Oscar Wilde was looked on as a demigod, today his rare and great quality of mind is misunderstood; he is considered out of date. What would he say about this, he who talked so well about "fashion" and knew all about its revenges and feared them?'

There were no more letters from Dieppe to Maria until Reynaldo sent a hurried note to Paris on 29 August: 'We

are all leaving tomorrow, I shall arrive home at 5.00 p.m.
– when and in what direction shall I be setting off again?'
He was at home only a few days, just time to collect clean
linen and some medicaments, and dedicate a song to
Mme Proust, and then he and Marcel were away, to Belle-
Ile in Brittany. The holiday did not begin well. The day
after their arrival Maria got an angry note from le Palais,
the port and largest village on the island, which they
disliked intensely. The hotel was dirty and dark, the food
– always a major consideration with Reynaldo – was
uneatable, everywhere smelt of fish and they were leaving at once for Beg-Meil, which was not far away and said
to be delightful.

A few days later Maria received an enthusiastic
description of Beg-Meil, written on pages torn from a
school exercise book and dated 6 September 1894. The
scenery was admirable, the sea on one side calm and
fringed with islands and the Concarneau peninsula,
extraordinarily like the Lake of Geneva, while the other
side was quite different with a rough sea and infinite
horizon. Apple trees everywhere, no village, just the
hotel, so primitive it was like a farm, but the rooms were
clean and airy, the food less satisfactory – it was all very
casual, and cheap at two francs a day each; also Mme
Hahn sent them hampers of delicatessen.

None of Marcel's usual daily letters to his mother have
survived; paper and ink were difficult to buy, but he
wrote briefly to Montesquiou's secretary and companion
Yturri, describing, as Reynaldo had done, the apple trees
'mingling the scent of cider with the perfume of sea-
weed, on the shore of a fantastic Lake of Geneva'. To
Robert de Billy he announced the imminent publication
of his short story 'La Mort de Baldassare Silvande'; his
holiday reading was Balzac's *Les Splendeurs et misères*

des courtisanes and Carlyle's *On Heroes and Hero Worship*. He thought the Balzac novel stupid and not to be recommended to a married man.

There is one other long letter from Reynaldo to his sister at the end of September which is headed 'Thursday, 11.00 a.m. on top of a rock surrounded by the sea'. 'As always happens,' he wrote, 'it is now that we have to think of leaving this wonderful place we are completely pervaded by it and are utterly content . . .' They had done hardly any work and Marcel's stomach wasn't too good but he looked splendid 'and dazzles me all the time with an incomparable display of intelligence and a heart of gold'. They had met a talented painter, an American, Alexander Harrison, who spent nine months of every year at Beg-Meil and never got tired of it. 'I have devoured the two volumes of Balzac's *Les Splendeurs et misères des courtisanes* – I got through it and must even admit that I enjoyed it, in spite of many things which would be absurd in another author. In any case, it isn't suitable reading for Maria!'

He went on to discuss the good qualities and failings of a friend in the composition class at the Conservatoire, whom they all knew – a student who was quite aware of his weaknesses and made excuses for them but did nothing to correct them. 'Since I believe that one must make one's own life, and that the will should be put above *all other qualities*, I cannot, in spite of the real affection I feel for X, rate his character very highly. The profoundest satisfaction on earth lies, I believe, in self-respect! But it must be earned . . . we spend so little time here that the idea of contributing as much as we can to its radiance should be our first concern. There is no true radiance except in genius or goodness. These two words comprise everything we should always aim for . . . Here's a philosophical effusion for you!'

Beg-Meil was the paradise they had dreamed about when they were in Dieppe. Now they could spend all day on the beach, separately or together, reading, smoking, dreaming, talking and, in the evening after dinner, gazing at the moon-lit sea from the dunes, talking and dreaming again. They did not want to leave. Marcel wrote to the Mazarine Library asking for an extension of leave, which was granted; they renewed their railway tickets and stayed on for another idyllic month.

Reynaldo was reading Mme de Sévigné's letters as background for his second opera, which was to be on a more ambitious scale than *L'Ile du rêve*. Its heroine was Louise de la Vallière, the girl Mme de Sévigné called 'the little violet'. Her story was a sad one: she had fallen in love with Louis XIV and he with her when they were both young. She loved him truly, not for his royal grandeur but for himself, remaining at court at the king's insistence for some years after he had transferred his affections to Mme de Montespan. Louise paid for her few years of intermittent happiness with more than thirty years of remorse when she became a Carmelite nun.

As for Marcel, the beauty and peace of the Breton countryside, the isolated hotel where they had only themselves to please, with no family or social obligations, compounded with Reynaldo's appreciative and loving companionship – all these factors inspired him, in spite of the shortage of paper and ink, to start writing something quite different to anything he had done before – drafts for an autobiographical novel which foreshadowed in many interesting ways the work which was to make him famous. He never gave a title to this eventually voluminous manuscript. Its first editor, Bernard de Fallois, called it *Jean Santeuil* after its young narrator.

In two months at Beg-Meil he wrote eighty-eight pages of manuscript on the cheap squared paper Reynaldo had used for his long letter to Maria at the end of September. From this it is not difficult to guess what they talked about during the long, lazy days on the beach, the books they were reading, their hopes for the future, the good and bad qualities in their own characters and those of their friends. Both Jean Santeuil (the hero of Marcel's autobiographical novel) and the narrator of *The Search* make lack of will-power an excuse for not getting down to work.

Jean was a highly strung, delicate child, unable to go to sleep without a goodnight kiss from his mother. In this early version the scene is set in Saint-Germain, on another page it became Auteuil, where Marcel had been born and where many summer days had been spent; M. and Mme Santeuil were entertaining a dinner-guest, a famous doctor, in the garden; Jean, sent up to bed, braved his mother's anger by summoning her from the bedroom window, but neither her kiss nor her kindness could prevent a hysterical outburst of sobbing. Mme Santeuil excused her son's lack of self-control by explaining that he was suffering from nerves, thereby absolving him from responsibility for his outburst, so that 'instead of having to avoid a fault, he had only to think of nursing an illness' – only gradually, as a result of constant effort, could his will-power have overcome his nerves. This passage is repeated almost word for word in *Swann's Way*; in *Time Regained* Proust again refers to the evening when M's mother abdicated her authority, the evening from which dated the decline of his health and will.

In spite of his laziness and ill health, Jean is a more energetic and tempestuous character than M in *The*

Search. He goes sailing and fishing, he takes long walks in the wind and rain, and enjoys a great storm at Penmarch, travelling there on the little train from Pont l'Abbé with two of the local fishermen. With considerable verve and humour, Proust set out to describe, using the third person, his childhood and schooldays, his parents and their friends, and the little girl he had fallen in love with when they played together in the Champs-Elysées.

It was no coincidence that he and Reynaldo should have chosen *Les Splendeurs et misères des courtisanes* to read on holiday, after their discussion of Oscar Wilde's disgrace while they were staying in Dieppe. A sordid melodrama of high and low life in the Paris of 1830, it was a sequel to the story of Lucien de Rubempré in *Les Illusions perdues*, and his relationship with a middle-aged criminal, the sinister Vautrin, an equivocal friendship which had a tragic outcome. Parisian high society as depicted by Balzac was very different from the Faubourg Saint-Germain glamorized by Proust in *Jean Santeuil* – for Balzac there was no glamour, only a preoccupation with money, power and sex, and a great deal of corruption and venality. Decidedly not a book for Maria!

It is taken for granted today that Reynaldo and Marcel were lovers; if so, they were very discreet about it for the sake of their families. Although both of them had many women friends it is unlikely that either ever had a more than casual physical relationship with a woman. Marie was not the only girl to fall in love with Reynaldo, but there is no record of anyone falling in love with Marcel. He, in a letter to his school friend Daniel Halévy, described pederasty as an amusement allowable to adolescents, citing Socrates and (mistakenly) Montaigne as advising young men to 'amuse themselves' in order to experience every sort of pleasure and so find an outlet for their feelings of tenderness – such sensual as well as intellectual friendships were better for young people than relationships with low, corrupt women!

In *Cities of the Plain* he wrote about homosexuality with a compassionate detachment, not as something to be condemned but as an incurable disease, resulting from a lack of balance in the nervous system. While susceptible to all the pleasures of the senses, and with an excitable imagination, he was an onlooker, a compulsive voyeur, needing to satisfy his compulsion to know. The importance of the relationship between Reynaldo and Marcel is that it was a lasting one, based on a real affection and respect for each other's character and talent – as Reynaldo had written to his sister in his second long letter, genius and goodness.

It was nearly the end of October and they had to go back to Paris. They had no regrets at leaving; they hoped to return the following year to Beg-Meil – but they never did. Marcel visited the north coast of Brittany briefly in 1904, while Reynaldo, in spite of his strongly expressed dislike of Belle-Ile, became a frequent visitor there. He now went to Réveillon to join the Lemaires. Suzette had written to Maria Hahn in mid-October: 'You have a brother of whom I'm beginning to get very fond – this is a charming link between us . . . he and Marcel Proust are amusing themselves by giving us false hopes and writing several times to ask if we are expecting them. You can guess that we replied with enthusiasm and since then, complete silence! . . . If they linger too long, winter will be here, our big house will be full of draughts and melancholy, and mama would be quite capable of putting them off!'

Marcel joined the party two days after Reynaldo. His story, 'La Mort de Baldassare Silvande', dedicated to Reynaldo, 'poet, musician, singer', was published in *La Revue hebdomadaire* at the end of the month. He wrote a last short paragraph for his book about the autumnal chestnut trees in the park, to follow the woodland rhapsody he had written in Dieppe. Reynaldo was thinking of translating into French an unspecified work by Carlyle – perhaps *Sartor Resartus*, a book popular with the Symbolist poets, a good-humoured satire on German philosophy and erudition which would appeal to his sense of humour. He summed up the year's activities as 'fertile en agitations'; he was appalled how quickly it had passed: 'One must be free, only work is good, however hard it may be. To love very little, to make oneself useful if possible, and resign oneself to the sadness which is the inevitable daily bread of every intelligent being, and finally, as Mme de Sévigné said, to look higher so as not to be impatient.'[1]

4
Pleasures and Days

A note in Reynaldo's journal reads: 'To the Louvre with Marcel. Pastels by Chardin and La Tour. Haunting portrait of Chardin in a scarf; that right eye, tired, puffy, an eye that has seen everything and knows how to look . . .' Marcel now offered two articles to the editor of *La Revue hebdomadaire*, one on Chardin, a philosophical study describing how great painters initiate us into knowledge and love of the exterior world, and one on the young poets of the Symbolist school, of which Mallarmé was the acknowledged leader. The latter was accepted by *La Revue blanche* and appeared the following year as 'Contre l'obscurité', but the article on Chardin was not printed until 1954; unfinished and unrevised, it showed Proust's ability to look closely at paintings and learn from them: the life and colour in Chardin's representation of simple domestic scenes make the spectator look more closely at his own domestic surroundings.

Reynaldo went back to the Louvre again and again to look at pictures and sculpture of the seventeenth and eighteenth centuries. He also went to Durand-Ruel, the picture dealer who did so much to promote the Impressionists, and there met Mallarmé whom he already knew well. Together they admired a painting by Manet – Mallarmé had watched the artist working on it. Reynaldo enjoyed going to the Tuesday evening gatherings at 87, rue de Rome where Mallarmé lived with his German wife and their daughter, and where for the past ten years they had welcomed poets, painters and writers both French and foreign. Mallarmé, standing in front of the stove as Whistler had sketched him, would deliver a three-hour monologue. There were not many women visitors – occasionally, perhaps, the composer Augusta Holmès, or Rodin's pupil Camille Claudel. Whistler and Mallarmé were old friends, as were Mallarmé and Manet.

Every day for many years, on his way home from the lycée where he taught English, Mallarmé called at Manet's studio. Here he met Méry Laurent, Manet's favourite model, of whom he did numerous portraits. Méry was a young actress from Nancy; shortly before the Franco-Prussian war of 1870, when she was in her early twenties, she became the mistress of a wealthy dentist, Thomas Evans. The generous allowance he made her enabled her to live in luxury and also to show generosity to the poets and painters whose company she enjoyed. Her good-natured, uncomplicated character, red-gold hair, sapphire-blue eyes and generously curved figure made her an enchanting companion; she was, like the elegant Laure Hayman, friend of Marcel's great-uncle Louis Weil, a high-class demi-mondaine. After Manet's death in 1883 Mallarmé got into the habit of calling in to see her at her flat, 52, rue de Rome, not far from his own home. In 1895 she moved to a house called Les Talus on the Boulevard Lannes, overlooking the Bois de Boulogne, where Reynaldo, introduced by Mallarmé, became a frequent visitor.

By the end of March 1896 Marcel's book reached the proof stage at last and the title, perhaps at Mme Lemaire's request, was changed from *Le Château de Réveillon* to *Pleasures and Days*. The new title was certainly more distinctive; Proust may have taken it directly from Hesiod's poem, 'Works and Days', or he may have been inspired by Emerson's essay on the same poem, in which the meaning of the Day was explained: 'Ancient

men, in their attempts to express the Supreme Power of
the Universe, call him The Day . . . We hope for long life,
but 'tis deep life or grand moments that signify . . . Let
the measure of time be spiritual, not mechanical . . . It
is the depth at which we live that imports.' In Marcel's
drafts for his novel, page after lyrical page described
such 'grand moments', moments of vision, of profound
illumination, when he struggled to understand why the
solitary contemplation of flowers, trees, countryside and
seascape should bring him such happiness that his writing became incoherent with the urgency of what he had
to say. It was as though the hours of discussion and meditation at Beg-Meil had released a hidden spring of
poetic memories.

The speed at which he wrote, sometimes in pencil,
often illegibly, makes the manuscript difficult to
decipher. The loose papers and exercise books that he
numbered in 1896 have disappeared. The longer sections, the scene of the little boy longing for his mother's
goodnight kiss, Jean's education and adolescence, his
friendship with the Duke and Duchess de Réveillon, the
holiday at Beg-Meil with their son Henri, his love affairs
with Charlotte Clissette and Françoise, and the old age
of his parents, formed a rough framework for the future
novel. Themes and characters which would be worked
out later in *The Search* appeared in embryo, maturing
slowly throughout the years he studied and translated
Ruskin.

Marcel was working on his drafts while staying with a
friend from his university days, Léon Yeatman, who read
the opening pages and thought them typical of Marcel,
'très poney'! 'If it is too much so,' Marcel told Reynaldo,
'you must help me to put it right. I want you to be in it
all the time, but like a god in disguise whom no mortal

will recognize. Otherwise you would have to write "Tear this up" on every page.' One of the disguises was that of the friend who went to Brittany with Jean Santeuil, Henri de Réveillon, a young nobleman, not as some commentators have surmised because Proust was a snob, but because Reynaldo had the manners and bearing of a natural aristocrat. When Jean and Henri first met as schoolboys, before they became friends, Jean noted the aristocratic ease of his manners, the vivacity which informed his entire being, an elegant bearing, a pleasant, smiling face and a charm both teasing and subtle, which made his former school friends seem unbearably coarse. Here was the longed-for true friend, *l'ami véritable*, whose loving companionship would bring him solace and inspiration.

Another of Reynaldo's disguises was as 'the Marquis de Poitiers' entertaining the young officers in their mess at Provins where he kept a cigarette in his mouth while he sang because he believed it was not necessary to move the lips for the words of the song to be completely audible. 'Poitiers' as a performer quite simply summoned his listeners' recollections, recalling to their memories this tune or that word, suddenly remembering some piece of comic business or complaining that he could not quite remember exactly the way in which an actress had played a certain scene or reproduce the little musical phrase played on the violins.

When Marcel fell in love with 'the little phrase' in the sonata by Saint-Saëns, it was Reynaldo who had to play the piano arrangement repeatedly; in *Jean Santeuil* it was Françoise who played the same piece almost every evening, ten or twenty times, 'in the heyday of their happiness'. After they quarrelled and their affair was over, the music brought Jean unbearable pain, but ten years later he had forgotten Françoise and the little phrase reminded him not of the woman he had loved but of all the places where they had been happy, that summer long ago, by the lake in the Bois de Boulogne, on the terrace at Saint-Germain, at Versailles, wherever she had played for him.

On Tuesday 26 May Reynaldo's choral piece, *Là-bas*, written at Beg-Meil, was performed before an appreciative audience in Mme Lemaire's studio. There was another musical evening at the Princesse de Polignac's, and Reynaldo asked Marcel not to go if he was invited. Marcel appealed to Maria Hahn to intervene – her brother had a horror of surprises and was already in a bad mood, which would not improve when he was confronted with Marcel and the Lemaires! And there was a misunderstanding with Mme Stern: an injudicious word, a sign of impatience, occasioned another apology and a charge of insensitivity from Maria. 'I have apologized twice and sent off a humble and charming letter with the ms of a song . . .' Reynaldo told her. 'You see, I'm not as *insensitive* as you think, only I don't always like to say what I'm doing – we all have our funny ways, don't we?'

Les Plaisirs et les jours was published in June in a luxury edition with facsimiles of Reynaldo's music for the poems, *Portraits de Peintres*, as centrepiece and several full-page illustrations, as well as chapter headings, by Mme Lemaire. There were six short stories, the poems, and a number of short prose pieces under two headings, 'Fragments de Comédie italienne', sketches of society people in the manner of Saint-Simon or La Rochefoucauld, and the more lyrical 'Regrets, rêveries couleur du temps'. Copies of the book were sent, with appropriate dedications, to the author's many friends and influential acquaintances, but sales were meagre and the few reviews lukewarm. This was very disappointing. In addition there were two bereavements in the family. In May Mme Proust's uncle, Louis Weil, died, and at the end of June her father, Nathée Weil, followed after only one day's illness. And then, too, Marcel's hay fever and choking fits had been particularly bad.

It was some consolation that in mid-July *La Revue blanche* published his article 'Contre l'obscurité', written six months before, about the difficulty of understanding modern Symbolist poetry – a curious exercise, as Proust himself noted, from a writer aged twenty-five putting a middle-aged point of view. He thought that as poetry is not, like philosophy, concerned with logic or reasoned arguments, the language it uses should awaken echoes in the reader's sensibility by a sort of hidden music. Mallarmé offered an oblique reply in the September issue of the same review: 'I know people want to limit Mystery to Music, when the written word lays claim to it . . . the tune or song beneath the text guiding the instinct of divination from one point to another.' Carlyle, as Proust would have read at Beg-Meil, in the essay 'The Hero as Poet' said the same thing in less abstruse terms: 'A poem is a musical thought . . . spoken by a mind that has penetrated to the heart of things, detected the inmost mystery of it, namely the melody that lies hidden in it.' Marcel took up these ideas in his drafts of 1908–9.[1]

Reynaldo's days as a student at the Conservatoire were over. Ambroise Thomas, the director, had died, and the post was offered to Massenet, who refused it on the grounds that he wished to devote himself to the writing of operas and supervising their production. He resigned in June and Reynaldo left at the same time, hoping he would find an acceptable libretto for his second opera.

When Reynaldo returned from Hamburg in July, he and Marcel had a serious quarrel. Now no longer a student and able to accept more professional engagements, he felt constrained by Marcel's obsessive questioning and his capacity for self-torture. In June he had made a promise to tell Marcel everything; he swore now there would be no more confidences. Marcel pleaded: 'I try to fill the gaps in a life which is dearer to me than anything – [to know everything] is the fantasy of an invalid and should not therefore be contradicted . . .' Reynaldo rebelled against this emotional blackmail. He refused to leave a supper party to go home with Marcel, and bitter words were exchanged. Marcel quoted sadly a line from a favourite poem by Victor Hugo: 'How short a time it takes to change the face of things.'[2] He had not yet reached the stage when he could write, as he did in *The Fugitive*, that we do not succeed in changing things according to our desires, but gradually our desires change. The situation we hoped to change because it was intolerable becomes unimportant – we do not manage to surmount the obstacle, life has taken us round it.

The honeymoon may have been over, but the relationship between Reynaldo and Marcel was as close as ever. They had now known each other for over two years and their relationship during this time, when they had met or corresponded almost daily, had been fruitful for both of them. The letters Marcel wrote to Reynaldo between the end of 1896 and September 1904, with the exception of a bare half-dozen, have disappeared, lost, destroyed or withheld perhaps, but it is apparent from his correspondence with other friends that they had reached a satisfactory understanding.

At the end of December 1896 Reynaldo found a new, engrossing interest. On Wednesday 9 December a 'Sarah Bernhardt Day' was organized by Mme Sarah's admirers. Reynaldo had hoped to attend the celebration but was kept at home by illness. He sent Mme Sarah a letter expressing his disappointment and telling her of his profound admiration for her art. Through Mme Lemaire, perhaps, or Georges Clairin, a meeting with Mme Sarah was soon arranged, and Reynaldo became a member of her inner circle of friends and collaborators; he went regularly to her dressing-room during and after her performances, had lunch at her home in the Avenue Péreire, travelled with her to London and on her tours, helped to prompt at rehearsals (even appearing sometimes on stage) and was commissioned to write music for her productions.

Exceptionally, Mme Sarah did not tour abroad during the early months of 1897. On 28 June Reynaldo, ten years younger than Mme Sarah's only son, Maurice, wrote in his journal: 'With some emotion I have just written a letter to Sarah in which I tell her of my deep admiration, my gratitude for what her genius has given me, my hopeless longing to go to her, to be near her always, to follow her everywhere, to write about her every day, minute by minute, to describe the thousand episodes of her life day by day.' His book, *La Grande Sarah*,[3] did exactly this; its mixture of gossip, loving description of her different roles, her clothes, her jewels, friends and family, their travels and the holidays he spent with her at Belle-Ile, gives a more living picture of the actress and woman than many closely documented biographies about her.

She was now at the height of her power, the extravagances of her early days behind her. There is remarkable unanimity among the admirers who described her in her two greatest roles, as Phèdre, and as Marguerite in *La Dame aux camélias* – Reynaldo never tired of seeing her in these plays. What was the secret of her fascination, apart from her professional mastery? She had immense vitality and gaiety as well as a compulsive need to work, partly to keep up with her own extravagance, largely with that of her son, whom she adored and spoilt. Reynaldo wrote of her: 'How extraordinary it is, the predisposition to gaiety of this woman, whose life has been more active and tempestuous than that of any statesman or victorious soldier, who gives of herself continually . . . always feminine in the midst of men and events, but dominating both, serious and teasing at the same time, perspicacious and understanding, mocking and compassionate, sometimes extravagantly imaginative yet gifted with an unmistakable common sense.'[4]

Sister Maria's reaction to her young brother's devotion to such a notorious woman – and an actress! – was predictable. Corresponding to her from Switzerland in July 1898, after he had gone to London with Mme Sarah for a short season, he wrote: 'As a result of getting to know this great woman so well, I have begun to feel a real friendship for her, all the more so because the people who surround her are not really worthy of her . . . I try to suppress my feelings when they start to run away with me. All the same, in a tight spot, Sarah could count on me, because she is a *very good person*.' He sensed that beneath the public persona there was a shy and susceptible woman. In a brief introduction to the book he wrote about her, he explained that he found it difficult to capture in all their variety those 'minutes profondes' that he experienced when she was at the height of her artistic power. This was Proust's phrase which Reynaldo borrowed on two other occasions (with due acknowledgements) to describe experiences they shared.[5]

If Marcel felt himself temporarily neglected, he consoled himself by seeing more than he had done hitherto, at concerts and picture galleries, of Lucien Daudet, now eighteen and a pupil at Julien's studio. Their companionship was noticed by the journalist Jean Lorrain who, always ready to work off a grudge against Alphonse Daudet, wrote a malicious gossip paragraph in *Le Journal* at the beginning of February 1897. Marcel challenged Lorrain to a duel, which took place on 6 February when two shots were exchanged without damage to either party. Reynaldo recorded the event: 'Today Marcel fought Jean Lorrain, who had written an odious article about him. He has shown, for the past three days, such sang-froid and firmness as would have appeared incompatible with his nerves but which did not surprise me at all.' Two versions of the duel were duly drafted for Marcel's novel. Shortly before these excitements, Reynaldo's Manchester cousin arrived in Paris with her aunt.

5
The Young English Cousin

Gladville, Victoria Park, Manchester – Proust was mystified by Marie's home address, because, he told her, he could not visualize it. He may have imagined Victoria Park to be some sort of country estate. In fact, as Marie explained, it was part of a town-planning scheme well ahead of its time, begun in 1836 on a site of 150 acres about a mile and a half south of Manchester town centre, with houses intended for professional families, a surrounding wall, and lodges to control entrances and exits at appropriate places. There were gate-keepers in uniform, and residents paid extra rates for special Park police.

'The postal district of Victoria Park was Rusholme,' Marie wrote, 'and what, not long ago, had been a village on the edge of farmland was, during my youth, the nearest local shopping centre, half-an-hour from the city in a lumbering three-horse omnibus. Gladville was a large, semi-detached, three-storied, brick, conventional Victorian house, approached by a wide gravelled drive with a lawn on the right, tall trees on the left, a large yard and garden with sand-pits for the children, at the back.'[1]

Proust evidently liked to think of Marie as typically English – yet her family background was half German and half Italian. Her father, Selmar Nordlinger, was born in 1832 in the Canareggio district of Venice when the city was under Austrian rule. The family may have originated in the little medieval town of Nordlingen in Bavaria, spreading from there in many directions; one branch dealt in antique tapestries and textiles in Paris, another had a modern business in Hamburg, and still another settled in Bradford in the Yorkshire woollen trade. After leaving school in Trieste, Selmar Nordlinger was sent round the various relations to gain business experience; from 1862 to 1867 he was with the firm of Jacob Behrens in Bradford. Having acquired British nationality, he took his younger brother, Charles, into partnership and they settled in Manchester as S. & C. Nordlinger, shipping merchants.

'Lancashire's expanding cotton industry in the middle of the nineteenth century,' Marie wrote, 'attracted business men from many European countries. The practical good sense and tolerance in the Mancunian merchants' attitude towards these strangers led to the establishment of numerous foreign communities in the city where, by 1876, fourteen nationalities were represented. Manchester owed a great deal in its educational and cultural life to these Europeans. One observer remarked, as early as 1836, that "Manchester is full of life and intelligence . . . the minds of men are in a state of electric communication of ideas."'

During his travels, Selmar Nordlinger visited Hamburg and fell in love with Helene, daughter of Clara and Felix Seligman. They were married in 1867 and came to Gladville where they lived for the rest of their lives. Marie-Louise, the second of their three daughters, was born on 31 May 1876; her sisters were Connie and Clara, her four brothers Charlie, Albert, John and Harry. Marie could barely remember her Italian grandmother who visited Gladville just once, but the Hamburg relations came frequently, especially her mother's only sister, Caroline Hinrichsen. Her husband had died after only six weeks of marriage, leaving her a very young widow with a substantial fortune that made it possible for her to help her nieces. She took great interest in Marie and early recognized her gifts and potential. Without Tante Caro's encouragement and financial help, Marie's career would have been very different.

Life at Gladville was typical of the Victorian middle class in Manchester, liberal and hard-working. There were servants, and a beloved and devoted German governess. Marie's memoir continued: 'My parents spoke English, French, German and Italian. They made a point of speaking English with us and were critical of our pronunciation. We were brought up as free thinkers, as they had been, with their sanction to follow any religion if and when we earnestly desired it. We paid regular visits to our grandmother, Frau Seligman, in Hamburg, sailing across the North Sea from Grimsby down the Elbe to the Hamburg docks; her eldest brother, Carlos Hahn, was the father of Reynaldo, whom I met first in Hamburg when I was a shy schoolgirl of twelve and he, two years older, was already a composer and a sophisticated Parisian.'

Two Anglo-German high schools for girls were established in the north-west in the 1870s, one in Bowdon, Cheshire, the other at Ladybarn House, in Fallowfield, where Marie and her sisters were educated. 'Languages were the best taught subject at the private day school I attended,' Marie wrote. 'French and German history, literature, grammar and geography were taught from the books used by French and German children; we read and recited the French classics and the same method was used by our German master. From school I proceeded to the School of Art in Cavendish Street, Manchester, to take a diploma course under the aegis of the South Kensington School of Art in London – drawing, design, painting, historic ornament, anatomy and modelling, with the concurrent lectures and examinations. My first year, 1894–5, coincided with Walter Crane's last as director. He was too shy to be successful as a teacher, but left his mark as a designer and lecturer. He was invariably kind and encouraging to me and when he left invited me to call on him whenever I was in London.' What was unusual for girls with Marie's background was that she and her sisters were encouraged to be independent – her elder sister, Clara, was secretary to the Director of the Manchester Museum until her marriage in 1902.

As the Courtois studio was in the suburb of Neuilly Marie took her bicycle with her when she went to Paris. 'My aunt and I arrived in Paris just before Christmas, 1896, for me to study under Gustave Courtois. Our first call, of course, was on the Hahns at 6, rue du Cirque, off the Champs-Elysées. When the family moved to Paris from Caracas in 1877, they brought with them the cook, Mrs Nelson, the valet de chambre, Auguste, and the coal black nanny, Nicolassa. There was also Margherita, the elderly Spanish duenna, who accompanied my only unmarried girl cousin, Maria, wherever she went, whether to Mass, to sittings for her portraits by Boldini or La Gandara, or to buy a yard of ribbon at Les Trois Quartiers.'

Marie soon became very much part of the Hahn family circle. She was devoted to Mme Hahn. Marie's published accounts show how stimulating she found the eighteen months of her first stay in Paris and how much she enjoyed the occasional companionship of two young men who evidently appreciated her liveliness and independent views. Marcel too was completely at ease in the informal Hahn household; he greatly admired Reynaldo's sisters, especially Maria. He often called in for a chat before he and Reynaldo went out for the evening. 'My daytime hours were fully occupied at the studio,' Marie's memoir continues, 'but, with other young artists and friends we used to foregather at my cousin's in the evening and on Sunday mornings he and Marcel occasionally joined me in the Louvre. If they had no prior engagement, they stayed at home and, joined by Coco, his older cousin Rafael de Ochoa (both of them aspiring artists), with other friends and relations, played old fashioned guessing games or charades, at which Marcel excelled. We amused ourselves (as Swann was to do in *The Search*) by attributing portrait painters to our acquaintances and friends. El Greco for Coco, of course, but we never quite succeeded for Marcel – Carrière, early Courbet, perhaps Pisanello, or Whistler? To my mind none of his portraits is like him. The pencil sketch by Jacques-Emile Blanche done at Trouville in 1891 concentrates on the eyes; the large portrait in oils by the same artist was originally three-quarter length and included the hands – in any case Marcel looked very different when I first knew him. My personal preference is for a somewhat pathetic likeness taken in Cabourg, probably in the summer of 1907.

'Marcel's looks naturally varied with the state of his health, more especially when he was suffering from hay fever. At all times, his eyes were his most striking feature; they were large and brown, strangely luminous, omnivorous eyes I can recall alight with fun and mimicry, or suddenly, unashamedly, suffused with tears. He was not well proportioned, his head being unduly large for his shoulders. Although expensively dressed (possibly not more so than others of his social status) and well-groomed, his appearance lacked elegance. For a man of his medium height, he was well-built, but his hands were small and ineffectual. His voice was indescribable, darker than his hair, more luminous than his eyes – I have never heard another like it.

'A favourite pursuit was graphology, much in vogue at the time. We analysed contemporary handwriting in the light of books on the subject, comparing them with autographs of well-known people. Reynaldo already had a large collection, beginning with a superb Louis XIV – some of the best of them, framed, were hung in his study.[2]

'But by far the best of all our diversions was Reynaldo's music-making. He would go to the piano and keep his audience spellbound for hours, starting perhaps with an operatic chorus, then, according to the cast available, he would conduct, lead and accompany an entire opera or improvise a pastiche, 1830s style. I heard *Così fan tutte* more than once in this way, and endless Gounod, Gluck, Offenbach, Lully, Massenet. He was inexhaustible, expounding his latest theories and enthusiasms before giving way to clamour for his own *mélodies*, *Les Chansons grises* or a new rondel. Although his *Etudes latines* did not appear until 1900 they symbolize for me those evenings long ago because the collection contains pieces dedicated to Massenet, Coco, Marcel and to me.'

The evenings she remembered most vividly were those when the three of them were alone, talking, reading, arguing – about art and aesthetics, music and literature; classical versus Gothic architecture, the Impressionist painters, the recently imported arts of China and Japan, and the theatre in all its aspects. They recited prose and poetry from ancient and modern literature; Marcel had an astonishing memory, and a single page read aloud evoked a whole host of others by dead or living authors.

'I listened to them eagerly, amazed at meeting, as it were in flesh and bone, people who had hitherto been nothing but names in print. "Heures propices à nos jeunesses en fleurs!" Halcyon days of their enchanted springtime!

'Sometimes they talked about personal problems and preoccupations. They both told me about their memorable Breton holiday with its difficulties and delights, so they naturally also spoke about their meeting with Alexander Harrison. Being myself much addicted at this time to sketching the seas and skies at sunset, Reynaldo asked Harrison if he might take me to the artist's studio in the rue Campagne Première. "It would give me the keenest pleasure to see you and your cousin," Harrison replied. "Come any Friday after three o'clock . . . " He showed us countless canvases and drawings, notably sea and skyscapes of Beg-Meil at different times of day. I little suspected that I had, on that Friday at the end of July, 1897, taken tea and chatted with the prototype of Elstir-Monet, Proust's personification of Impressionism.

'In March, 1897, I find an entry in a note book of Paris impressions: "Proust was really extraordinary this evening. R and I were sitting opposite to him at R's table with the oil lamp between us when, staring at me, Marcel suddenly exclaimed "Madamoiselle, has anyone ever told you that you resemble Titian's mistress – you know, the portrait in the Salon Carré (at the Louvre)?" To which I replied, "No, never, Monsieur." "Yes, indeed, it's the hair – I know hers is undone, but all the same . . ." Whereupon R got up and looked at me across the table. We were tired, worn out by the rarefied atmosphere in which we had been immersed during long discussions on the subject of Ruskin. If I quote this incident, which at a later time when I knew Marcel better would in no way have struck me as extraordinary, it is because of the allusion to Ruskin.

'It was a revelation for me to meet a young Parisian obsessed with the writings of Ruskin. He had not only read every word available in translation, but could quote at length from what he had read. And was it not a strange coincidence that I, a devotee of Ruskin, steeped in Pre- and Post-Raphaelite doctrine, whose Manchester postal district was in fact Rusholme, where, as Marcel knew, Ruskin had delivered the lecture on reading printed in *Sesame and Lilies*, should have been at hand when Marcel needed help and advice?

'Very little of Ruskin's work had been translated into French before 1895. Brief extracts had appeared in the *Bulletin de l'union pour l'action morale*, a publication to which Marcel subscribed because it was edited by a family friend, Paul Desjardins, a lecturer in literature and philosophy at the Sorbonne. Between December, 1895, and April, 1897, *La Revue des Deux Mondes* published a series of articles on Ruskin's life and work by Robert de la Sizeranne for which he translated long extracts from Ruskin's autobiography, *Præterita*, also from his first great work *Modern Painters*, from his most popular one, *Sesame and Lilies*, from *Lectures on Art* and *The Queen of the Air*, as well as shorter passages from *The Seven Lamps of Architecture*, *Val d'Arno* and *Mornings in Florence*, *The Stones of Venice* and *St Mark's Rest*. In 1897, La Sizeranne's articles were published as a book with the title *Ruskin et la religion de la beauté*; it must have been from La Sizeranne that Marcel quoted at such length because he had not yet read Ruskin in English, a language with which he was not familiar.

'My uncle's health was failing. To escape from the intense Paris heat of 1897, the Hahns moved to 11, parc de Montretout, above Saint-Cloud. I sometimes cycled there in the evening and always spent Sunday with them.' Carlos Hahn died during the evening of Thursday 15 July. Reynaldo informed Marie at once and their visit to Harrison's studio was postponed until he and his mother returned from Hamburg where they went immediately after the funeral.

During her two months' summer holiday in Manchester, long letters reached Marie from Aix-la-Chapelle where Reynaldo and Mme Hahn were taking a cure. He was engrossed in a book about Leonardo da Vinci, whom he thought 'the most captivating companion of all, greater than Voltaire, Goethe or even Michelangelo . . . he was both scholar and artist, a universal man'. The motto of his school in Milan was 'Fuyez les orages' ('Avoid all storms'), which was, according to Reynaldo, the most beautiful, complete and artistic formula: 'These three words encapsulate all the eternal laws of art.'[3]

At last came the offer for which he had waited so long. The Director of the Opéra-Comique died, and the man appointed to succeed him, Albert Carré, decided to inaugurate his tenure of office with a new work by a young composer. He chose, no doubt with Massenet's encouragement, *L'Ile du rêve* for production in March 1898, in a double bill with an established favourite, *Le Roi l'a dit*, by Delibes.

'There were many fascinating first nights about this time,' Marie wrote, 'Rostand's *Cyrano de Bergerac*, Messager's *Les P'tites Michus*, Réjane as Napoleon's independent laundress in *Madame Sans-Gêne*. Some music-hall performances were not considered proper, even for an English girl; all the same, I heard Fragson and Mayol, but never, alas, Yvette Guilbert. My greatest theatrical experience of all occurred on January 2nd,

1898, when my cousin sent me a note: "Dinner will be early, Mother wants you to go with her to the dress rehearsal of Sarah's P*hèdre*." In the interval, he took me round, for the first of many times, to her dressing-room. *Phèdre* was her greatest triumph. Reynaldo thought it would need an entire book to give the details of her interpretation. In a diary entry dated London, June 18th, 1898, he described her first entrance: "How beautiful she is! In the whole of Greek art there is no more imposing or touching figure . . . During the invocation to Venus (in Act III), her gesture endows her whole personality with an almost sacerdotal bearing. The gesture is quite simple: her right arm is stretched out almost straight, letting the white, gold, embroidered cloak fall, the left hand on her heart, her eyes lifted to heaven . . . In the fifth act, Sarah is transformed, she has chosen a terrible death . . . After the performance, in her dressing-room, Sarah talks to me through a curtain as she takes off her jewels. She is satisfied with the fourth act."[4]

6

A Celebrated Affair

In the New Year of 1898 Marie Nordlinger's sister, Clara, spent a short holiday with her in Paris; she remarked on the change in Marie, who knew, after a year in France, that she had found her true homeland, as she noted in her album (writing always in French). She loved Paris and she was in love with Reynaldo, though she was under no illusion that his feelings for her were more than those of cousinly affection. She confided to her album the heartaches of an attachment which was never declared; she thought he was in love with Cléo de Mérode and resigned herself, characteristically, to what she called 'the dignity of reticence', something that lasted to the end of her life.

She knew she could not compete with Reynaldo's other women friends – Mme Sarah, Mme de Polignac, Lady de Grey, Cléo – nor did she mention, if she ever knew about, his relationship with another notorious beauty, Liane de Pougy, dancer, actress and courtesan. According to her published notebooks, she adored him for thirty-five years. She loved everything about him – his voice, which she described as warm and slightly husky, his good looks, his style and culture, his cool sensibility. She had many wealthy lovers and told him all about them. He was the one man she wanted but he was not interested, much as he admired her beauty, elegance and intelligence; she thought he loved only his family. She sent him long passionate letters. It was a game they played which he enjoyed as much as she did. Her liaison with Natalie Barney, one of a glittering group of feminists and lesbians (which included several aristocratic ladies), was well known; no doubt Marcel was kept up to date with the gossip about them by Reynaldo and over the years built a background for M's suspicions about Albertine's lesbian relationships.

Marie lived in the very different world of impecunious, hard-working art students. She was struggling to find a philosophy of life and art and thinking about the future. She was far from the conventional idea of an English girl finishing her education by taking a course in art before finding a suitable husband. She was determined to be independent and find work of some sort for which she would be properly trained. By hard work and courage, and with the firm support of Reynaldo and Mrs Hinrichsen, she found the necessary confidence to make a career for herself, first as a craftsman, then as a 'travelling sales-man' in America, and finally as a writer, translator and business woman.

Both Marie and Clara had vivid memories of the excitement caused by new developments in the Dreyfus case; they devoured the daily issues of *Le Siècle* and *L'Aurore*, both pro-Dreyfus papers. Dreyfus was an artillery officer and the only Jew serving on the French General Staff. He was accused of selling military secrets to the Germans. During the three years since he had been tried and condemned, his brother, Mathieu, had been working to prove his innocence. The case against him hinged on a handwritten note (the *bordereau*) found in a waste-paper basket at the German Embassy in Paris. His handwriting was similar to that on the *bordereau*, which had been written not by an artillery officer but by an impecunious infantry officer, Major Esterhazy.

In November 1897 Mathieu Dreyfus published a fac-simile of the *bordereau* with new evidence from expert graphologists. On 11 January 1898 Emile Zola, a prolific journalist as well as a powerful novelist, who had already written in defence of Dreyfus, decided that the only way to force the government to take account of the new evidence was to provoke a civil trial, so he wrote an open letter to the President of France, a 4,000-word indictment which was published by Clemenceau in *L'Aurore* under the heading 'J'accuse'. 300,000 copies of the paper were sold, many of them burnt in the street by the Nationalists; there was a wave of anti-Semitic riots, and French society was divided into factions which set families, old friends and colleagues against each other.

The Dreyfusards formed the League for the Rights of Man and drew up a petition for revision, the 'Protest of the Intellectuals', which appeared first in *L'Aurore* the day after the publication of 'J'accuse', with 104 signatures. By the end of the month 3,000 people had signed it. This was the petition for which Marcel and Robert Proust, with Jacques Bizet and his cousins, the Halévy brothers, were busy collecting names. Dr Proust, who was firmly on the side of the government, as he knew and worked with many of its ministers, refused to speak to his sons for a week.

The trial of Zola began in the Palais de Justice on 7 February and lasted sixteen days. He was found guilty by the narrow margin of seven votes to five, fined 3,000 francs and sentenced to a year's imprisonment. When his appeal was rejected in July, he was persuaded to take refuge in England. Every day during this exciting fortnight Marcel and a journalist friend, Louis de Robert, were in the crowded public gallery, provided with small packets of sandwiches and a thermos of coffee so as to miss nothing of interest. Afterwards Marcel wrote some sketches for his novel which captured the feeling of comradeship and the feverish atmosphere of uncertainty, curiosity and excitement in the courtroom. Reynaldo was busy with rehearsals for his opera, but he read the papers avidly and the new developments were discussed at length in the rue du Cirque and at Méry Laurent's.

In December 1897 Alphonse Daudet died suddenly after much pain from syphilis contracted as a young man – a disease suffered by many of his contemporaries, Baudelaire, Maupassant, Verlaine and Manet among them. His friends and family mourned him sincerely, and particularly Reynaldo, who was full of gratitude to the man who after Massenet had encouraged him to write for the stage. For three days he and Marcel did not leave Lucien Daudet's side. The friendship with the family thus cemented lasted throughout the years, in spite of their opposing views on the Dreyfus case and Léon Daudet's ferocious anti-Dreyfus, anti-Semitic diatribes in *Le Gaulois* and *La Libre Parole*.[1]

L'Ile du rêve opened on Wednesday 24 March 1898. André Messager was the conductor, and the part of the heroine, Mahénu, was sung by Julie Giraudon, a young soprano who had appeared with Mme Calvé in Massenet's *Sappho*. The story was similar to that of *Madame Butterfly*. A young Frenchman, Georges de Kervan, on a visit to Tahiti, was baptized with flowers, and re-christened Loti; he married Mahénu and then left her. *Le Temps*, in its review the following morning, praised Mlle Giraudon but considered the music too much influenced by Massenet and the libretto so lacking in action and characterization that the young composer was fatally confined to creating a sort of cameo effect in mother-of-pearl. Loti himself recalled in his memoirs that the musical interpretation of his novel exactly matched the intentionally languid atmosphere he had wished to evoke when he wrote it.

After the performance Reynaldo wrote to Coco de Madrazo that 'the press were not able to subdue my heroine with their blows, nor trample on my little Polynesian flowers with their dirty, clumsy feet . . . They hold all the good qualities of the work against me, that's to say, its languor, grace and lack of action . . . Thanks to Massenet all the old rigmarole of opera production has been swept away; the orchestra is in semi-darkness, and so is the auditorium; the chorus moves about and acts; the moonlight is blue, not white as it traditionally is at the Opéra-Comique; the singers in the chorus are made-up – unprecedented innovation, etc., etc.'

Marie went to the first night with Mme Hahn and the family party; she remembered meeting Pierre Loti when he came to congratulate her aunt. 'He was in naval uniform and I was immediately impressed by the charm and sincerity of his eyes, but quite taken aback to find that the face of the author, whom we all more or less idolized, was very much made up and that he was wearing high, very high heels!'[2]

When Clara returned to Manchester after her holiday, Marie went with her to discuss her plans for the future with the family. She was doubtful about a career as a painter; although making steady progress at the Courtois studio she felt she should learn some craft which she could pursue at home. M. Courtois, while commending her enthusiasm and hard work, agreed that she should join a life class in sculpture on the Left Bank; so, in April 1898, she moved for the first and only time, over the Seine to live in the rue Notre-Dame des Champs and work every morning in the Colarossi studios, and on two evenings a week to take a diploma course in what she called 'decorative-design-sculpture' at a nearby municipal school.

Marie enjoyed exploring her new *quartier*. She made Sunday excursions into the countryside, to Amiens and Chartres, and to Senlis where, recommended by Marcel, she visited the church and its lovely spire, and made a little sketch of a group of trees which she later sent to him. 'I never went to Réveillon, but, having been introduced to Mme Lemaire and her daughter soon after my arrival in Paris, the rue Monceau has always been associated with some of my happiest memories. I was privileged to be invited frequently to the Tuesday evenings in May. Everybody who was anybody, of whatever nationality, rank or profession, even nonentities like myself, could be met in the celebrated studio, where the guests often overflowed to the garden and the street. On one of those mild, lilac-scented evenings, when Mme Emma Calvé had electrified us with her "incandescent voice", Marcel, seeing me home, recited the whole of *La Maison du berger*; the following day Reynaldo presented me with a first edition, autographed by Vigny himself – they seemed to vie with one another in spoiling me.'

On her way back to Manchester in July, Marie stayed for two days in Rouen at the invitation of Mme Hendlé, wife of the Prefect, relatives of her father. She explored the town and the cathedral where she talked, as Ruskin used to do, to the craftsmen and stonemasons repairing the porch and she also happened to meet the aged Jullien Edouard who had acted as guide not so many years before to Ruskin and his friends. Proust later met him at the church of St Ouen, during his visit to Rouen.

In June Reynaldo was in London with Mme Sarah and her company and kept daily notes of his conversations with her; he attended rehearsals, acted, very efficiently, as prompter, and studied her in every role. At the National Gallery he was in ecstasy before the Poussins, writing to Marie at length about them and adding: 'Your letters are a delight to me and I'm glad to hear that you are working hard . . . I've seen Irving as Shylock and shuddered. I saw Tree in *The Vagabond* and it made me yawn. Yet here they prefer Tree to Irving. It's the old, old story, mediocrity taking precedence over genius! Oh, ye gods, how stupid people are! Au revoir, work and dream.'

Some time during the summer, his sister Maria was unhappy about the progress of her relationship with Raimondo de Madrazo and Reynaldo wrote to her with tender understanding: 'Chère petite . . . Small disappointments are frequent and cruel when one loves deeply; but they are also *without any real importance* – there are bad moments in all serious love affairs . . . No more tears; have courage, smile, hope and show firmness before the enemy. This is the message these roses bring you, from someone who knows only too well *the deep grief of an impossible love!*' Ten years later, in October 1908, when the newspapers published a false story of Mme Bernhardt's death, Marcel described her in a letter to Reynaldo as 'the admirable friend who loves and understands you and knows how to please your difficult, melancholy heart'. Maria and Raimondo de Madrazo were married on 28 June 1899; Reynaldo wrote a wedding march for the occasion – and left it in the cab on his way to the ceremony.

Reynaldo spent the autumn in Versailles at the Hôtel des Reservoirs in a quiet street on the north side of the Palace with direct access to the park through a private gate. This was the first of many visits; he went there year after year, to work quietly, to walk in the park alone, with

Marcel, Marie or other close friends, at sunset, in snow or summer heat. He loved the long vistas, the fountains and groves, and wrote about them often. On this first visit he wanted to immerse himself in the atmosphere of the seventeenth century for his opera, although he knew that the romance between Louis XIV and Louise de la Vallière had flowered at Fontainebleau and not Versailles, which until 1668 had been a simple hunting-lodge. The Palace went through many changes after Louis' death but the park, laid out by Le Nôtre, stayed essentially the same.

In September Stéphane Mallarmé died, aged fifty-six, at his country home, Valvins, near Fontainebleau, the great work he planned still unfinished. Reynaldo, with unobtrusive kindness, now devoted himself to Méry Laurent, who was already a sick woman and survived Mallarmé only by two years. Early in the summer he had taken Marie Nordlinger to see her pictures. Marie remembered, in the salon, 'a slanting easel draped with plush on which stood Manet's enchanting pastel of his beloved, wearing a little toque with a veil, from which emerge her dreamy eyes, her slightly tilted nose and small pursed mouth'. There was also a superb Lautrec, paintings by Whistler and Manet's portrait of Mallarmé, now in the Louvre. Marie was the first to realize that Odette de Crécy's house in *Swann's Way*, which Proust situated in the rue la Pérouse (a street at one time inhabited by both Laure Hayman and Liane de Pougy), was very similar to Mme Laurent's villa at 9, Boulevard Lannes, with its Oriental décor, chrysanthemums and Japanese lanterns lit by a gas-jet.

7
Apprenticeships

Owing to her mother's ill health, Marie did not return to work in Paris after her summer holiday. She was exploring the possibility of training as a silversmith and had been to see Lalique, to whom friends had given her an introduction. He was just becoming well known and was emphatically against employing a young woman in his workshop. He suggested she might try Mr Ashbee's Guild of Handicraft and the Arts and Crafts Society in London, but 'I had seen the Guild's work,' she wrote, 'and was embarrassed to admit that I thought the metalwork technically amateurish and was not greatly impressed by the designs. The interview ended by M. Lalique saying "Let me know how you get on."'

Eventually a solution was found in Hamburg and she was taken on as an apprentice in the workshops of two young Munich silversmiths early in 1899. She settled down at her grandmother's home at 100, Mittelweg, a twenty-minute bicycle ride from Herr Schönauer's workshop. 'This, of course, was a very different life from Paris,' she continued, 'but I hardly had time to think about that, the work was interesting and intensely strenuous, the atmosphere friendly and encouraging, my teacher a highly qualified technician. The only drawback was my dislike of the Teutonic art nouveau work being produced. The Museum of Decorative Art was only a stone's throw away and I usually spent part of my dinner hour there, reading in the library or studying the collections that the director, Dr Brinckmann, was extending in various directions; his museum was one of the first to collect really fine oriental art and integrate it with the best modern European craft work – a Morris tapestry, a Carriès pot, Lalique jewellery and glass – at a time when they had hardly been seen, much less appreciated.'

Before she left Manchester for Hamburg in the New Year, Marie sent Christmas greetings to Marcel and received an elegantly written letter, apologizing for the delay in replying due to his own ill health and his mother's three-month stay in hospital after a serious operation. 'Mademoiselle,' he wrote, 'Your Christmas card gave me great pleasure. If we were nothing more than creatures of reason, we would not believe in anniversaries, in festivals, holy relics or tombstones. But as we are also made up of a small amount of matter, we like to believe that it, too, constitutes a part of reality and that it has its own material symbol, as our soul has in our body; also, we would like whatever has a place in our hearts to take up a little space around us as well. And so, as Christmas gradually loses some of its truth for us as an anniversary, it takes on an increasingly intense reality by a gentle emanation of accumulated memories, in which the light of its candles, its snow – melancholy obstacle to some longed-for visitor – the scent of its mandarin oranges drinking in the warmth of the rooms, the gaiety of its frosts and its fires, the perfumes of its tea and mimosa, are all conjured up, imbued with the delicious honey of our own personalities, which we had unconsciously deposited during years of preoccupation with our own affairs, blinding us to the reality of Christmas; and now suddenly, this reality makes the heart beat faster . . . Although I envy you your English life, I hope you will come back to Paris soon. I shall be so happy to renew acquaintance with your delicate, unusual mind and your grace as fresh as a spray of hawthorn . . .'

Was Marie surprised or amused, in 1899, to be compared to so unpretentious a flower as a hawthorn, being
unaware, then, of its special significance for her correspondent?[1] When *Jean Santeuil* was published in 1952,
ten years after Marie's *Lettres à une amie*, she immediately noticed the similarity between phrases in this letter
and passages in the early drafts. Memories of Christmas
and the scent of mandarin oranges were incorporated
into some pages he wrote for his novel about another
young woman, Anna, Comtesse de Noailles, whom he had
met the previous year. His vivid, affectionate portrait of
her as 'la vicomtesse Gaspard de Réveillon' reflected the
fascination exerted on him by her intelligence, gaiety
and wit. She was the same age as Marie Nordlinger,
twenty-three, and had been brought up by her widowed
mother, the Princesse de Brancoven, partly in Paris,
partly at the family villa at Amphion on Lake Geneva,
with her sister, Hélène, Princesse de Chimay, and her
brother, Constantin. She had married in August 1897,
and her first published poem appeared the following
February in *La Revue de Paris*. Her unconventional
behaviour, volubility, and especially her support for
Dreyfus, met with the disapproval of the older generation
who found her self-assurance intolerable. Proust was
charmed by her; he felt she shared his own awareness of
other people's idiosyncrasies, and that she too had the
poetic gift of seeing beneath the surface of things, a gift,
he noted, 'which exists in people of superior powers' –
such people, he thought, betray their superiority in the
difficulty they find in sleeping, in laziness, in squander-
ing their talents, also carelessness, outbursts of temper,
neuralgia, egotism, passionate tenderness and excessive
nervous sensibility.[2]

*

Just before Christmas Reynaldo and his mother moved from the rue du Cirque to No 9, rue Alfred de Vigny, not far from Mme Lemaire's studio in the rue Monceau. He kept Marie up to date with the progress of his opera, *La Carmélite*, which he had begun so nervously. The song he wrote for Mme Sarah's revival of an old play by Octave Feuillet, *Dalila*, was appreciated, though the production was not a success. In May, however, her performance of *Hamlet* brought her rave notices from some critics, while others disagreed about her interpretation. When the company went to London in June, the reviewer in *Punch* thought parts of it excellent – Mme Sarah began as a precocious child brought up by an injudicious mother and grew in dignity as the play progressed. Reynaldo found her unforgettably lovely as she lay dead in Osric's arms at the end of the evening.

In May, too, there was another first night, of a new opera by Massenet at the Opéra-Comique. Reynaldo had just taken over the music column in *La Presse* and reviewed *Cendrillon* as one of his first professional engagements as a journalist. With all he owed to Massenet in friendship and encouragement, his reaction can only be called lukewarm. In further articles he pleaded for more French music to be performed, and more support for young musicians; also for more operettas at the forthcoming Paris Exhibition, especially work by Offenbach, Lecocq, Hervé and Chabrier. He thought Paris had too few theatres suitable for music making. There were, in effect, only three, the Renaissance, the Opéra-Comique and the Opéra. He heartily disliked the Opéra – he thought it nothing but a monument, a meeting place for socializing, its acoustics were appalling and it was too big to enable artists to make contact with the audience.

On 3 October Wagner's *Tristan und Isolde* was performed at the Opéra, conducted by Lamoureux, with Félia Litvinne and Brema in the title roles. Reynaldo was evidently stunned by the passion and surge of the music; he praised 'this stupendous work' – the marvellous prelude to Act I, the Love Duet in Act II, and the Liebestod at the end of Act III. As Reynaldo's Tuesday column appeared each week, a copy of *La Presse* was sent to Hamburg where Marie meticulously mounted each cutting on a handsome piece of taffeta, chintz or Liberty print, so that in a year or two, when Marcel suggested that some of the articles should be reprinted in book form, Reynaldo, who had kept no copies himself, appealed to Marie for the loan of hers.[3]

In August Marie went home for a holiday in the Isle of Man, and Reynaldo spent the month working quietly at Versailles. To Maria de Madrazo, back in Paris with her husband after their wedding journey to the United States, he sent two impassioned letters about the retrial of Dreyfus, which began on 9 August in the Breton garrison town of Rennes. All the old recriminations were reawakened. The retrial lasted twenty-five days. At the end of it, by a vote of five to two, and in spite of the evidence of the handwriting experts, Dreyfus was again found guilty but with 'extenuating circumstances'. Ten days later the President of the Republic remitted the rest of his sentence, but it took a further seven years before justice was finally done.[4]

Marcel and his parents were in Evian; Dr and Mme Proust returned to Paris on 9 September, the day of the Rennes verdict, leaving Marcel at the Hôtel Splendide for a further month's holiday. The twenty-one long letters to his mother which have survived give an entertaining and detailed commentary on his activities, as well as showing the close communion of mind and heart between son and mother. Marcel's affection for his mother, and her unselfish devotion, are evident in the drafts he wrote for his novel about the old age of Jean's parents.

On holiday at Evian, Marcel's time was almost entirely taken up with social entertainments and visits while his letters to Mme Proust were full of complaints about his health and his inability to keep within his allowance. In matters of finance and health, he wrote as though he were an unsophisticated adolescent instead of a man of twenty-eight. His writing was making little progress. In four years he had accumulated an inchoate mass of material, character sketches and poetic ideas, and what had originally been intended as the story of a writer's development (the author C whom Jean and Henri met in Beg-Meil) had become instead a semi-autobiography, a saga without focus or plan.

The theme of unconscious memory recapturing through the senses the eternal essence of time, with which he would frame the narrator's story in *The Search*, was clearer in his mind after the weeks spent at Evian. In a hastily written draft for his novel, he described Jean driving despondently into Geneva one afternoon. He could see the lake at the end of the road in all its length; the streaks of white foam left on the water by the boats suddenly reminded him of carriage drives by the sea, alone or with Henri, or with Henri's parents, and memories of their holiday in Normandy or Brittany which he had thought unusable filled his mind, so that he no longer needed to try and discover beauty in the lake scene actually in front of him. It had become an image of a life lived long before, imprinted on his heart and brought back, not by a conscious effort of mind but fortuitously – it was 'the transmutation of memory into a reality directly felt'.[5] There are other drafts of involuntary memories in *Jean Santeuil*, using the pronoun 'I' instead of 'Jean'. Did the secret of happiness and joy, he wondered, lie for the poet 'in that invisible substance we call the imagination . . . which is perhaps the source of all our joy, something we find in books but only with difficulty in things around us . . . something which gives us a glimpse of eternity?' Here was more than a hint of the discovery made in *Time Regained* of salvation through art – the writing of an original work.

For the task Proust had set himself, the search for a way to express his ideas and feelings about memory and imagination, he found inspiration and guidance in Ruskin's work. By the end of September, when the season at Evian was over, he had more time for reading. He asked his mother to send him La Sizeranne's book about Ruskin so that he could 'look at the mountains through the eyes of this great man'. There is no evidence that the book was ever sent to Evian. What is certain is that as soon as Marcel got home he immersed himself in the study of Ruskin's work, reading his autobiography, *Præterita* (literally, *Time Past* – a prophetic title), Collingwood's *Life of Ruskin*, *The Seven Lamps of Architecture* and *Lectures on Architecture and Painting*.

Early in December Reynaldo, busy with preparations for a long stay in Italy with his mother, wrote in haste to Marie. 'Marcel will write to you one day soon . . . he wants to ask for I don't know what information about Ruskin. He is much occupied with this personage and is translating the fourth chapter of his book on Amiens.' A week or so later Marcel's letter reached her in Manchester: 'Mademoiselle, How annoying that you are not in Paris, and how annoying that when you were here we knew each other so slightly and I benefited so little thereby.' He thanked her for a charming and sympathetic letter, confessing that, in spite of his poor health, he had been working 'for a considerable time on a very long and exacting piece of work, but without completing anything. And there are times when I wonder whether I am not, like Dorothea Brooke's husband in *Middlemarch*, amassing ruins.'[6] During the past fortnight, he told her, he had been busy with something quite different to what he usually wrote, about Ruskin and certain cathedrals, and he promised to send her a copy of his article if it ever appeared in print.

The fourth and final chapter of *The Bible of Amiens* is the only one directly concerned with the cathedral, and then principally with one section of it, the quatrefoils of the west porch and façade, because Ruskin hated the modern restoration of much of the building. The first three chapters give the historical background to the building of the cathedral by the Franks in the thirteenth century; then the history of the Franks and Saint Geneviève, patron saint of Paris; and, in Chapter Three, an account of Saint Jerome and his translation of the Bible into the vernacular. Amiens was the only cathedral to which Ruskin devoted an entire book.

With the help of his mother Marcel began work on his translation. At the beginning of December he asked Pierre Lavallée, who worked at the Bibliothèque de l'Institut, for the loan of a copy of Ruskin's *The Queen of the Air*. The book was not available, so Marie, at Reynaldo's request, sent her own annotated copy to Paris. Reynaldo thanked her on Marcel's behalf in a brief letter dated 23 December: 'I'm hoping to leave for Rome in a week. Marcel was very touched at receiving a book with annotations. He would have thanked you before now if his wretched health didn't play fiendish tricks on him every day. Sarah is sublime every evening. How many of us can say the same? Affectueusement à toi, R.'

While La Sizeranne's book contained only a passing reference to *The Bible of Amiens*, it did include several long passages from *The Queen of the Air*. Marcel must have been grateful for Marie's notes as an aid to understanding what Ruskin himself called 'the coruscation of a perpetually active mind'. He copied into the school exercise book he used for his notes a passage from Collingwood's *Life of Ruskin*: 'In 1865 Ruskin had told his listeners at Bradford that Greek religion was not, as commonly supposed, the worship of Beauty, but of Wisdom and Power. They did not, in their great age, worship Venus but Apollo and Athena.' Athena, goddess of wind and clouds, was the spirit of creation and will, a formative and decisive power, directress of the imagination.

In a chapter on Ruskin's aesthetic and political ideas, La Sizeranne paraphrased Ruskin's definition of the imagination in *Modern Painters*[7] – its role was 'to reach by intuition and intensity of gaze (not by reasoning but by its authoritative opening and revealing power) a more essential truth than is seen at the surface of things'. Paragraphs like this, echoing the thoughts Proust had tried to put into words in the drafts of his novel, together with Ruskin's poetic descriptions, his love of Gothic architecture and the craftsmen who made it, his insights into the great innovative artists, Giotto, Veronese, Tintoretto, above all Turner – these attributes were more than enough to make him the object of Marcel's close study for the next four years. They were both engaged in the same search for the reality behind appearances and the nature of the creative act. What they shared, and Proust acknowledged his debt to the

79

end of his life, was a quality of vision, a love of language, a compulsive need to know – they saw, felt and wrote in the same way, with an emphasis on imagination and instinct and the importance of memory.

8

A Passion for Ruskin

John Ruskin died at Brantwood, his home near Coniston, on 20 January 1900, in his eighty-first year. Marcel wrote to Marie at once, apologizing as usual for not replying sooner owing to ill health and thanking her for *The Queen of the Air*, which she had sent him. 'When I heard of the death of Ruskin it was to you, more than to anyone else, whom I wished to express my sorrow, a healthy sorrow nevertheless and full of consolation, for when I see how mightily this dead man lives, how much more truly I admire him, listen to him, strive to understand and obey him than I do many living men, I know how slight a thing death is . . . Just imagine that when you sent me the little book by Ruskin with your graceful annotations interspersed on every page, I had just written some sentences about a work of Ruskin's which I have now forgotten (but will send you when they appear and which went something like this: "In this way he gives us pleasure, as do those people who send us something they have used for themselves for a long time without ever intending to give it away, and it is these very presents which are most prized by sensitive souls." And a moment later, I received a book bearing the signs of your personal use, so delicate a gift – and actually a book by Ruskin – O pre-established harmonies![1] Has Reynaldo told you how, owing to that wicked Ruskin having forbidden his books to be translated into French, my poor translations cannot be published?[2] But I shall quote long extracts from them in some articles I am doing about him.'

On 27 January a brief obituary notice on Ruskin by Proust was published in 'La Chronique des arts et de la curiosité' in *La Gazette des beaux arts*; this was followed by a short article in *Le Figaro* on 13 February in which he wondered what Ruskin would have written about the cathedrals of Rouen and Chartres if he had continued the series of books of which *The Bible of Amiens* was the first. By a combination of luck and hard work, and with the wholehearted collaboration of his mother, Marcel had found a subject – and a market. In the four months since his return from Evian the previous October he had read in English (and claimed to know by heart!) five of Ruskin's books, as he told Marie in a letter postmarked 8 February. He thanked her again 'for everything, so many exquisite thoughts and for the precious articles you sent . . . What interests me most just now is what he [Ruskin] has written about French cathedrals (except Amiens) and apart from *The Seven Lamps of Architecture*, *The Bible of Amiens*, *Val d'Arno*, *Lectures on Architecture and Painting* and *Præterita*, for I know these books by heart. But if you should ever read anything of his about poetry or architecture in other works or lectures about Chartres, Abbeville, Rheims, Rouen, etc., this would greatly interest me . . . All my work is finished and if, even ten years hence, you were to come across a single line by him on these subjects, it would still interest me just as much as it does today.' Marcel was mistaken in thinking his work on Ruskin was finished – it had only just begun and was to occupy him for the next five years, during which time he read, and meditated upon, nearly all Ruskin's vast oeuvre, and much else besides.

With her reply to Marcel's letter, Marie enclosed some verses she had written after her visit to Chartres in July

1898. Marcel wrote at the end of February to thank her. 'Your verses are charming and evoke in my memory the lovely spring posy you once brought me from one of your excursions, which my hay fever prevented me from imitating. But you are a poet and need not go into the fields to gather flowers. Don't complain about not having learnt. There is nothing to know. Even what is called technical facility is not strictly speaking knowledge, because it does not exist outside the mysterious associations of our memory and the intuitive skill of our inventiveness when dealing with words. Knowledge, in the sense of something that can be learnt, as in science, something ready-made and extraneous to ourselves, is non-existent in art. On the contrary, it is only when the scientific relations between words have vanished from our minds and taken on a life in which the chemical elements are forgotten in a new individuality that the technique, the skill that discerns their dislikes, gratifies their wishes, recognizes their beauty, handles their forms, groups their affinities, can begin . . . Victor Hugo, whose Shakespeare I'm afraid I do not like, says: "Car le mot, qu'on le sache, est un être vivant." You know it. Moreover you love words, you do them no harm . . . And your horror of yellow is an altogether exquisite symphony in yellow.'[3]

'The mysterious associations of our memory and the intuitive skill of our inventiveness when dealing with words . . . Knowledge is non-existent in art . . .' Proust had already expressed similar ideas in his article 'Contre l'obscurité' in 1896. Theories, he maintained, were no use to poet or novelist. An artist probed as deeply into the nature of things as a metaphysician, not with the help of philosophy or reasoning but by an instinctive power. 'It is the age-old and mysterious affinities between our maternal tongue and our sensibility which create a sort of hidden music . . .'

In April the *Mercure de France* published the first of Proust's essays on Ruskin; in 'Ruskin à Notre-Dame d'Amiens' he quoted, in a footnote, a comparison between the statues on the west front of Chartres cathedral and the Madonna of the Hawthorns at the door of the south transept at Amiens. This came from a lecture by Ruskin in *The Two Paths*, which had been mentioned in the *Bulletin de l'Union pour l'action morale* in July 1896. Proust commented on Ruskin's preference for the dignified, delicate charm of the sculptured queens at Chartres and added: 'If I allude here to Ruskin's preference, it is because *The Two Paths* dates from 1858 and *The Bible of Amiens* from 1885 . . . I thought you would enjoy *The Bible of Amiens* more when you realized that he had meditated these things over a long period of time, so that they expressed his deepest thoughts and the gift he was offering to you was one of those most precious to people who love, consisting as it does of objects which he had used only for himself, with no intention of ever giving them away. In writing his book, Ruskin was not writing for you, he was simply publishing his memories and opening his heart to you.' Marcel referred to this passage in his letter to Marie in January.

When the preface to *La Bible d'Amiens* was published in 1903, the comparison between the statues at Chartres and the Amiens Madonna was no longer a footnote but included in the preface, and in the complete book (1904) Proust translated five paragraphs from the lecture in a three-page footnote to Chapter Four, showing how much importance he attached to it. The affinities he now discovered between his own thought and Ruskin's fired his enthusiasm, especially the significance of memory for an artist. He realized that Robert de la Sizeranne was mistaken when he described Ruskin as a lover of beauty for its own sake rather than a moralist who thought of beauty as a revelation of divine purpose and a means of discovering truth.

Sincerity, dedication and enjoyment are necessary for the creation of a work of art, Ruskin wrote in *The Two Paths*: 'Ask yourselves what is the leading motive which actuates you while you are at work – If it be love of that which your work represents . . . then the Spirit is upon you . . . But if, on the other hand, it is petty self-complacency in your own skill, trust in precepts or laws, hope for academical or popular approbation, or avarice of wealth – it is quite possible you may win the applause, the position, the fortune you desire, but one touch of the true art you will never lay on canvas or on stone as long as you live.'

Here was one answer to a question Marcel had asked himself in *Jean Santeuil*: Could what he wrote be any good if he enjoyed writing so much? He had already chosen what Ruskin called 'the true path' – he had written about what interested him and the things he loved – memories of his childhood and adolescence, the pleasures of the mind and the senses, the fascinating behaviour of other people, but he had not been able to weld them into a story. Ruskin gave him a clue: 'You observe that I always say interpretation, never imitation . . . Good art rarely imitates – [it] always consists of two things: first, the observation of fact; secondly the manifesting of human design and authority in the way that fact is told. Great and good art must combine the two' (para. 19). A choice between the two paths must be made; yet, as Proust read later in *St Mark's Rest*, Ruskin insisted that no true disciple of his would ever be a

'Ruskinian' – an artist must follow his own instincts and find his own truth.

Henry James was once asked at a dinner party where he got ideas for his novels. He explained that a stray suggestion, a word, even a vague echo could start a train of thought in a novelist's imagination as though it had been pricked by a sharp pin – 'one's subject is the merest grain, the seed transplanted to richer soil'.[4] The two paths described in *Swann's Way* are very different from Ruskin's, yet they are an illustration of Ruskin's precepts. The path to Méséglise and the path to Guermantes were, Proust wrote, the deepest layer of his mental soil, the firm ground where he felt secure and where he began his search for the truth which he and Ruskin believed lay in unconscious memories which could only be brought to light by hard work and love. The two paths eventually lead to the discovery of his vocation.

In *Præterita* Ruskin described how, when he was nearly forty, he had had a moment of revelation, an experience of heightened perception, which led him to reject the rigid Calvinism in which he had been reared. One Sunday morning during the autumn of 1858, after attending a simple service in a country chapel on the outskirts of Turin, he walked back into the city and went into the art gallery where Veronese's painting of *Solomon and the Queen of Sheba* glowed in the afternoon light; through the open window floated the sounds of military music from the courtyard below. The perfect colour and sound gradually asserted their power on him, and convinced him 'that things done delightfully and rightly, were always done by the help and in the Spirit of God. Of course that hour's meditation in the gallery of Turin only concluded the courses of thought that had

been leading me to such end through many years.'[5]
There was no sudden enlightenment for Proust either;
his attempts to describe his own 'privileged moments'
went back to the very beginning of *Jean Santeuil* in 1895
and culminated in the brilliant *coup de théâtre* of the biscuit dipped into a cup of lime tea in *Swann's Way*. His
'search' for his vocation took almost as long as Ruskin's
in *Modern Painters*, which, like *The Search*, was published in several volumes over many years – 1843 to 1860
– with other works and collections appearing in the
meantime.

Marcel celebrated his cult of Ruskin by visiting the
cathedrals which Ruskin loved; Chartres he had known
since childhood, Amiens was easily accessible, and a few
weeks after Ruskin's death he went off to Rouen with his
friends Léon and Madeleine Yeatman, to try and find a
tiny sculptured figure, lost among hundreds of other
little figures, above the Bookseller's door of the cathedral, described and drawn by Ruskin in *The Seven Lamps
of Architecture*. The crude carving was a memorial to the
pleasure taken in his work by the unknown medieval
craftsman, and to Ruskin's own pleasure in it. Marcel's
description of the vast cathedral soaring into the sunshine, with its angels, kings, saints and apostles, 'the
stone hosts of the mystic city', has a distinct Ruskinian
flavour. 'What is individual in each of us,' he wrote, 'does
not die but lives in the memory of God and will rise
again . . . Who is right, the gravedigger or Hamlet, when
the one sees a skull, and the other remembers a man of
fantasies? Science may say the gravedigger; but it takes
no account of Shakespeare, who kept alive the memory
of the fantasies long after the skull had crumbled.'

*

Reynaldo's tribute to Marcel's interest in Ruskin was a wordless chorale for women's voices with harp accompaniment, *Les Muses pleurant la mort de Ruskin*.[6] This was probably written during his four months' stay in Rome. He and his mother arrived at the Grand Hotel del Quirinale early in January and he wrote at once to Marie to say that he had already found much to admire but, like other illustrious travellers before him – Ruskin, George Sand, George Eliot, Goethe – he was less than enchanted with modern Rome and expressed himself forcibly on the subject in his letters to Marie and to his sister.

He was reading Stendhal's two books on Italy, also Suetonius, Saint-Simon and the Abbé Fénelon, the last two authors as background for his opera, which was making slow but steady progress. He finished a collection of songs, *Etudes latines*, settings of ten poems from an early volume by the Parnassian poet and scholar, Leconte de Lisle. Marie remembered a discussion with Reynaldo and Marcel two years previously about his *Poèmes barbares*. Their 'harmonieuse volupté', which had been a revelation to her, was familiar to Marcel since his adolescence when Leconte de Lisle had been his favourite poet. Reynaldo's music, echoing ancient instruments, was in a very different mode to that of *Les Chansons grises*.

To Marie he wrote in the middle of March: 'I've been spending my time here correcting the proofs of my *Latin Studies,* and I've ventured to inscribe your name on one of them, after I finally fixed on "Salinum", in which the poet is celebrating quite simply the pleasures he enjoys when he is at leisure, the cult of the Muses and a peaceful country existence. The accompaniment is for one hand only!'

In the Vatican he particularly admired the statue of a youth in the Sala Rotunda – Antinous, beloved of Emperor Hadrian, drowned in the Nile at the age of seventeen. 'The Graces saved him from growing old,' he wrote in his journal; 'this throng of heroes and gods is a bittersweet pleasure of mingled regrets and vain hopes, like Ganymede, who, carried away by the Eagle of Genius, caught a brief glimpse of Olympus. But a cultured, solitary spirit, who suffers the misfortune of not being like all the others, is less fortunate than the shepherd, he struggles free and falls to earth.' There is no hint of melancholy in the postcard of the Sala Rotonda he sent to Manchester on 17 April, not knowing that Marie was already on her way to join her aunt, Mrs Hinrichsen, in Milan.

On 26 April an invitation arrived from Reynaldo and Mme Hahn. 'Maman would be happy if you would come and spend a few days in Rome with her und mich,' he wrote. 'Ist es möglich? If you agree, I think the best arrangement would be that you come away at once and spend a few days here, then I shall take you back to Florence, probably with Coco, who is anxious to go there; you can finish off your holiday there, and I may perhaps (though there is a large question-mark here) go on to Venice where I know Marcel intends to go . . . Attention! Je prévois que la télégraphe va fonctionner!!!' All was resolved in the end and Marie joined her cousin and aunt in Rome for a few hectic days, as Marie explained: 'Mrs Hinrichsen, who knew Rome well, preferred the cooler air of Florence and Fiesole, where her friends, the art historian Abe Warburg, and his wife, were then living. Rome was certainly anything but cool, the more so since we didn't waste a minute . . . My cousin was a perfect guide, ruthless regarding standardized sight-seeing, but we saw the Campagna at sunrise and the Coliseum by moonlight.

'And then, one night, we took a train for Florence, to collect my aunt Caro and proceed to Venice. I little suspected the surprise in store for me when, during the journey, at dawn, my cousin roused me with: "Wake up, we're getting near to Pisa, why not spend the morning there?" After the heat and tumult of Rome, this was refreshment indeed. We walked in silence, drinking in the pure morning air, far aloft the song of a rising lark, the sound of a distant angelus. Gradually we approached the spot where, as he said, four flowers of marble and of stone cluster in the city's centre; from the Baptistery, beyond the Leaning Tower, into the cloudless sky – he sang, hailing the age-long echo, again and again until the heavens rang with man-made melody.

'During the fifty years of our friendship we walked together many times, in many places, many moods, in sunshine and in rain; in London, Rome and Venice, by Hamburg's northern waterways; in Paris, most of all, in every corner of the park at Versailles, in Rheims from the chalky Champagne caves to the top of the tall cathedral towers, from Dieppe down to the lonely graves in the cliff top cemetery at Varangeville. Still, now looking back, our walk in the Paradise garden of Pisa remains beyond compare.'

Marie Nordlinger; pastel portrait by Federico de Madrazo, Hamburg, 1902

Above: Reynaldo Hahn; portrait
in oils by Federico de Madrazo,
Hamburg, 1902

Right: Reynaldo Hahn in Hamburg with
Herr Lutz, tutor to his sister Isabel's
children, c. 1902

Marie in her studio at Gladville, working on the coat of arms
for the Manchester Technical College, 1902

Marcel Proust in Venice, 1900

9
Venice

A letter from Marcel, sent to Florence, followed Marie to Venice. It began: 'Chère amie, I have been so ill I couldn't write . . .' Had he thanked her, he asked, for *The Queen of the Air*? He had intended to send her a copy of the magazine with his April article on Ruskin, as her name was mentioned in one of the footnotes, but, he added in a PS: 'I have this moment received your card saying you are in Florence. So as not to delay in sending the Review I am simply enclosing a cutting . . . Let me know if you go to Venice, for it is possible that I may go there. Alas, hay fever and the flowers forbid Florence.' The cutting read: 'Miss Marie Nordlinger, the distinguished English artist, has brought to my notice a letter by Ruskin in which Victor Hugo's novel, *Notre-Dame de Paris*, is described as the scum of French literature'! Marie pasted the cutting on to the letter and noted: 'Received in Venice – he arrived next day.' He and Marie set to work in the shadow of St Mark's on the translation of *The Bible of Amiens*, though she could not remember afterwards which part exactly they were translating. Her memories of Venice were coloured by the fact that it was Reynaldo and not Marcel with whom she was emotionally involved. If she was disappointed in the Venetian episode in *The Fugitive* it was perhaps because her Venice, and Ruskin's, were enshrined in the preface and notes to *La Bible d'Amiens* and not in *The Search*.

This was her first visit to the city where her father had spent his boyhood. We do not know where she and her aunt stayed though her sister, Clara, remembered that

Tante Caro always went to one of the German *pensioni* – there were two along the Riva degli Schiavoni and one near the Rialto Bridge. Nor do we know whether Reynaldo was with them. He may have stayed with the Fortunys at their Venetian home, as Signora Fortuny was a sister of Reynaldo's new brother-in-law, Raimondo de Madrazo. Marcel and his mother were probably at the Danieli, just near the Piazzetta.

For Reynaldo it was the first of many visits. He fell in love with Venice the first morning when, standing on the Piazzetta, he looked at St Mark's Cathedral: 'At first sight (that's just a *façon de parler,* for I have looked at everything) all this piling on of richness and colour which is so much to my liking, is eclipsed by those four heavenly horses, so redolent of the ancient world . . .' Four poetic paragraphs on the colours and shapes of the glorious façade end with the irreverent comment: 'vestibule (first cupola on the right) above the door, a curious bedroom scene. This lady is in danger of committing an indiscretion!' As well as looking, Reynaldo listened, with his musician's ear; he absorbed the Venetian dialect so that he could reproduce it perfectly. For him it was the true language of love, eternally youthful, amorous, racy and graceful; he learnt to speak it like a native and the following year used it for his song cycle, *Venezia*. He would have liked to write a work for the theatre using it.

As for pictures, he and Marie were especially enthusiastic about those of Tintoretto. Ruskin had a great deal to say, in the Index to *The Stones of Venice,* about the series of paintings by Tintoretto in the Scuola di San Rocco. He advised visitors to San Rocco to go there early in the morning, as this was the only time when some of them could be seen. It was unlikely that Marcel accompanied his friends and the early-rising Tante Caro to San Rocco. When the cousins visited the Canareggio district, the old Jewish quarter, where Selmar Nordlinger's family had lived, they were thrilled to find Tintoretto's parish church, Santa Maria dell'Orto, one of the finest Gothic churches in the city, in which the artist had been buried. It contained four important paintings by him, one of which Reynaldo admired more than any of the others. He devoted a whole page of his journal to *The Worship of the Golden Calf.* They went, of course, to the Accademia to see the pictures by Veronese, Tintoretto and Titian. In Room VIII there hung Bellini's *Procession in the Piazza San Marco* of 1496, and Carpaccio's *Miracle of the Holy Cross,* painted two years before. There was no mention of Carpaccio in *The Stones of Venice* because Ruskin had only discovered this painter in 1869, but a whole chapter in *St Mark's Rest* was devoted to him. When Marcel came to write about Venice and Carpaccio in *The Fugitive* he gave a detailed description of *The Miracle of the Holy Cross,* with its panoramic view of the Grand Canal and the old, wooden Rialto Bridge, showing Venice at its most colourful and crowded. Young men in rich brocades (which Fortuny had reproduced for his ladies' gowns) stand beneath the loggia, on the canal itself elegant gondoliers in plumed caps ferry gaily dressed passengers. Banners flutter and pink chimneys shaped like tulips punctuate the blue sky.[1]

While Marie and Reynaldo were busy every morning visiting churches and palaces, several afternoons were passed by Marie and Marcel in the Baptistery of the Cathedral, 'whose astonishing coolness,' wrote Marcel, 'is so delightful on a scorching hot Venetian afternoon. It is, in its way, a sort of Ruskinian Holy of Holies'; they could not have chosen a more appropriate place in which to work. Marcel's longing to visit Italy had been aroused by Ruskin's books – the *Val d'Arno, Giotto and His Works in Padua,* as well as *The Stones of Venice* and *St Mark's Rest.* 'Those blessed days when, with some other disciples in spirit and in truth of the Master [Ruskin], we went round Venice by gondola, listening to his preaching at the waters' edge, and landing at each of the temples which seemed to rise from the sea to offer us the object of his descriptions and the very image of his thought, so as to give life to his books, whose immortal reflections shine over these temples today.' Marie added: 'These lines might well be attributed to Ruskin, were they not to be found on page 245 of *La Bible d'Amiens,* in one of the most striking of Proust's many striking footnotes. Nor can I forget, and this he recalls in his preface, how, during an afternoon of sudden darkness and storm, we sought sanctuary within St Mark's, and while I read an appropriate passage from *The Stones of Venice* Marcel stood motionless, wholly rapt, entranced.' The vast church was described by Ruskin in the chapter about St Mark's in *The Stones of Venice* as 'a great Book of Common Prayer; the mosaics were its illuminations, and the common people were taught their Scripture history by means of them . . . they had no other Bible.'[2] Marie improvised a translation for Marcel of Ruskin's majestic prose and read the last paragraph of the chapter which he quoted afterwards in his preface.

However, as Marie noted, their holiday was by no means Ruskin all the time. 'We explored the galleries and churches, enjoyed endless sights and sounds, meeting Marcel's mother and my aunt at Florian's on the Piazza for an ice, "un granito", or coffee at Quadri's across the way. Nothing escaped Marcel, grave or gay, he revelled in every minute. It was there he dubbed the pigeons "lilacs of the animal kingdom". At sundown we met again, "per una sgondolata" on the lagoon, with Reynaldo singing Gounod's 'Biondina Bella', "Venise la rouge, pas un bateau qui bouge," or some old Venetian folk-song. Venice, for Marcel, was a dream come true, a "fountain and a shrine". For me, as my father's birth-place, it was endowed with much reality, and for Reynaldo, reality and dream merged in the possibility of an opera. We climbed one day to the top of the Campanile, Marcel perambulating below, and from our vantage point planned scenery, costumes – should it be fifteenth or eighteenth century, we wondered? We gave auditions alternately to Carpaccio, Caruso, Guardi, Longhi, Calvé and Canaletto, and then we came to the eternal, inevitable problem of a librettist and – "there is no da Ponte today" brought us down to earth.'

The 'blessed days' came to an end. Mrs Hinrichsen and Marie were the first to leave; they went on to Munich before returning to Hamburg. Reynaldo and Marcel paid a quick visit to Padua to see Giotto's frescoes in the Arena Chapel, and those by Mantegna in the nearby Eremitani, and then Reynaldo rejoined his mother in Rome. Sadly he wrote in his journal: 'Venice is a city which should be contemplated with a mind empty of pre-occupations. At the moment, mine is too tormented to enjoy the charm of everything here to the full.' And Marcel was not well; he had difficulty in breathing, could not sleep and had to stay in bed, as a Paris friend, Abel Hermant, reported when he paid a courtesy call on the Prousts at their hotel. Before the end of May they were back in Paris, which was now full of visitors for the Great Exhibition of 1900.

*

After Venice, Munich was an anticlimax, and Marie was glad to get back to work in Hamburg. 'I was now participating in some of the general work,' she wrote, 'and occasionally executing a design of my own, a buckle, a bonbonnière, for instance, in the lid of which was set an antique cameo, and a cigarette box decorated with enamelled autumn leaves. The largest individual object I made was a circular copper alms-dish about eighteen inches in diameter. It combined a variety of techniques, thus constituting a sort of metalworker's sampler. An enamelled disc, bearing a champlevé, heraldic cock on a field of blue, with white flowers, occupied the centre. Marcel, who once saw the dish in Paris in 1903, described it in the verses he wrote for me in 1904 and which exemplify the accuracy of his observation and memory when he described the central plaque and the gilt frame round it. As my technical ability increased, I became increasingly critical of my work artistically, and the urge to be independent was coupled with the need for some stimulus other than that provided by my surroundings.'

Reynaldo had been disappointed in Florence, as Marie was. After Venice, Florence seemed grey and desiccated, in spite of its prodigious picture-galleries. A card on 7 June announced that he was back in Venice, and his next long letter referred to the frustration they both felt with the circle of family and friends in Hamburg. 'Chère amie,' he wrote, 'Your letter didn't appear to me as malicious as it ought to be! You must be surrounded by horrors and grotesques! . . . Venice is still there, in her elegant and ferocious melancholy. I have spent long hours in St Mark's . . . You are surprised at my latest ideas on religion. Alas! So am I . . . Rome left a very nasty taste in my mouth and this disgust with

Catholicism has led to a profound disbelief in Christianity as a whole.'

In October Marcel returned to Venice while his family moved from 9, Boulevard Malesherbes to a flat in a quieter district, 45, rue de Courcelles. As Reynaldo was busy with his second opera, Coco de Madrazo went to Venice with Marcel for a week. Coco had been immersed in his painting studies in Rome in May and was now free and happy to act as Marcel's companion while Mme Proust arranged the new flat. They stayed at the Hôtel de l'Europe, a fifteenth-century palace, on the Grand Canal within easy reach of St Mark's.

They spent some time in the Scuola San Giorgio, examining the series of pictures by Carpaccio which cover its walls. Marcel was working on Chapter III of *The Bible of Amiens*, as he wrote at the beginning of a long footnote: 'The best place to read this chapter is the church of San Giorgio degli Schiavoni in Venice . . . where you can see, when the sun shines on them, the pictures which Carpaccio devoted to St Jerome. You must take with you *St Mark's Rest* and read the entire chapter of which I give here a long extract.' Ruskin's description of the little chapel, tucked away on its narrow canal from the busy Riva degli Schiavoni, admirably captured the atmosphere of this delightful place, which had hardly changed since Ruskin was there in 1876–7. Proust – and Ruskin – were charmed by Carpaccio's colours and intricate patterns, and his humour, especially in the picture showing St Jerome introducing his lion into the garden of a monastery. Marcel translated six dense paragraphs of Ruskin's amusing description of timid monks flying in terror from 'the delicately smiling lion, his left paw raised, partly to show the thorn wound, partly in deprecation'.

'Carpaccio is precisely a painter I know very well,' Marcel wrote to Maria de Madrazo in 1916, when he wanted her advice on Fortuny gowns. 'I have passed long days at San Giorgio de' Schiavoni and in front of St Ursula (in the Accademia), I have translated everything that Ruskin has written on each of his pictures . . . there isn't a day in which I don't look at reproductions of Carpaccio.' Marianito de Fortuny was Coco's cousin; he had just begun to design the fabrics which became immensely fashionable. He discovered a way of reproducing the medieval patterns which Carpaccio showed on the garments worn by young people in fifteenth-century Venice. Marie had been asked to stay in Venice and work with Fortuny on the new designs, but the family did not consider him a suitable employer for her.

Marcel and Coco made another Ruskinian pilgrimage during their October holiday, to the little island of San Lazzaro, where Marcel signed the visitors' book on 19 October. This had been one of Ruskin's favourite retreats. It was quiet, there was a lovely view of Venice over the lagoon, and the oleanders in the cloister garden were superb. Ruskin enjoyed speaking Italian with the Armenian monks and kept in touch with them when he returned to England. In 1900 there still hung in the library a framed letter from Ruskin to Father Jacopo, in which he jokingly suggested that the monks should leave Venice and build a monastery on an island in Lancaster Bay. Just as in Rouen Jullien Edouard talked about Ruskin to visitors in the church of St Ouen, so at San Lazzaro there were probably members of the fraternity who remembered conversations with Ruskin twenty-five or thirty years before.

10
Work in Progress

The Great Exhibition in Paris, 1900, celebrated the new century with a display of French achievements in the Arts and Sciences. The pavilions of thirty-nine different nations were on the Quai d'Orsay; those of the French colonies and protectorates, a source of great national pride, were grouped round the Trocadéro. One of the most surprising pavilions, however, was in the commercial section near Les Invalides. Its exterior walls, facing the river, were decorated with paintings of elegant Parisiennes in graceful attitudes, representing Architecture, Sculpture and Painting, under a frieze of enormous painted orchids. The artist was Georges de Feure and the building Bing's Maison de l'Art Nouveau.

Siegfried Bing, of German-Jewish origin, had made a name for himself as a dealer in oriental prints, porcelain and objets d'art from the Far East. His galleries at 22, rue de Provence displayed examples of the modern decorative art in which he now dealt, much of it made in the studios and workshops at the back of the building – furniture, jewellery, ceramics, paintings, leather craft and textiles. The exterior of the shop was decorated with frescoes by Frank Brangwyn, who had worked with William Morris and Burne-Jones.

The Far East was greatly in favour. The Ceylonese pavilion was crowded at teatime and the Japanese Gardens were filled with beds of iris, peonies and hydrangeas. But the Exhibition as a whole was not as successful as the one held in 1889 – while parts of it were illuminated at night, the rest was badly lit and evening attendances were poor. Theatres and places of entertainment profited by this.

The indisputable theatrical success of the year, both artistic and financial, was Sarah Bernhardt's performance in a new verse-drama written for her by her friend Edmond Rostand, author of *Cyrano de Bergerac* and *La Samaritaine*. *L'Aiglon* told the sad story of the young Prince Imperial, only son of Napoleon I. It was romantic, sentimental and brilliantly theatrical. All Parisian high society went to the first night on 17 March to applaud Mme Sarah. For an actress well over fifty and not as slim as she had once been, *L'Aiglon* was a *tour de force*. Reynaldo thought her exquisite in a white uniform in the third act. He noted how natural her performance was – magnificently so in the death scene of the last act, but even he considered that the uniform she wore in the fifth act did nothing to make her look slimmer![1]

The social success of the season, according to *Le Figaro*, was the costume ball for 600 guests given by Madeleine Lemaire on Tuesday 30 May, the culmination of her Tuesday entertainments during May. The theme was, of course, the Exhibition. The hostess received her guests in front of a representation of the Porte Monumentale wearing a costume personifying the Exhibition – her cloak had a bird's eye view of the Exhibition plan and her blue and gold helmet was topped by a model of Binet's gateway with la Parisienne above it; a photographer took 300 photographs. Reynaldo and Marcel certainly missed a notable occasion.

Back in Paris at the beginning of July, Reynaldo found time in the midst of many activities to answer a long philosophical letter from Marie in Hamburg: 'On certain questions a man who is also an artist simply must not equivocate . . . What has never changed in me, and will never change, is a love of art, a passion for everything that shines and soars, a hatred of anything that lurks in the shadows.' He was working on his second opera and sent her some material he had found in Venice for the set of Act II 'so that you can continue what you have so well begun'. Another of his projects was an orchestral piece for the Concerts Colonne, a *Prometheus Triumphant* inspired by the great machines he had seen at the Palais de l'Industrie.

Much of his time was spent with Mme Sarah, who remained in Paris playing to packed houses until November when she and Coquelin took the company on an American tour. Two of the seven chapters in his book about her are devoted to his notes on their conversations from July to September – her lively, sensible, often unconventional opinions on many subjects, including her childhood, her performances and her friends, among them Oscar Wilde. In December 1898, after a performance of *Tosca* in Nice, Madame Sarah had renewed acquaintance with her former admirer and they had embraced each other in tears. Wilde had been in Rome too in 1900 for a month while Marie, Marcel and Reynaldo were in Venice, and gossip about him had spread. Wilde died on 30 November 1900, in the little hotel on the Left Bank which had been his home for the last three years of his life; he was buried in the suburban cemetery at Bagneux. On 28 November another once glamorous figure in the literary-artistic world of Paris died after a long illness. Since Mallarmé's death Reynaldo had become a close friend of Méry Laurent; in her will she left him her furniture, her papers and her country house.

During the autumn Marie's sister, Clara, announced her engagement to a distant cousin, Otto Hahn, a landowner in Mecklenburg. Early in November Marie surprised everyone by becoming engaged too, to the son of an old friend of her Tante Caro's, a young man who worked at the Arts and Crafts Museum in Hamburg. Reynaldo was staying at Versailles and wrote to her from the Hôtel des Reservoirs: 'Ma chère Marie, Do I need to say how surprised I am? No news could have surprised me more, nor given me greater happiness. I can't overlook the fact that former friendships will suffer from your marriage and that I'm losing a true friend. These good wishes come to you from Versailles, Versailles the tomb of the old world, ignorant and cruel, Versailles so blameworthy and so beautiful, today nothing but a cradle of forgetfulness and death.' Sombre thoughts for a letter of congratulation on a dear friend's engagement.

Marcel did not write to Marie when she became engaged – nor did he send her a copy of his essay on John Ruskin, published on 1 August in *La Gazette des beaux arts,* although it contained an account of his visit to Rouen with the Yeatmans about which he had written to her in February. However, their holiday in Venice and the work they had done together there was at the forefront of his mind as he continued with the translation and notes of *La Bible d'Amiens.* As frontispiece to the August article there was a reproduction of Charity, one of the Virtues painted by Giotto beneath the great frescoes in the Arena Chapel at Padua. There are fourteen allegorical figures, each Virtue facing its attendant Vice, Charity with Envy, Justice with Injustice, Faith with Infidelity and so on. In his notes to Chapter 4 of his translation Proust compared the way in which they were depicted at Padua with the figures on the capitals of the Ducal Palace which he and Marie had examined in detail, and then with those in the quatrefoils at Amiens where Faith is opposed not by Infidelity but by Idolatry, an important theme for Proust's future work.[2]

While Dr and Mme Proust went off to Evian early in August, Marcel was left at home with his books. After his return from Venice the routine of his life was gradually established. To mitigate the attacks of hay fever and asthma caused by dust or sunshine, he went to bed in the morning after the arrival of the post and daily newspaper, slept all day, and got up in time for dinner in the evening; if he was not going out to a theatre, dinner party, or to meet his friends, he worked all night at the dining-room table, with its red plush cloth, a large fire burning in the grate, his books spread out round him under the soft light of an old-fashioned Carcel lamp. Lucien Daudet remembered how he would chat with his visitors while continuing to make notes on what he had been reading. This regime meant that if he had an engagement during the day he went without sleep for thirty-six hours and was consequently exhausted and ill afterwards. Mme Proust had the task of seeing that the servants and tradesmen did not make too much noise to disturb his rest.

Marie's plans for her wedding were not going smoothly. She and her fiancé had intended to move to Paris in the spring if they could find somewhere to live. Reynaldo advised her to get in touch with the father of Edouard Risler, who was the architect for the factory at Sèvres, as her future husband, evidently a ceramics expert, would be working there. The wedding was postponed and Marie went home to Manchester in a miserable state of indecision. Reynaldo tried to cheer her up:

'Why is life so difficult for you? Are you not happy, and completely so? If you trust me you must tell me. My own life, as I've already told you, consists in producing as much as possible and being free . . . I must sacrifice everything which might put restrictions on my heart, my imagination or my actions. I can't suffer a little; I can only suffer a great deal, and deeply; so I have decided not to suffer at all . . . I hope I'm not an egoist. Here's a psychological letter for you! In reply to something you wrote, the truth is that a terrible misunderstanding arises from the fact that a man's life and a woman's cannot be happy under the same conditions . . . I've written some Venetian songs which I hope will soon appear in print and I'll send them to you as soon as they do.' He described them as 'vulgar, sentimental, extremely Grand Canal – neither the Venice of the Doges nor that of Byron or Guardi (except No. 3). This is banal, cosmopolitan, pleasure-loving Venice, floating on a tide of indolence and facile love affairs.'

Having stated his own problems he proceeded in his next letter to deal with hers. 'You know me well enough to anticipate the advice I might give you in this struggle between your heart and your reason . . . I think perhaps you were over-hasty in your decision.' Marie broke off the engagement. She returned to Manchester and to the School of Art there to work for a South Kensington diploma in metalwork.

Entries in Marie's album for 1902 show how bitterly unhappy she was; she longed to confide in her mother but did not want to worry her. There was nobody else she could talk to, so she concentrated on her work. Early in the New Year she won her first professional commission, to make the light fittings and switches for the great hall of the new Manchester College of Technology in Whitworth Street. Reynaldo as usual gave her strong encouragement: 'You will finally get the better of the family's scepticism; a number of connoisseurs have admired the photograph of your plate[3] – you are now known simply as Benvenuta,' and he began his letters to her 'Ma chère Cellina'.

In February he and his mother went to Monte Carlo so that he could work on the final pages of *La Carmélite* and attend the première of Massenet's opera *Le Jongleur de Notre-Dame*. He had taken only two books to read, he told Marie, two volumes by Sainte-Beuve because 'I can't live without this old scoundrel!' He did not return to Paris until the end of April and so missed the first night of Debussy's *Pelléas et Mélisande* at the Opéra-Comique on 29 April.

The performance was not received with enthusiasm by the critics. The reviewer in *Le Figaro* picked out six singable tunes and condemned the rest of the music as 'a nebulous ocean of sound'. Debussy's treatment of Maeterlinck's dream world, with its understated menace and unhappiness, its strong sensuality and mythical medieval setting, appealed far more to Marcel's imagination – quite apart from its links with the magic lantern story of his childhood – than it did to Reynaldo's. The latter found the experience disturbing, as he wrote to Marie: 'It is an unusual and powerful work, but in essence it is a dangerous one and has upset a lot of people, me included. All the same, I am so attached to what I have always loved – purity of form, grace and charm of expression, plain, unvarnished truth – that I shall persevere and the poor *Carmélite* will carry the weight of all my mistakes.'

He wrote from Versailles where he was preparing the score of the opera for publication and production at the end of the year. The composition of the four-act work had not been an easy task because he was scrupulous to the point of obsession – no sketches, no rough drafts, very few second thoughts, as he told Edouard Risler, his father confessor in musical matters. 'My uneasy nature would not be able to resist the written indecision of a draft, I should go demented in a week . . .' He had been browsing in the library at the Opéra where he had found, in the score of *Ascanio,* an early opera by Saint-Saëns, a musical device – the underlining of a passage for strings with tremolo – which he had recently discovered for himself.

Marie remembered an evening soon after she had been to a Sunday concert at the Conservatoire to hear a performance of Saint-Saëns' *Nuits persanes*; Reynaldo was at the piano 'picking out some of the Master's songs and waltzes to clarify some technical point for me, and Marcel, not for the first time, expressed his lack of admiration for Saint-Saëns, while Reynaldo, not for the first time either, launched into his enthusiasm for Saint-Saëns' immense technical talent (talent in the French sense of the word, implying a natural gift, plus its conscious artistic and technical skill). Reynaldo explained how, in this particular work, the technical skill was the starting point, the framework, as it were, which once established, the composer proceeded to fill with incredible masterly elaboration, whereas many composers work in the reverse way, contriving a setting after stating the basic musical idea. From the outset of their friendship, their tastes and inclinations differed widely. This is clearly borne out in their musical likes and dislikes. Nevertheless, the musical motif which permeates

The Search suggests that in spite of his comparative ignorance of the technical art of music, Marcel was a musician. The development of "the little phrase" first described in *Jean Santeuil* and culminating in the triumph of the Vinteuil septet, would virtually not have attained its perfection but for his close association with the trained composer.'

Saint-Saëns' passion for the music of Mozart had been communicated to Reynaldo, who conceived a new project – to establish an authentic French text for *Don Giovanni* which, like Mozart's other operas, was usually presented in a mutilated and truncated form. This was the beginning of a lifelong commitment to the presentation of Mozart in France. With an introduction from Saint-Saëns, Reynaldo went to see Pauline Viardot, one of the greatest singing actresses in operatic history. In 1901 Mme Viardot was eighty. In spite of growing blindness, she was full of life and enthusiasm; her voice was still strong although she had retired from the stage in 1861 and had devoted herself to teaching, first in Baden-Baden, then in Paris. She took immediate charge of the interview. 'They tell me you are Spanish,' she said and began to speak pure Andalusian at great speed. Reynaldo tried to steer the conversation to questions which interested him, but Mme Viardot wanted to hear him sing. She approved the simplicity of his style and they went on to talk about her interpretation of Donna Anna in *Don Giovanni*, a role she played as though the unhappy girl were in love with the Don, although there is nothing in the libretto to support this view.[4]

With Reynaldo away in Hamburg for the whole of the autumn in 1901, and again in the south of France from

February to April 1902 and then busy with his opera, Marcel, still working at his translation of Ruskin, made a number of new friends. Chief among them were Emmanuel and Antoine Bibesco, whom he had met several years before at the home of their Brancovan cousins, Mme de Noailles and her sister, the Princesse de Chimay. The elder brother, Emmanuel, delicate and reserved, was particularly interested in architecture and photography. Antoine, seven years younger than Marcel, had recently returned to Paris after a year's military service in his native Romania, and was studying for the diplomatic service.

Another young diplomat with whom Marcel became friendly through the Bibescos was Comte Bertrand de Salignac Fénelon. Still another new acquaintance was Comte Georges de Lauris, a writer of novels and short stories. They met at dinner parties in their favourite restaurants, Webers in the rue Royale or Larues in the place de la Madeleine, and were joined there by several young aristocrats, Armand de Guiche, Gabriel de la Rochefoucauld, Prince 'Loche' Radziwill, Louis d'Albuféra – all of them except Albuféra Dreyfusards and individualists. Marcel enjoyed their discussions and gossip, they admired his erudition, wit and psychological insights. They formed their own 'little clan' with its private language, special code words, spellings and nicknames. Fénelon was 'Nonelef', Antoine 'Téléphas', and Marcel 'Lecram', an idiom stemming perhaps from Reynaldo's youthful letters to his sisters, as Marcel made clear in a letter to Antoine on 11 November 1901, when Reynaldo was expected back from Hamburg. At Marcel's request, Reynaldo had submitted Antoine's play, *La Lutte,* to Mme Bernhardt (she rejected it). 'Reynaldo's first visit will be to Haras [Mme Sarah], his second to me,' Marcel wrote. 'If you like, I will rehearse you in our "shocking" language, so that you can surprise and charm Reynaldo.'

He and Reynaldo had their own nicknames for each other, dating at least from 1898, when Marcel wrote to 'mon petit genstil', or simply 'Genstil', and then more elaborately as 'Mossieur de Binibuls', 'le marquis de Bunibuls' and other variations such as 'Bunchnibuls', 'Hibuls', 'Buncht' and 'Puncht', and using a childish form of spelling, 'moschant' for 'méchant', 'phastigué' for 'fatigué' and so on. Many lively young people have used the same device to show their intimacy, Mozart and his sister, for instance, the Keats family and the Mitford sisters. The letters from Marcel to Reynaldo are quite different to those he sent to his other correspondents – he wrote to amuse Reynaldo, the style is relaxed, sparkling often with affection and humour (sometimes malicious), with gossip and inventive play with words. Reynaldo was aware of their special nature and always intended to publish a selection of them; as he remarked to a friend in 1938, they would show admirers of Proust's work 'something of his real nature'. Shortly before his own death in 1947 he discussed with Marie the possibility of publication.[5]

Some time during the autumn of 1901 Marcel borrowed from Robert de Billy a copy of Emile Mâle's book on medieval church architecture. In his letters to Reynaldo he now enclosed playful sketches copied from the illustrations in Mâle's book, with explanations in doggerel verse. The sketches survived without the letters; some of them were reproduced in the 1956 edition of the correspondence.

When the fine weather came in the spring, Marcel joined his friends in excursions by car to see churches and castles in the Ile de France. On Good Friday, 28 March, he, with the Bibesco brothers, Georges de Lauris, Robert de Billy and Bertrand de Fénelon, went to Saint-Leu d'Esserent near Chantilly, then on to Laon with the huge stone oxen high on the church towers and to the thirteenth-century castle at Courcy where they climbed the tower, Fénelon helping a breathless Marcel by humming the Good Friday music from Wagner's *Parsifal*.[6] Proust wrote over 100 letters in 1902 and more than half of them were to Antoine Bibesco, many of them concerned with arrangements to meet, and with his obsessive attraction to Fénelon. Even Reynaldo had not been told about the anxiety Marcel felt – he was worried that his affection for the elegant, athletic young diplomat might be interpreted as a homosexual one.

By the end of June Marcel had completed his documentation on *La Bible d'Amiens* and most of the preface. He asked Mme de Noailles if he could borrow a French bible belonging to her husband in order to finish his notes as his own bible was badly translated. In his notes he made use of Emile Mâle's meticulous scholarship, which compared each small figure or scene at Amiens with similar representations on other French cathedrals. Marcel's research into Ruskin's aesthetic and moral teaching was just as meticulous. The longer notes to the four chapters chart Proust's journey towards understanding his own mental processes as well as Ruskin's. He enjoyed Ruskin's humour in Chapter One, and in Chapter Three where he quoted at length the descriptions of Carpaccio's paintings in *St Mark's Rest*; Marcel thought that this was far from being one of the old man's best books as it was written when he had already begun to suffer from the recurrent bouts of insanity that prevented him from working in the last decade of his life.

'To what extent my spirit has been paralysed by the failures and sorrows of life is beyond my conjecture or confession,' Ruskin wrote. Proust's comment was that sorrow, according to Ruskin, was an obstacle to the full exercise of our faculties, instead of something to be used by the artist in the exercise of his craft, an idea he developed in *Time Regained* as 'fertilization by unhappiness'.

In October Marcel and Bertrand de Fénelon travelled together to Holland via Bruges. Marcel went to Dordrecht and Delft, rejoining Fénelon in Amsterdam for a week which included visits to Haarlem to see portraits by Frans Hals, and the Hague for Vermeer's *View of Delft*. Fénelon was a charming companion and Marcel's health was excellent, with not a sign of asthma; he was often out in the morning by ten o'clock, returning late in the evening, but his emotional state was still 'disastrous', he told Mme Proust, and he feared to spoil his friend's holiday with his complaints and moroseness. Soon after their return to Paris, and before Fénelon left to take up a post at the French Embassy in Constantinople, Antoine Bibesco's mother died at the family estate in Romania. He suggested complicated arrangements to meet Antoine – in Romania, or Munich perhaps, even Constantinople – but there were difficulties. Marcel's brother, Robert, had just become engaged, and the wedding, at which Marcel was to be best man, was to take place early in February 1903. Marcel had also agreed to write several articles on Paris salons for *Le Figaro*.

He had written 'portraits' for his novel too, like those he had done of Reynaldo and Anna de Noailles – one of 'Mme Jacques de Réveillon' based on the extravagant appearance and deplorable manners of the Prince de Broglie's new wife;[7] 'Miss Smitson' (*sic*) was a middle-aged Englishwoman, in real life companion to two widowed French ladies. Jean was fascinated and charmed by her accent and background; and there is a draft Marcel wrote late one evening alone in the unheated dining room of the Château d'Ermenonville, the country home of Prince 'Loche' Radziwill, when he tried to describe the faults and virtues, moral, intellectual and physical, of his friend and the uncertainties of their relationship.[8]

The longest 'portrait' – ten manuscript pages[9] – described Jean's friend Bertrand de Réveillon, who had a passion for knowledge, progress and equality, and was totally lacking in snobbery or condescension. His good breeding was inherited and unselfconscious. This was proved by his behaviour one evening when, dining with Jean in a crowded restaurant, he borrowed a fur cloak to keep Jean warm and delivered it by running along the tops of the benches along the wall, jumping gracefully over the light flexes on the way. Fénelon had performed this acrobatic feat and Proust used the episode again in *The Guermantes Way* on the foggy evening when Robert de Saint-Loup took M out to dinner.[10] There was another occasion which Proust rewrote for *The Search* when, in an angry tantrum during a visit from Fénelon and de Lauris, Marcel jumped on Fénelon's top hat and ripped out the lining. In *The Guermantes Way* M, goaded into fury by M. de Charlus' insults, did the same to the Baron's new hat.[11]

'All I am doing is not real work,' he wrote to Antoine just before Christmas, 'but simply documentation, translation, etc. It is enough to awaken my thirst for producing something – without, of course, gratifying it in any way. From the moment . . . I turned my eyes inward, towards my thoughts, I feel the complete emptiness of my life, while hundreds of characters for a novel, a thousand ideas ask me to give them body like the shades in the *Odyssey* who ask Ulysses to let them drink a little blood to bring them back to life and whom the hero disperses with his sword. I have awoken the sleeping bee and I feel more keenly his cruel sting than his impotent wings.' If ideas and characters for his 'real work' so haunted him, there were no hints in any of his letters or articles as to its nature.

He was still busy with Ruskin, negotiating with the director of *Le Mercure de France*, M. Vallette, for the publication of *La Bible d'Amiens*, at his own expense if necessary. Extracts from *La Bible d'Amiens* were to appear shortly, he hoped, in a monthly magazine. Besides his translation work, there were the celebrations in connection with Robert's engagement, and, on Wednesday 16 December, the first night of Reynaldo's opera.

André Messager conducted an excellent cast in *La Carmélite* – Emma Calvé in the name part, Marie de l'Isle as Madame de Montespan, Dufresne as Bossuet and M. Muratore as Louis XIV. Catulle Mendès' libretto did not treat the story historically but as 'une grande chanson populaire', for which Reynaldo's music can hardly have been robust enough. The critic in *Le Figaro* wrote that, while every page revealed the composer as a pupil and disciple of Massenet, with quite a few reminders of Gluck, he appeared to lack the staying-power to keep an audience interested for several hours at a stretch. As Reynaldo had anticipated, Mme Calvé was thought unsuitable as the young Louise, but the production and décor were highly praised. *La Carmélite* was the only new work in the winter season at the Opéra-Comique.

In a personal letter to one of the reviewers, written with ironic elegance, Reynaldo raised the age-old question of the competence of critics who are not practising artists: 'Reread – for I do not doubt that in your capacity as a critic you have already studied him in depth – reread Sainte-Beuve, [and] imitate the effortless grace and breeding which make his judgements so forceful, and his mockery so insolent . . . The day when you have completed, without help from anyone, a work in four acts and it is judged, you will realize what disproportion there is between what you have accomplished and what has been done by those who speak about your work, unless they are your peers . . .'[12]

Reynaldo wrote to Marie in Hamburg, where she was spending Christmas with her grandmother and aunt. '*La Carmélite* will be given at least during the whole month of January. I hope you will be able to hear it.' She arrived in Paris early in the New Year; her programme of the opera is dated 7 January 1903.

11
The Art Nouveau

'Throughout the past two years my cousin had kept me informed of the progress and impending performance of his opera,' Marie wrote, 'and I was homesick for Paris. It was with alacrity that I accepted Tante Caro's Christmas present of a couple of weeks there in January. With me went the alms-dish and one or two other things I intended to show Lalique.' She did not, after all, return to Hamburg when the two weeks were over. During January and February she and Reynaldo met frequently: notes, cards, letters and *petits bleus* flashed between her pension and the rue Alfred de Vigny, invitations to lunch, to dinner, to meet at a restaurant or the Bibliothèque Nationale, offers of theatre and concert tickets, advice on what to see and where to go.

On 10 February he wrote: 'Will you go to the theatre tonight with Coco, Rafael and me? . . . I have seen Clairin. Lalique is in Saint Louis for the exhibition and won't be back for three weeks; Clairin will then write to him and you will go to see him at once . . . How are you and do you need anything?' As soon as Lalique returned from America, Marie went again to his studio: 'He was genuinely interested and encouraging, but obdurate about giving me a job; on the other hand, he admitted conditions were changing and there was quite a possibility for an opening for a woman in the States,' and he gave her introductions to Tiffany and others. The mention of Tiffany produced a brainwave from Reynaldo: 'Go and see old Bing, tell him you're my cousin; we met at the Goncourt sale when I bought the Kakemono, tell him what Lalique said, and don't be prejudiced by some of his Art Nouveau stuff.' 'So off I went to 22, rue de Provence, and, as luck would have it, was ushered into the presence of its moving spirit. M. Bing examined my work, asked me a few patient questions and added: "We have a metal workshop upstairs, my son manages it, he is not an executant but does quite a lot of designing . . . If you care to leave your things with me he might be interested."

'Siegfried Bing had come to Paris from Hamburg as a young man and became a traveller for a firm of importers of modern Japanese pottery and lacquer. On a business journey to Japan, Mr Bing fell under the spell of the classical Japanese art to which henceforth he devoted himself wholeheartedly. His volumes of *Le Japon artistique* and other writings bear witness to the depth of his knowledge and his literary skill. Museum directors, scholars, collectors from far and wide – Messrs Burty, Goncourt, Gillot, Freer, Havemeyer, Vever, Chas J. Morse, Atherton Curtis, Koechlin, Gouse among many others – all consulted Monsieur Bing.[1]

'Within twenty-four hours of my call on M. Bing, his son, M. Marcel, telephoned, asking me to come and see him. He had obviously studied my work closely and soon enquired as to the possibility of my entering his work-shop.'

Marie started work at the Art Nouveau at the beginning of March. 'There is no denying it, the entry of a young Englishwoman into the metal-shop created some surprise, but once again, my fluent French proved the best of passports. One afternoon I was busy at the work-bench when a message came from M. Bing: "Would I please come down to the Gallery?" There I found him talking to the director of the Hamburg Kunst gewerbemuseum, Dr Brinckmann, whom I knew well, and a stranger, a slight, fairly tall figure, with a reddish Vandyck beard. We were introduced and he, in American style, repeated my name while I, reciprocating, said "Mr Freer". Apologizing for having interrupted my work, M. Bing explained: "Miss Nordlinger is a silversmith and a far better linguist than I." He begged me to interpret for his visitors: "Dr Brinckmann knows some French but no English; Mr Freer as good as no French and not a word of German and they have a good deal to say to each other." I had heard of the Detroit millionaire, the collector and friend of Whistler, and here he was, deep in discussion about Chinese and Japanese pottery, Korin, Kenzan tea-bowls, Korean Tammoku glazes. What were the Fates spinning on that afternoon in Paris? Who could have guessed that a few years later I should be the bearer of a priceless, green celadon bowl, a gift from Mr Freer to the Hamburg Museum of Decorative Art?'

In the early months of 1903 Marie did not see Marcel, occupied as he was by his brother's wedding on 2 February and the need to prepare extracts of his Ruskin translation for publication. Her memories of their col-laboration during this time were vague, but she kept some of the scribbled notes Reynaldo sent her – 'Marcel would be grateful for the meaning of tempera painting' or 'Marcel would like to know if you would be good enough to go and work with him this evening at nine. Please send word on your way home.' When she started work at the Art Nouveau studio she was, of course, fully occupied during the daytime when Marcel was usually asleep; very occasionally he went to work with her at her *pension*, and she remembered one or two sessions with him in the dining-room at the rue de Courcelles; Robert d'Humières was also giving him some help.

Parts of *La Bible d'Amiens* appeared in the February and March numbers of *La Renaissance latine*, whose editor, Constantin de Brancovan, upset Marcel by remarking that as he (Marcel) did not know any English, the translation must be full of mistakes. Marcel wrote an eight-page letter to Prince Constantin, explaining in detail the care with which he had worked: 'I do not know a word of English and I do not read it well. But after four years of working on *The Bible of Amiens* I know the whole thing by heart, and I have achieved that degree of assimilation, of absolute transparency wherein the only cloudy patches to be seen are those due not to our inadequate vision but the hopeless obscurity of the thoughts we are contemplating.' (Marcel exaggerated the time he had spent on Ruskin – it was just over three years, not four.) The letter ended: 'If there are mistakes in my work, they are in the obvious, easy parts, because the obscure parts have been meditated on, recast, thoroughly examined, for years. Yet, if you asked me in English to have a drink, I shouldn't know what you were asking me because I learnt English while I had asthma and could not speak, I learnt it by sight and don't know how to pronounce the words, nor recognize them when they are spoken. I don't claim to know English. I do claim to know Ruskin.'

Reynaldo, in an article in *Le Figaro* (1945),[2] explained Marcel's successful translations of Ruskin by attributing them to inspired guesswork, or *divination surnaturelle*; this also accounted for his ability to read the inmost thoughts of other people with great clarity and speed, not by any process of psychological discernment but by a brusque illumination, like a probing searchlight. 'I am certain,' Reynaldo wrote, 'that it was by one of these miracles that he understood the language of Ruskin, which was otherwise foreign to him. When Marie Nordlinger was not there, he turned to me to verify something he was not sure about, but of course I could not compete with my cousin, a well-educated and cultured Englishwoman, who was familiar with Ruskin's purposely esoteric style and who, in addition, had specialized technical knowledge . . . The work done with the invaluable help of Marie Nordlinger was based on a text already dictated to Marcel by *an unknown intermediary*.'

The first of Marcel's articles on Paris salons, that of Princess Mathilde, had been published in *Le Figaro* in February; the second, 'La Cour aux Lilas et l'Atelier des Roses; le Salon de Mme Madeleine Lemaire', appeared on 11 May (both were signed 'Dominique'). On the surface this article, like others in the series, was the usual gossip-columnist's mixture of anecdote, flattery and name-dropping, but readers of *The Search* can recognize without difficulty characters and episodes which would find a place in the novel – the arrival of guests at a social gathering, the vivacity and, often, the vacuity of the conversations, the reactions of the hostess, or the way in which a fashionable audience half listens to a concert while weighing up the other guests and thinking what to say about the music afterwards – all this was repeated and transformed in the seven or eight parties which punctuate the course of the novel.

Marcel was thinking of his 'wasted' youth and lost illusions – he would be thirty-two in July! 'We who for so many years now past have attended these Tuesday festivals in May – in a perfumed springtime, soft and scented then, now frozen for ever . . . In this memory-filled studio, there was once an enchantment whose lack of reality and deceptive illusion has gradually been revealed and dissipated by time.' Time, memory, illusion – the main themes of *The Search* are here, and love – in the description of Reynaldo at the piano, head thrown back, mouth melancholy and slightly disdainful, 'the most beautiful, warmest and saddest voice . . . never since Schumann has there been such beautiful music for depicting grief, tenderness and the tranquillizing effect of Nature'.[3]

Mme Lemaire's Greek ball was certainly the social event of the summer. 'The invitation was for ten o'clock on the ninth of June,' Marie wrote, '"Athens in Pericles' day", banquet, procession, dancing – costume strictly classical. Every star in every Parisian firmament was present; among the breathtakingly beautiful young women, Madame Marcel Ballot as Diana of the Chase, and Madame Letellier; famous artists like Albert Besnard and Mme Besnard, their unusual girth swathed in purple and blue. Reynaldo as Apollo, majestically bearing a lyre, and I, a multicoloured Tanagra with a tall, pointed white straw hat, slip in to the studio. And what about Marcel? Though uncertain to the last, he would surely come, and how attired? But he was nowhere to be seen until suddenly from behind a heavy velvet curtain, past which I was dancing with Guiraud de la Rivière, the unmistakable voice stopped me in my tracks, saying: "Dieu, que vous êtes belle" – and there stood Proust, in evening dress and fur-lined overcoat – better disguised that night than any other of the motley crowd!'

At the beginning of June Marcel asked Antoine Bibesco if he would help to correct the proofs of *La Bible d'Amiens*, 'which I haven't had time to go over with d'Humières and which I'm going to do with Mlle Nordlinger (a young English girl who is very fond of me) . . .' Antoine, knowing Marcel's scrupulous attention to detail, evidently could not spare the time, so Marie was enlisted to help check the manuscript and the proofs. She described her visits. 'When I first went to work with Marcel in the rue de Courcelles Mme Proust received me graciously in the heavily furnished salon, with its bronzes, plush and mahogany, but she always effaced herself, and soon Félicie would take me straight to his room, returning with an orangeade or an ice-cream and petits fours from Rabattet for me, and boiling hot coffee for Marcel. I carefully poured out the skin with the milk, having been admonished, "It's the cream, it's the best part!" Whatever the season, his room was oppressively warm and he would be swathed in Jaeger woollens and thermagene wadding.

'Our sittings lasted well into the night, scrutinizing or revising a chapter, a sentence or a single word. Orders had been given and observed that no one but M. Hahn be admitted and he rarely came. Reminiscing with Antoine Bibesco shortly before his death in 1951, he reminded me how he had once gate-crashed, but never again! Marcel preferred to keep his friends in separate compartments. Our conversations ranged far and wide. One evening I sensed his gaze riveted to a long chain I was wearing, from which hung a pair of exquisitely wrought Japanese cloisonné earrings. Without any preamble he asked: "May I touch them? No, don't remove them, tell me about them, where did Reynaldo get them? Yes, go on, I'm listening." So Ruskin was abandoned for the time being and I had to expatiate on the craft, origin, history and the various techniques of enamel. Now and again he would comment: "Yes, of course, the plaque in the centre of your alms dish, the cock on the blue ground, that's champlevé? You remember the big reliquary, was that Rhenish?" I looked at him enquiringly – "The one we passed that Sunday morning in the Louvre when we went to see the Tiara?" and he laughed long and low – he had so many ways of laughing! "The Tiara of Saitapharnes – oh what a Tiara!" Six or so years had elapsed since that Sunday when we had inspected the costly fake of which now nothing worthwhile remained save the memory, and a word added for a while to our vocabulary.'[4]

That Marie should be received so informally at the rue de Courcelles is a measure of her acceptance as a friend and helper and Marcel's need for someone reliable and sympathetic of whom his mother approved. She was now twenty-seven, independent, always conscientious, full of energy and curiosity; brought up in a liberal, free-thinking family, with innate good taste, she was never a 'feminist' or 'suffragist'; she was used to living frugally, whether as student or silversmith. She dressed simply, made her own clothes and jewellery, she loved dancing ('Alas! Reynaldo never, never danced,' she wrote in her album!) – she had brothers, was used to being teased and always to the end of her life enjoyed the company and conversation of intelligent men. Like Reynaldo, she was a loyal and generous friend.

During June and July Marcel and Marie worked steadily on the proofs of *La Bible d'Amiens*, which went to the printer at the end of August. In spite of his hay fever and social engagements, he finished the preface by the end of June – the major part consisted of the two articles already published in 1900 in *La Gazette des beaux arts*, 'Ruskin à Notre-Dame d'Amiens' and 'John Ruskin', slightly amended. Marcel wrote a brief foreword and a longer postscript to follow the second article, which ended with the sentence: 'Under what touching and tempting forms falsehood may have crept into his intel-

lectual sincerity is something we will never know . . .' In
the postscript Proust explained what he meant by this.
One particular phrase of Ruskin's had struck a chord in
his mind. In a lecture to Oxford undergraduates in 1870
on 'The Relation of Art to Religion' Ruskin had deplored
'the deadly function of art in its ministry to what, in hea-
then or Christian lands . . . is truly to be called idolatry
– the serving with the best of our hearts and minds some
dear or sad fantasy which we have made for ourselves'.
Meditation on this text would supply a major theme for
his novel.

He remembered how he and Marie had taken shelter
in the basilica of St Mark's on a stormy afternoon during
their Venice holiday and she had read to him from *The
Stones of Venice* a passage about the decline of the
Venetian Republic. 'The sins of Venice, whether in her
palace or in her piazza, were done with the Bible at her
right hand' – because St Mark's was next door to the
palace of the Doges![5] There was no logic in this, Marcel
claimed – Ruskin had been carried away by enthusiasm.
He too had stood spellbound by the glory of the mosaics
gleaming in the half-light, proud of his own erudition in
understanding the texts on the ceiling. He too had been
over-enthusiastic in his admiration for Ruskin's work –
too lazy and too respectful to discover the cause of the
confusion in Ruskin's mind when he wrote about aesthetic and moral values. Although he constantly
preached the doctrine of sincerity, Ruskin was guilty of
insincerity. The quality of his mind, the tremendous
mental energy which led him into so many digressions,
resulted in a struggle between idolatry and sincerity
which, according to Proust, takes place all the time in
those buried, unrealized regions of our personality
'where images are imprinted by the imagination, ideas

127

by the intelligence, words by the memory, and which by the continual choice we make of them determine the shape of our spiritual and moral life'. In these hidden depths Ruskin committed the sin of idolatry, not in what he said but in the way he said it – his love of words and familiarity with the Bible blurred or distorted his ideas so that he was no longer true to himself – he was not sincere. In his own attempt to take intellectual sincerity to its furthermost limits, Proust was exposing a weakness not peculiar to Ruskin but one inherent in human nature, which could be overcome, as Ruskin always taught, by discipline, dedication and love. He knew now how a writer can be misled by an undisciplined imagination, how laziness and habit can prevent him from discovering the truth about his deepest feelings. From his study of Ruskin he learnt the discipline which is the beginning of liberty. 'There is no better way,' he wrote, 'of finding out what one feels oneself than to try and recreate in one's own mind what a master has felt. The endeavour, hard as it may be, brings one's own thoughts as well as his into daylight.'

When he tried to recapture the state of mind in which he had first come to enjoy Ruskin, Marcel found he could remember only facts and nothing 'of the past buried deep beyond recall'.[6] His memory of that earlier self was frozen and could not be revived because conscious memory could not recapture the enthusiasm he had once felt. How could frozen sensations be thawed, the reality of the past be recaptured? Could the self who had read Ruskin with such uncritical pleasure be brought back to life, or the child who had walked on a spring evening along the river bank at Illiers with his parents, or the schoolboy absorbed in reading Loti and Augustin Thierry?

At the end of the preface he wrote: 'It is only when

certain periods of our life have closed for ever, when we are incapable of placing ourselves again in our former state, even for an instant, it is only then we refuse to accept that such things could be totally abolished.'[7] In the brief foreword he again took up the theme of memory. The many long notes in which he quoted passages from other works by Ruskin were to serve as a sort of improvised memory, 'a sounding board where the words of *The Bible of Amiens* could gather more force by awakening fraternal echoes'. It is only in the study of more than one work by any artist that what is permanent and fundamental in his thought becomes apparent, so the critic's task must be to help his reader grasp the essential characteristics of a writer's genius. In fact, he must go further and try to recreate the spiritual life of the artist, but, Proust added, he had not attempted to go so far in the present work. He needed, as he would show in the preface he wrote for the translation of *Sesame and Lilies*, to go beyond commentary on Ruskin's ideas and begin creative work of his own.

Before she went on holiday at the beginning of August to join her sister Connie and friends at Varengeville, near Dieppe, Marcel told Marie that he had lost all the bits of paper on which he had noted her corrections to his proofs, but he hoped to see her before she left Paris. The letter began: 'Dear Mademoiselle Marie, or would you mind "Dear Friend"?'[8] He returned some 'fine aesthetic impressions' she had sent him which, as he was so bad at languages, he found rather impenetrable! Reynaldo was staying with Mme Lemaire and Suzette in Dieppe; one of several postcards he sent Marie during the month was of the ruined eleventh-century abbey of Jumièges, which overlooks the Seine not far from Rouen, already known to Marie from her previous excursions in Normandy and certainly familiar to Marcel who wrote, in a later draft, some revealing pages about the layers of history on this enchanted site. Reynaldo was working on his revised French text for *Don Giovanni*, which he planned to give as a concert performance in Paris. He had hoped that Félia Litvinne would be able to sing for him, but she was not available so he was busy trying to replace her by an even more famous soprano, Lilli Lehmann. Mme Lehmann had sung Isolde at the Paris Opéra during the 1903 season and had met Reynaldo during her visit. She was a legendary figure in the opera world – she had been one of Wagner's original flower maidens in *Parsifal*, and both she and her mother had known the composer well. She had an enormous repertoire and was renowned as much for her Mozart performances as for those in Wagner's operas, or Offenbach, Donizettiand Beethoven. Though her voice was light she was a formidable personality, inclined to impatience with less gifted colleagues and very conscious of her abilities and experience. With Jean and Edouard de Rezské she was one of the first international opera stars to insist on singing in other languages besides her own. Reynaldo was delighted when she agreed to sing Donna Anna for him.

While Marie returned to Paris and the Art Nouveau studio after her holiday, Reynaldo went to Versailles to work without interruption and Marcel set out for Evian, stopping on the way to visit Avallon and Vézelay. After a night made sleepless by fever, he caught a train to Dijon at 6.00 a.m. to see the tombs of the Dukes of Burgundy. On the journey back from Evian in mid-October he visited Beaune and was enchanted with the fifteenth-century hospital, describing it enthusiastically in his preface to *Sésame et les lys*. In a letter to Marie he was rather less enthusiastic: 'Ma chère amie, do not think I have either forgotten the bright Rose of Manchester or scorned the withered heather of Varengeville, but I have trailed an ardent curiosity and an increasingly ailing body the length and breadth of France from Roman vestibules to Gothic apses. Of all the monuments I visited only the hospital at Beaune suited the acute state of my illness . . . Viollet-le-Duc said it was so beautiful that it made you long to fall ill at Beaune. He obviously didn't know what illness means!'

Late in November, Reynaldo was off to Berlin to meet Lilli Lehmann and discuss *Don Giovanni*. From Berlin he went on to the Mozartian cities of Prague, Vienna and Salzburg. A telegram from Marie followed him to Prague with news about Marcel's father. Dr Proust had collapsed at the Medical School, was taken home to the rue de Courcelles on a stretcher and died on the morning of 26 November without regaining consciousness.[9]

As Marcel, his mother and brother were observing a period of strict mourning, Marcel was not able to go to the three concert performances of *Don Giovanni* given at the beginning of December. Marie acted as 'dresser' for Mme Lehmann and was rewarded with an affectionately signed photograph. It was now a matter of haste that Marcel should correct the proofs of *La Bible d'Amiens* and get them to the printer for publication in February. His mother insisted that Dr Proust had been waiting from day to day for the book to appear and the deadline must be honoured. When it came out in March Marcel dedicated it to the memory of his father instead of Reynaldo, as he had originally intended. In a letter to Mme de Noailles he praised his father's kindness and simplicity: Mme Proust was showing her usual energy – 'the kind of energy that doesn't look like energy and in no way suggests the exercise of self-control,' Marcel wrote in the same letter, 'but I, who know the depths, the intensity and duration of this drama, cannot help being afraid'. As Mme Proust's health was not good, Marie Nordlinger was called in again to help with last-minute problems on the proofs of *La Bible d'Amiens*.

12

Japanese Water Flowers

In January and February 1904 Marie and Marcel finished correcting the proofs of *La Bible d'Amiens* which they had begun the previous summer. His uncertain health made it difficult to arrange meetings, and the disorder of the papers he kept in his bedroom and on his bedside table meant that he was continually losing her corrections.[1] Fresh scruples about the translation beset him. How, he asked, should the title of a book quoted by Ruskin be translated – did *Legendary Art* mean *L'Art légendaire* or would *La Légende dorée* be more accurate? What did Ruskin mean when he explained the name 'Eisenach' as 'significant of Thuringian armouries' – the word 'armouries' was not in any dictionary? His exasperated haste showed in his handwriting: 'It doesn't really matter either way to me' (*'Du reste, cela m'est tout à fait égal'*); *'tout à fait'* runs right off the edge of the paper as he wrote on his knee in bed. 'This old man is beginning to bore me,' he added.

His impatience with Ruskin's etymological concerns and his eagerness to get on with the translation of *Sesame and Lilies* is apparent. Marie did a first draft in school exercise books (*cahiers*) similar to those Mme Proust had used for her drafts of *La Bible d'Amiens*. *Sesame* contained two lectures; the first, 'Of Kings' Treasuries', given by Ruskin (as Marcel liked to remind Marie) in December 1864 at the Town Hall in Rusholme, Manchester, was a plea for public libraries; the second lecture, 'Of Queens' Gardens', concerned the education of young women. As this was one of Ruskin's best-selling works there were many editions, some of which included a third lecture, and there were prefaces from different dates. Marie was working on the first lecture in which Ruskin spoke of books as a means of communication with great minds; in fact he referred to books and reading only in the first fourteen paragraphs, the remaining thirty-six covered a great variety of subjects – language and pronunciation, the meaning of words such as 'pastor' and 'bishop' (and how Milton applied them in *Lycidas*), the need for discipline, the inequity of 'Free Trade' and a plea that money should be spent, not on armaments, but on galleries for art, natural history and libraries.

'You are so good to me that I venture to ask you to solve some last grammatical and archaeological doubts,' Proust wrote at the end of January. 'Would you be free to come round on Monday evening about 9.30 . . . or I could come to you, but not before 11.00 p.m. on Tuesday. Or what about Wednesday? Or if that's too inconvenient would you rather not at all?' By the following Saturday he had redone ten pages of the beginning, changing every word; 'Still, I think the French isn't quite so bad and allows a smaller number of fugitive English meanings to escape its finer mesh. But if I entertain so many scruples it will take us ten years and never was "well and quickly" more necessary!' A week later, increasingly ill, he sent 'a little message of impatient friendship'. She had taken some of her watercolour sketches to show him and he, appreciating her work and her patience with him, had given her a copy of Whistler's book *The Gentle Art of Making Enemies* which had belonged to Robert de Montesquiou – a luxury edition bound in scarlet leather, gilt-tooled. She had probably told him about her meeting with Whistler's friend,

Charles Freer; the spelling of the painter's name became a private joke, Marcel wrote it as the French pronounced it, Wisthler.

The Gentle Art of Making Enemies was published in 1890 and included an account of the libel suit Whistler had brought against his arch-enemy, Ruskin, twelve years previously. Ruskin had chosen Whistler as a target for an attack on the new aestheticism when, in June 1877, he had gone into the Grosvenor Gallery in London to be confronted by Whistler's pictures. Ruskin was appalled at what he considered the disparity between workmanship and price, accusing Whistler of wilful imposture and ill-educated conceit. The famous letter in *Fors Clavigera* continued: 'I have seen, and heard, much of Cockney impudence before now; but never expected to hear a cox-comb ask two hundred guineas for flinging a pot of paint in the public's face.' Similar criticisms had been made years before of Turner, whom Ruskin had ardently defended in *Modern Painters*.

Marcel continued to misspell 'Wisthler' in his letters to Marie. (As many commentators have pointed out, the name of Elstir, the famous painter in *The Search*, is almost an anagram of Whistler – only the difficult 'Wh' is omitted.) He explained to her that while Ruskin and Whistler despised each other because their systems were in conflict they shared one truth. In the libel suit, Whistler said: 'You say I painted this picture in a few hours. But I painted it with the knowledge of a lifetime'; at the same time Ruskin had written to Rossetti: 'I pre-fer the things you do rapidly, immediately, your sketches, to what you labour over. What you do at one go is the culmination of many years of dreaming, of love and of experience. Here the two stars strike at the same point with a ray, perhaps hostile, but identical. A case of astronomical coincidence.'[2]

'Thanks to Reynaldo (everything I have ever done has always been "thanks to Reynaldo"), I met Wisthler one evening and he told me Ruskin knew absolutely nothing about pictures. That is possible, but in any case when he rambled on about those of other people his very mistakes depicted and retraced marvellous pictures of his own which must be loved for themselves. And you and I will try to reveal and acclimatize these in France in the form of scrupulous and impassioned reproductions. Affectueusement à vous, Marcel Proust.'

'Thanks to Reynaldo (everything I have ever done has always been "thanks to Reynaldo")': a sweeping statement! What had Marcel done? He had begun, at Beg-Meil, encouraged by Reynaldo, to draft a semi-auto-biographical novel, which he abandoned several years later to write about Ruskin. Their discussions, arguments, exchange of gossip, the concerts, operas, musical and other soirées they went to, contributed to his writing – short stories, journalism, 'portraits'. Reynaldo's constant support gave him confidence to continue, in the face of family scepticism about his ability to produce something worth while. Through Reynaldo he met Marie, who took his mother's place as collaborator for the translation of *Sesame and Lilies*, as well as many artists and musicians, the Daudets, Mallarmé (and Méry Laurent), Massenet, Risler, Mme Bernhardt, the music-hall performer Fragson, and many others. Music became increasingly important for him – it inspired dreams and revelations; it had, he wrote more than once in *The Search*, an even more potent effect on him than subconscious memories and impressions – in *Time Regained* the last works of Vinteuil 'combined the quintessential character of all the sensations of involuntary memory' that he had experienced;[3] but he was not ready yet to make use of this idea in his work.

He was ill again after going to see an exhibition of oriental art at Durand Ruel. He had worked 'like a nigger' at *Sesame* and revised the beginning again, and all of the first exercise book, with a commentary to serve as preface or notes. 'I am all on fire for *Sesame* and for you,' he added at the top of the page. She sent him some balsam seeds, another private joke, a mark of her sympathy for the continual ill health he complained about, a memory, perhaps, of the balsam offered by Kundry to the wounded Amfortas in the first act of *Parsifal*. He wrote a poem for her to put into the book by Whistler, instead of a dedication on the flyleaf; 'You are sublime, marvellous, incredible; I won't let you do the ten pages . . . I am determined to do them . . . and the Milton as well.' 'How is Reynaldo?' he asked, and added, in the 'joke' spelling they used in their letters, 'Vous seriez gentille de dire à Coco que sa jolie cannch est chezzz moi'! (Would you kindly tell Coco that his handsome walking-stick is here.)

The poem, written on a separate sheet, was a verse of twenty-seven lines about her enamelling work; it began:

Thy hand, like unto water, mirrors the shadows
Of thy mind and its own fantasies . . .
Beneath thy hand, O Marie, the glaze doth all reveal
From proud cock crow to laughing orchard's song
Within the wondrous dish where I still see
Lapis enamel bound in gold filigree! . . .
Substance is sealed; re-open it, Sesame!
And with thy hands still nobler and serene,
On Treasures of the Kings, plant Lilies of the Queen! . . .

Recapture stained glass windows in thy dreams.
Mingle with stones of Venice rubies red of Rheims!

He could go on indefinitely with such doggerel, he told her, but she might not care for it. In any case, 'I cannot accept this marvellous flower and after extracting all its beneficent balm, I shall send it back to you, or rather, bring it back. Many grateful, respectful and admiring regards, Marcel.' In her notes to Lettres à une amie Marie explained that the 'flower' she had sent him was a hawthorn blossom in translucent pink enamel.4

At the end of February *La Bible d'Amiens* was published. Autographed copies were sent off at once to all the author's friends, to Mme Daudet as well as Léon and Lucien; to his former philosophy tutor, Alphonse Darlu; to Louisa Mornand with a mildly suggestive note. To Reynaldo he sent an apology: 'Dear old Ruskin, who cannot thank you in person for the enchanting tears you made the Muses weep when he died, has asked me to express his gratitude and admiration for your fraternal genius. And I thank you, too, my dear Reynaldo, the great affection of my life; you know this little book was dedicated to you as long as my dearest Papa was alive . . .' Instead, the first lecture in *Sésame et les lys* was dedicated to Reynaldo, the second to Suzette Lemaire, and the preface to Princess Alexandre de Caraman-Chimay. Reynaldo was one of Marcel's friends who did not share his enthusiasm for Ruskin.

The translation of 'Of Kings' Treasuries' was almost complete, except for some notes and the verses from *Lycidas*. Ruskin's long footnotes were no problem, but the verse and the paragraphs that preceded it gave a lot of trouble. Marcel sent Marie detailed instructions – doubtful words were underlined, gaps were for words he did not understand; she should use a special pencil to underline all mistranslations, writing the real meaning above them. Ruskin quoted twenty-two lines from Milton's poem, ending with a dismal description of a rural feast, the translation of which made no attempt to reproduce the rhythm of the original:

The hungry sheep look up, and are not fed,
But swoln with wind, and the rank mist they draw,
Rot inwardly, and foul contagion spread;
Besides what the grim wolf with privy paw
Daily devours apace, and nothing said . . .

After a short holiday in Manchester at the end of March, Marie returned to making buttons[6] and buckles in the rue de Provence, and to helping Reynaldo with his research on Mozart. He sent her two books in German on 8 April and asked her to summarize them for him, especially the one on *Don Giovanni*. He was busy planning concerts, performing, writing – he had recently been appointed music critic of *La Flèche*. He and Marie met frequently for lunch or dinner, often at home in the rue Alfred de Vigny; he lent her books, she mended his gloves, he had seats for the opera, the theatre – he had so much to do, so many people to see, she never knew when he would be free. Madame Sarah had commissioned him to write some choruses for girls' voices for her new production of Racine's play, *Esther*. He played part of the score for Dr and Mme Proust. Marcel described the scene in one of his notebooks: 'Reynaldo sang the choruses sitting at the piano while I was in bed, and Papa came quietly in and sat in the armchair while Maman stood listening to that magical voice. She ventured, timidly, to sing the tune of the chorus, like one of the little girls rehearsing with Racine. And the lovely lines of her Jewish face, stamped deeply with Christian gentleness and Jansenist courage, were like those of Esther herself, in this little family performance . . . which she had thought up to distract the despotic invalid lying there in his bed.'

Marcel was still not satisfied with their Ruskin translation when he wrote to Marie in mid-April to thank her for another simple gift. 'Chère amie, Thank you for the wonderful hidden flowers which enabled me, this evening, to "make a springtime", as Mme de Sévigné said, a fluvial, harmless spring.[7] Thank you, likewise, for the beautiful translation which I will examine closely and, with your permission, alter, albeit timidly, with affectionate deference, but alter none the less. You speak French not only better than a Frenchwoman, but like a Frenchwoman. But when you translate from the English all the native characteristics reappear; the words revert to type, to their affinities, their meanings, their native rules. And charming as this English disguise of French words may be, or rather this apparition of English figures and English faces breaking through their French trappings and masks, all this vitality will have to be cooled down, gallicized, further removed from the original, the originality extinguished . . . Mille respects, mille affections. Marcel Proust.'

Marie's simple gift of Japanese water flowers, tiny pieces of compressed, coloured pith (not paper) contained in little boxes or shells, which open in water, a childish toy bought for a few centimes in the course of an afternoon's stroll along the Seine embankment, gave Marcel a more than childish pleasure. It inspired him to use his talent for finding analogies – a talent, as he wrote in one of his notebooks in 1907–8, 'for discovering, at different periods of my life, a profound affinity between two ideas or two feelings . . . And it is often when I am most ill that this intermittently acknowledged self perceives such affinities . . . This young man has no need of food; the pleasure he draws from the sight of the idea he has discovered is all the nourishment he requires . . .'⁸ 'Analogies deliver us from the bondage of appearances,' he wrote in *Within a Budding Grove* and, in *Time Regained*, 'Intuition alone is a criterion of the truth . . . the beauty of images is lodged at the back of things.'

Marcel used the analogy of the Japanese water flowers in a draft for his novel, a sort of prologue for the whole work as he envisaged it in 1907–8. This began: 'Every day I attach less value to the intelligence . . .' and went on to describe how each hour of life, once it is past, is reincarnated and hidden, like the souls of the dead in popular myth, in some material object. They come to life again by chance when someone discovers them. He had only indistinct memories of the old house in the country where he had spent summer holidays in his boyhood until, one snowy day years afterwards, coming home chilled, the old family cook offered him a cup of tea and some pieces of toast. The taste of toast dipped into the tea gave him suddenly an extraordinary feeling of happiness, he could smell the scent of geraniums and orange trees. And then he remembered the house, his grandfather drinking tea and giving him a biscuit to dip into it. It was a magic pact which made a whole garden, with its forgotten footpaths, flower again, basket by basket, in the cup of tea, like those little Japanese flowers which open in water. In this early version, only the country garden was brought back to life. In *Swann's Way* the analogy was expanded and the whole town was recreated.

Marcel thought of *Gardens in a Cup of Tea* as a possible title for this first volume.

'By May 1904,' Marie wrote, 'my work at the Art Nouveau studio was becoming increasingly stale and I was growing restless, the more so since the plaster cast of a private commission for a cinerary urn was waiting to be turned into bronze. I plucked up my courage and approached M. Bing, who kindly gave me time off on two afternoons a week which I promptly proceeded to spend in a founder's workshop in Belleville, the district in which for generations metal workers had congregated.' She hinted at her dissatisfaction in a letter to Marcel, who replied: 'Chère amie, What a lovely letter you wrote me . . . I will send you word, not to come and work, but to pay me a little visit for a talk . . . What pleased me less than the lovely words and thoughts in your letter is a kind of vague allusion to some profound, unexpressed sorrow of which you perhaps never even thought while writing, but which seemed to confine and darken your letter like an unavoidable horizon. I am so slightly acquainted with your life, it may well contain troubles I do not know about, but even unknown they distress me . . . You have an extraordinary memory. I who can remember nothing about the previous day because of these horrible anti-asthma medicines, I envy you for keeping so precise a memory of the days in Venice . . . I feel that your letter itself is a charming trellis screening something sad that I cannot see. Chère amie, I would have you revel in life, at the cherry-laden dish, clamorous with the song of chantecleer, not weep sadly by an urn containing nothing but regrets. Your Marcel.'

With his acute insight into other people's thoughts and feelings, his own affection for Reynaldo and the happy days they had all spent in Venice, Marcel must have been aware of what lay behind Marie's unhappiness. She was fond of Marcel, she admired his work and enjoyed helping him, but she was never in love with him – he was simply 'not her style'.[9]

Marie commented on Marcel's reference to his poor memory. 'It is perhaps surprising to find this confession coming from the pen of a writer who was to make the phenomena of memory one of the principal themes of his work, but there is no real contradiction in this. The memory which recreates impressions and links them to one another by seemingly arbitrary or unconnected currents, is not the same as the purely quantitative memory which is usually called "good" or "bad" according to the number of facts it can retain.' Marcel himself remarked that 'a memory without fault is not a very powerful incentive for studying the phenomena of memory... just as someone who goes to sleep the minute his head touches the pillow can hardly be expected to make even cursory observations on sleep . . . a little insomnia is not without its value in making us appreciate sleep.'[10]

Marie was thinking of moving back to Manchester. Before the decision was made, however, she received from Marcel a most unexpected offer: 'As I can't see you I must write to tell you about an idea I had which, since you seemed sad about leaving Paris, might perhaps enable you to stay on a little longer. Here it is: Maman would like – however painful it might be for the most vivid and dear picture she has kept of my father to be confronted with a work of art, inevitably unfaithful – Maman would like, for those who come after us and who may wonder what my father was like, a portrait-bust at the cemetery to give as simple and exact a likeness as possible. And she intends to ask some young, gifted and amenable sculptor to try from photographs to give in plaster, bronze or marble the form of my father's features with an accuracy that, however far from our memories and perhaps even hurtful to them, would, to those who did not know him, give a better idea than his mere name inscribed in the stone. Would you like to be this sculptor? Tell me what you yourself think of the idea. Our *Sésame* will appear in *Les Arts de la vie* as soon as it is ready, but when will that be? I am overhauling it from top to bottom. I didn't ask what they would pay us but in this review I don't think it will be too bad. Just imagine, all my *Sésame et les lys* books have turned up (six books). By pure chance! . . . Votre ami, Marcel.' Marie dated this letter 27 May 1904.

The commission to do a portrait-bust of Dr Proust was a challenge which she, after some hesitation, accepted. As she explained: 'I had never met Marcel's father, it would therefore entail working from photographs and a life-size relief in bronze of the heavy features was a challenge – added to which I was enjoined, "You simply cannot omit the spectacles, they were so characteristic." Was I the "youthful, gifted and amenable sculptor" for the task? On the other hand, it would enable me to abandon what had become a routine job in the rue de Provence. It was an unusually warm summer; I welcomed the loan of a house and garden belonging to English friends in Auteuil, in the rue La Fontaine, complete with maid and dog and, what was more important, a studio workshop in the garden.'

Before she moved to Auteuil, Marcel found the missing exercise books with all his notes for *Sesame*, and was anxious to talk to her about them. The commission for a funerary urn was finished and Marie took it to show Marcel. His appreciative comments must have given her confidence for the new commission from Mme Proust. 'The urn is marvellous! The four harpocratic heads are exquisite, the symbolic serpent . . . the leaves . . . the flower petals and the serpent's knots are all wonderful. But more than all else I like the figure of sorrow so intimately joined to the beloved ashes to which she clings, her cloak like the one in *Middlemarch*, her reverie rapt and bitter . . . there is nothing of the conventional conception of sorrow, a real creation of your own.'[11] He had been ill for a week, he told her, unable to speak, eat, sleep, etc., etc., and had seen the urn for barely five minutes.

All the same, he wrote at the top of the letter, 'I have worked well'! The references to books consulted and read in the preface and notes to *Sésame* were proof of his industry; as well as verifications of biblical texts and further works by Ruskin such as *Fors Clavigera*, *Time and Tide*, the later volumes of *Modern Painters* and *On the Old Road* (with Ruskin's essay on 'Fiction Fair and Foul'), which were not mentioned in *La Bible d'Amiens*, and he referred to works as diverse as Schopenhauer's *The World as Will and Representation*, a book on *Diseases of the Will*, Fromentin's *Summer in the Sahara*, Gautier's *Travels in Spain* and his novel *Capitaine Fracasse* (which he had read so eagerly in the garden at Illiers), Renan's *Life of Jesus* and *The Origins of Christianity*, books by Maeterlinck and, particularly in the preface, a number of works by Sainte-Beuve, including the only novel he ever wrote, Volupté, a psychological study of an unhappy love affair, a book which failed because it was sixty years ahead of its time.

La Bible d'Amiens was apparently enjoying a moderate success with the French reading public. Three months after its first printing it went into a third edition and Marcel asked Marie to send him any corrections for the new edition so that he could give them to the publisher.

On the afternoon of Saturday 28 May, at the Institut de France, the best-known and most widely read philosopher in France, Henri Bergson, presented Proust's book to the members of the Académie des Sciences Morales et Politiques in a brief speech in which he laid stress on what Marcel had written about Ruskin's essentially religious character. M. Bergson described Ruskin as a man who believed that poets and artists were vehicles for transcribing a divine message, and his works could only be understood from the standpoint that his aesthetic ideas were inspired by religious feeling. As a student of philosophy, Marcel had read Bergson's book, *Time and Free Will* (1888), and his essay on 'Laughter, the Meaning of the Comic' (1901). In a later book, *Matter and Memory* (1906), Bergson emphasized the importance of time, memory and intuition in the search for reality. In the second chapter of *Matter and Memory* Bergson made a distinction between two kinds of memory: first, the habit of memory, like learning a poem by heart, and second, pure or spontaneous memory that stores up perceptions and impressions subconsciously, revealing itself in sudden flashes.

Proust always insisted that it was inaccurate to use the term Bergsonian to describe his work because the distinction he himself made between the two kinds of memory did not appear in Bergson's philosophy and was even contradicted by it. In the years between 1904 and 1913 he assimilated the work of both Ruskin and

Bergson and developed his own way of dealing with the problems of time, memory and reality. In 1904 he was still trying to clarify his ideas; he was thirty-three, ever conscious of precarious health and the years going by. With the late summer weather his hay fever improved and he was able to lead a more normal social life, particularly as two of his friends announced their forthcoming marriages: Armand de Guiche was engaged to Elaine, only daughter of the Comte and Comtesse Greffuhle, Louis d'Albuféra to Anna Masséna, daughter of the Prince d'Eseling.

Marcel reported these events to Fénelon, who was now in St Petersburg, and Antoine Bibesco, temporarily transferred from the Romanian Legation in Paris to London. 'I'm telling you about my life since you left from a purely frivolous point of view,' he told Antoine in mid-July, 'but you know, don't you, that "this is the apparent life" and that "the real life" is underneath all this?' Albu's engagement was announced just after his mistress, Louisa de Mornand, had gone away to Vichy with her mother and sister. Fond as he was of Louisa (and there are no grounds for suspecting that their friendship amounted to more than her own description of it as an *amitié amoureuse*), Marcel knew her to be extravagant, quarrelsome and not always faithful to Louis; with good sense and affection for both young people, Marcel acted as go-between, reassuring Louis, calming Louisa. 'I have been told what a devoted and loyal friend you have been in difficult circumstances,' wrote Fénelon from Russia.

Devoted and loyal both as friend and son he may have been, but Marcel knew he had another imperative duty, that of the artist to his work. What he must do now, he wrote in the preface to *Sésame*, was to choose solitude instead of friendship, books instead of conversation – reading was communication in the midst of solitude, it acted as a curative discipline and could introduce a lazy mind to the life of the spirit. This, for him, was 'the real life'.

13

A New Venture

'August in Paris was commonly referred to as "la morte saison", but it never seemed less so to me,' wrote Marie. 'The days were over full and the portrait of Dr Proust was a greater problem than I had anticipated. I rarely went into Paris except to meet Reynaldo at the Bibliothèque Nationale. He was preparing a series of concerts devoted to Rameau, Lully, Gluck and Mozart, and consulting a variety of German books which had not then been translated into French or English. He had a good knowledge of colloquial German, but was hampered by the printed Gothic type, and I had acquired a habit of extemporizing a rapid, *sotto voce* French translation. We thus came across all sorts of information unknown in France where the cult of Mozart in particular had been limited . . .' As for Lully, Reynaldo had to transcribe important fragments from the old seventeenth- and eighteenth-century editions by hand as no modern editions existed. He kept a watchful eye on the progress of Marie's plaque until he went off to Berlin again to work with Lilli Lehmann. While he was away Marie used to cycle from Auteuil to Versailles to stay with her aunt at the Hôtel des Reservoirs for a night or two.

Marcel wrote to her in Auteuil early in August to say that he was not well enough to visit her but would like to see the sketch of the medallion; unfortunately she had already destroyed it. She took the preliminary cast to show to Mme Proust and her sons before Marcel went off to join the de Billys for a brief cruise on the steam yacht belonging to Mme de Billy's father. If the commission from Mme Proust had been unexpected, Marie received an even greater surprise – from M. Bing.

Her memoir continues: 'Unexpectedly one morning M. Bing's niece, Mlle Léonore, turned up. "M. Bing says would you please come to dine tonight, it is very important for you – an idea he has had – he wants to tell you about it himself." I went to Vaucresson;[1] M. Bing certainly had something of interest to communicate and his concern for my welfare had manifested itself more speedily than I could have imagined.

'He had that day received a letter from Mr Charles J. Morse, of Evanston, Chicago, scholar and collector, informing him that some three hundred Japanese colour-prints were being forwarded to him from California by a friend to whom M. Bing had sent them and who had now made his choice. Should they be returned to Paris? This is where I came on the scene; I was to meet the prints in Chicago, collect the balance of a selection of pottery sent to Mr Freer in Detroit, and exhibit and sell them on my own initiative in the Middle West, where interest in oriental art was apparently increasing daily! Simultaneously I was to explore every opportunity for myself as a metalworker and, finally, stay in New York some weeks, seeing old clients and making new contacts.

'He would like me to go towards the end of October for a minimum period of three months. As far as I could judge the financial conditions appeared satisfactory – there was no mention of sharing the risks this time! I did not hesitate to tell him that I had absolutely no business experience, and ventured to ask: "But why do you want to send me?" To which he replied, smiling enigmatically: "I have sent men travellers now and then, but I have a feeling you will do better." I examined any qualifications that I might have as a "commis voyageur", and came to the conclusion that only my independence and enthusiasm might be worth something.'

In spite of insomnia, Marcel enjoyed his four-day voyage from Le Havre along the north coast of Brittany to St Malo; he sent cards to his friends, including two to Marie, from Cherbourg and Dinan. He went to Auteuil on Wednesday 24 August to see the medallion again but did not stay for lunch as she had hoped. Her address in Auteuil was 56, rue La Fontaine, the same district, the very same road in which Marcel had been born at No. 96, a house which had belonged to Mme Proust's uncle, Louis Weil, where the family spent many happy weeks when the boys were young. After M. Weil's death in 1896 the house was demolished and a block of flats was built in the garden. Marcel's visit to Marie must have revived memories of the old home with its big garden, of walks in the Bois de Boulogne, his mother's goodnight kiss, his grandfather's love of drinking tea.

In a letter to his mother written from Auteuil in September 1888, when he was just seventeen, he told her of the delight he felt in getting up early and going off into the woods with a novel by Loti to read: 'there was pleasure in breathing, feeling, moving my arms and legs, just as it was in Tréport or at Illiers, the year of Augustin Thierry'. The novel was *Le Mariage de Loti* and the 'year of Augustin Thierry' was at Illiers in 1886 when his grandmother's enthusiasm for *The Conquest of the Normans* had been shared with Marcel and he resolved to become a writer.

The joy of reading and the urge to write were equally the subject of his preface to *Sésame et les lys,* which he drafted during the next two or three months – by December it had been accepted for publication in a monthly magazine, *La Renaissance latine*. The little country town described in the first part of the preface was not given a name, but it is recognizably a preliminary sketch for Combray in *Swann's Way* where the young narrator knew the childhood pleasure of being absorbed in a book, of finding magic in a phrase and the fount of all wisdom in a particular author.

Some time during the summer Marie sent Marcel the little water-colour she had done at Senlis in 1898 (it hung by his bedside until, shortly before he died, he gave it to Reynaldo, whence it came back to Marie). His letter of thanks became, for her, another 'marvellous present'. 'Chère amie, The prettiest thing I ever saw was once in the country, in a mirror fixed to a window frame; a piece of sky and landscape with a cluster of trees standing like brothers in a group. And the necessarily fugitive delight of this moment, already distant, seems to have been given back to me now in a lasting present from you . . . How grateful I am to you for this wonderful present: a place in nature, an hour, a nuance, a moment of your own self, mindful of nature and the secrets that are hers alone. I truly thank you with all my heart. Votre Marcel Proust.'

The 'fraternal group of trees' reappear in *Within a Budding Grove* when M on a carriage drive near Balbec sees three trees which awake a memory he cannot identify – were they phantoms of the past, begging him to bring them back to life?The trees reflected in a mirror attached to the gabled houses on each bank of a Dutch canal were described in a paragraph of his preface explaining that truth is not to be found in libraries or in some folio in a Dutch convent – it can only be discovered by our own efforts of heart and mind.[3]

At the end of August Reynaldo returned from
Germany to the hotel at Versailles and just missed
seeing Marie who had left the same day to visit her
grandmother in Hamburg. In spite of a bad attack of ton-
sillitis he wrote to her at once about M. Bing's offer. A
letter from Marcel to Hamburg followed a fortnight later
with apologies for not writing since his visit to Auteuil
and thanking her for 'a very charming letter, though
from anyone but you it might well have appeared rather
ironic or scornful. For into my appalling physical state
broke the proud words, "I am overflowing with health,
with vitality, with strength, with the capacity for happiness." Chère amie, don't think that I read that with bit-
terness. Believe rather that I understand the charity of
these words which were like an offer of a moral blood
transfusion . . .'

He was very much in favour of her going to America,
provided that she enjoyed it and the money was good. 'I
think it is very flattering and something anyone who
loves the arts would be delighted to undertake.' He continued: 'Why don't you wish your name to be associated
with mine on the cover of *Sésame*? You only answered
evasively. Answer me, "dic nobis, Maria quid . . . ?
(Easter Day Service)".' And he recalled their walks in
Venice, *St Mark's Rest* in hand, 'à propos of which, isn't
this touching? A bookseller in the Piazza San Marco
writes that he has got my address from M. Maurice
Barrès and he wants me to translate *St Mark's Rest* for
him. I think I shall refuse, otherwise I shall die without
ever having written anything of my own.' Earlier in the
year he had written to Maurice Barrès in similar terms,
rejecting a suggestion that when he had finished with
Ruskin he should translate something by Walter Pater

because he wanted 'to try and translate my own poor mind, if it hasn't died in the meantime'. He had so many ideas, so many 'ghosts' begging him to give them life, characters in the novel going on perpetually in his head, but he still could not see how to transform his fantasies into a work of art. Was it, as he wrote in the preface to *Sésame*, 'a kind of laziness or frivolity' which prevented him from digging down into 'the deep regions of the self where the true life of the mind begins'?[4]

When Marie returned to Paris after a fortnight in Hamburg, Reynaldo was away, Mme Proust had gone to Dieppe with Robert and his family while Marcel tried to make up his mind whether to join her or stay at home to attend the forthcoming wedding celebrations of Albuféra and Guiche. He was trying to keep more normal hours, but rarely succeeded. He wrote briefly to Marie to say he was leading a miserable life, uncertain of his health from one minute to the next, adding after his signature: 'The idea of your visit during Mother's absence being "improper" strikes me as quite enchanting and made me laugh a lot. As if you were the young man and I the girl, and yet I have been to see you all alone at Auteuil. Still, it would be too silly to come if I were in bed or make any other sort of wasted effort.'

It was now October and Marie was preparing for her American visit. 'M. Bing kindly gave me access to his own print collection and spent many hours initiating me into their history, deciphering their signatures and memorizing special characteristics. The Hamburg relatives shared Reynaldo's reservations as to my "hawking Japanese colour-prints round the Middle West" with the difference that he as usual "favoured experiments". Meanwhile I had accepted M. Bing's offer, provided that the engagement could be terminated after three months should either of us wish to do so. I gave the medallion of Dr Proust some finishing touches and supervised its installation on the tombstone at the cemetery of Père Lachaise.'

'On October 24th, 1904, I embarked on the Hamburg–America liner *Prince Bismarck*, arriving in New York some ten days later. Mr Bing had announced my arrival to some of his clients whom he knew personally, and his former agent gave me a list of collectors and dealers in New York and Boston, among them Professor Denman Ross of Harvard and Mrs J. Gardner of Boston, whom I proposed to contact before setting off for Chicago. My first call in New York was on General di Cesnola, director of the Metropolitan Museum, whom M. Bing had known earlier as consul in Cyprus.

'Having drawn a blank in Boston, I proceeded straight to Chicago. A message from Mr Morse awaited me and a meeting was arranged for the following day. We checked over the 300 or so prints from California, discussed a lengthy list of collectors, and most helpfully, went into matters such as insurance, printing, publicity and display. He approved my scheme of taking a suite in a hotel for a month and showing the prints there. As Mrs Morse had invited me to spend Thanksgiving Day with them in Evanston, I was to see his own collection and hear about the book he was writing on Tibetan painting, the first ever undertaken.

'Chicago in those days seemed far less civilized than New York and yet it was more American and bursting with vitality. Wherever I went, I met with cheerful courtesy and interest, wonderful hospitality and helpfulness. One day, Mr Freer, whom I had already met in Paris, announced the arrival of pottery from Mr Bing. Only a couple of pieces were suitable for his collection but, he added, it would be a pleasure if I would accept "a bachelor's hospitality" and go to Detroit for the weekend and we would then decide what to do with the remainder. "Does he want me to accept or refuse?" I asked Mrs Morse. "Oh, of course, you must accept, his house is like a hotel, people coming and going all the time." So I cautiously packed a couple of bags and took the train to Detroit.

'Thanksgiving Day had been a glorious warm, late summer's day – now winter had set in and I barely recognized my host on the platform, his eyes and nose only emerging from an upturned fur collar. My luggage had gone astray so the carriage had to stop for me at a drugstore where I bought some essential items. Arriving at 33, Ferry Avenue, the Canadian housemaid, Minnie, was told of my dilemma and assured me of her help. Mr Freer added that under the circumstances he would not change for dinner.

'The dining-room was definitely Whistlerian, plain yellow walls, simple furniture and pictures by the Master on the walls. Later in the evening he read to me the famous "Ten O'Clock" which I confessed to not knowing.[5] By an extraordinary coincidence I came across quite a pile of the green paperback copies a few weeks later in New York and secured half a dozen of them for a trifling cost, despatching several post haste to Paris. When I showed my find to Mr Freer he instantly declared it a pilfered edition; he notified Miss Birnie Philip, Whistler's sister-in-law and executrix, whose solicitor had every available copy seized and destroyed and an abject apology published in *The Times*. Naturally I refused to hand mine over!

'Charles Lang Freer was born of Huguenot stock in 1856 in Kingston, New York. His parents were poor and he left school at an early age. A propitious meeting with Colonel Frank Hecker introduced him into the world of railways; they eventually founded a vast factory making railway trucks in Detroit, chosen for its geographical position in the Middle West and its proximity to the Lakes. They built the first refrigerated wagons, establishing a far-reaching industry (and corresponding fortune). The partners bought adjoining plots of land in Ferry Avenue. Colonel Hecker's title dated from the Spanish-American war; his mansion was typical of the owner, broad and high, ornate and inclined to pretentiousness; his neighbour's bachelor establishment, designed for him by the Philadelphia architect, Wilson Eyre, was of homelier, more modest dimensions, but it was elegant and comfortable. The stables were now empty awaiting modifications for the installation of Whistler's Peacock Room above which a new Gallery was to be built.

'A few months previously, in 1904, Mr Freer had decided to offer his entire art collection to the Smithsonian Institution in Washington, thus constituting the first national collection. His plan was that the government should reserve a plot of land on which, after his death, the gallery was to be built as he had laid down and at his expense; the building was to bear his name and be maintained by the governors but he would retain ownership of the collection during his lifetime.

'I was shown innumerable, undreamed-of masterpieces during the weekend. He also showed me the list of 250 items he was loaning to the Whistler Memorial Exhibition in Paris that summer. As I sat in the train reviewing the events of the weekend, I realized the opening up of a new dimension, and I pondered the strange chance that had led me from Marcel and Ruskin to the

Freer treasure-house of Whistler. And I knew how right I was to be "hawking prints in the Middle West".'

Charles Freer first met Whistler in March 1890, and came to have the highest respect and admiration for him, as both man and painter. He already owned a large number of Whistler etchings. As their friendship grew, first in Paris and then, after the death of Mrs Whistler, in London, Whistler introduced Freer to oriental art, infecting him with his own enthusiasm and encouraging him to build up a collection. In 1902 they went to Holland together, where Whistler fell seriously ill; Freer stayed at his friend's side for six weeks until the invalid was well enough to travel. After this Whistler began a portrait of Freer, a rapid sketch which was never finished – it made his subject look older than his forty-six years. 'He is making me look like a pope,' Freer told Colonel Hecker, 'but then, that is all right as there will of course be little of Freer in it. It will surely be all Whistler!' Exactly a year later, June 1903, Freer was in Paris dining with Siegfried Bing and buying oriental objets d'art from him. This was when Marie met him. In London the following week he bought some rare Whistler prints, but he was seeing nothing of London, he told his partner, except the museums and Whistler, whose physical condition had become so much worse that he could hardly speak. When Freer arrived to take him for a drive in the park on the afternoon of 17 July, Whistler had died a few minutes before.

Freer immediately became involved with the artist's executrix and sister-in-law, Rosalind Birnie Philip, to whom he gave all possible support. He went on adding to his collection of Whistler paintings and kept up his inter-

est until his own death in 1919. In 1903 he bought from
the Glasgow collector Sir William Burrell *The Princess
from the Land of Porcelain*, a 'portrait in rose and silver';
this had at one time belonged to the Liverpool ship-
owner F. R. Leyland and was to hang in the dining-room
of his house in Princes Gate, London. During the winter
of 1876–7, in Mr Leyland's absence, Whistler painted
over the walls of the dining-room, covered in historic
300-year-old Spanish leather, a motif of peacocks and
peacock feathers in blue and gold, so that what had been
intended as a Tudor-style room was given an oriental
character. Another famous quarrel ensued. After Mr
Leyland's death the house was sold, the room dismantled
in its entirety and re-erected in the galleries of Messrs
Obach & Co., New Bond Street, London, where Freer
inspected it on 14 May 1904, bought it at once and
arranged for it to be shipped to Detroit later in the year.
He never thought of his purchases as personal posses-
sions but as being held in trust by him for future generations of Americans.

Memorial exhibitions of Whistler's work were being
held in Boston and Edinburgh in 1904, and two more in
London and Paris in 1905. Freer decided that his pictures should go to Paris because he believed that
Whistler cared little for the English view of art and much
more for that of France. In January 1905 Charles Freer
was told that the trustees of the Smithsonian Institution
in Washington had at last accepted his offer to give them
his collections, together with the money to build the
gallery in which to house them.

'1904–1905 was a particularly severe winter with a great
deal of snow,' Marie wrote. 'From Chicago, where busi-

ness had been very good, I went to Cleveland and other places including a return visit to Detroit. In New York I rented a small studio-gallery at the top of an old building, No. 489, Fifth Avenue, living, or rather sleeping, in a quiet family hotel. Snow was still being dug out of Fifth Avenue in April. The Paris chestnut trees would be in bloom – it was high time I got back; I had no desire to stay on in America and did not use the letters of introduction which Lalique had given me.

'Mr Freer, who came to New York frequently and usually took me out to dinner, anticipated my departure for Europe by suggesting that I might help him with the catalogue of his collections for two or three weeks before leaving. I said I would consult M. Bing. Hardly had I done so when another surprise intervened in the shape of a letter from the Customs Office to the effect that they were holding a roll of ten Tibetan paintings addressed to me by M. Bing of Paris, and that in view of their having been declared to the extent of less than half their real value, they were confiscated; my presence at the Customs was requested urgently and I set off there at once. After some acrimonious discussion with the Customs Officer, I was ushered into the presence of the all-powerful Judge Thwaites. He listened to my arguments, thanked me for my co-operation and finally asked me to sign a couple of documents authorizing him to do what he had never done before, i.e. release an item confiscated by the New York Customs authorities "for the purpose of their expertise"!

'Some years later Mr Freer wrote to me: "I dined recently at the White House, only the family, Judge Thwaites and myself. The talk turned of course on the new tariff, and the Judge mentioned how only once in his long career had he released a confiscated article, and that had really been brought about by a young Englishwoman and so quickly that it never got into the papers. I reminded him of the ten Tibetan paintings and told him that I owned five and Mr Charles J. Morse of Evanston the other five." The Englishwoman's ears, and possibly those of the Customs Man, must have tingled that evening!' This episode certainly proved Marie's resourcefulness and expertise. She spent the last month of this first visit to America in Detroit.

These few pages, written at the end of her life, give little indication of the extent of Marie's friendship and collaboration with Charles Freer. She died before she had written any account of her second stay in Detroit, but it is clear from Mr Freer's letters and diaries (now in the library of the Art Gallery which bears his name in Washington, DC) that he had a high opinion of her abilities and enjoyed her companionship; nor can there be any doubt that she learnt a great deal about oriental art from him and from the work she did on his collections. On each of his visits to Europe – and until 1910 he came every year – she was there, in London or Paris, to greet him, to act as 'interpreter, counsellor and friend', often travelling with him, visiting collections, sales and exhibitions.

Mr Freer introduced her to dealers in Japanese art and visited salesrooms with her. In March they met in Boston and at the beginning of April she arrived in Detroit to work with Mr Freer on his collection of prints – he kept only those by Whistler, finally owning over 900 of them, all now in the Freer Gallery in Washington. Early in May they sailed together on the SS *Hamburg*, as Mr Freer reported to Colonel Hecker: 'The "eats" are good, the drinks all right, but the company, excepting that of Miss Nordlinger, is as uninteresting as the measles – however, she more than offsets all other short-comings.'

14

On Reading

Marie received several postcards from Reynaldo while she was in America and one long letter which followed her from Chicago to New York. He was planning some Mozart concerts with Mme Lehmann which were postponed because she had other engagements. Mozart was always Reynaldo's idol; to Risler he wrote: 'I do not like Bach, I find Palestrina a great bore and I adore Mozart. What a prodigy he was . . . a curious mixture of skill, depth and naïveté. I have been reading *Don Giovanni* a great deal recently . . . But whatever they say, *Don Giovanni* is, musically, much inferior to *Figaro*, itself inferior to the sublime *Così*.'

On a postcard of the Sainte Chapelle in Paris, postmarked 10 February, he thanked Marie for the little book by Whistler she had sent him. Marcel wrote the same evening to thank her for the booklet and with the usual apologies and excuses of ill health: '. . . I am afraid of their reaching your over-accustomed (and I don't mean incredulous) ears, faded and without the power to excuse and acquit . . . I have been thinking about you a great deal . . . I bless the Wisthlerian magician who has brought you happiness, for I do not think that things alone would have given it to you and I surmise that persons are involved.

'I am sorry that your new friend, since you were kind enough to mention me to him, must, as a good Wisthlerian, much despise an admirer of Ruskin, but actually I believe that, though their theories (the least intimate part of any of us) were antagonistic at a certain depth, they agreed more frequently than they suspected . . . I was given the magnificent new edition of Ruskin for Christmas. You will enjoy it when you get back, and you'll see some marvellous new illustrations . . .

'Tell your friend that in my intentionally bare room there is only one reproduction of a work of art, an excellent photograph of Wisthler's *Carlyle* in the coat with snaky folds like his Mother's dress. The more I think about Ruskin and Wisthler's theories the more I believe they are not irreconcilable . . . Wisthler is right when he says in "The Ten O'Clock" that Art is distinct from Morality. But I have talked on too long and send you without more ado my respectful and grateful affection.'

For Whistler art was 'a whimsical goddess and a capricious one, live we never so spotlessly, still may she turn her back on us'. For Ruskin great art was the expression, by an art-gift, of a pure soul, and the art-gift itself the result of the moral character of generations, but 'of course,' he wrote in *The Queen of the Air,* 'art-gift and amiability of disposition are two different things; a good man is not necessarily a painter, nor does an eye for colour necessarily imply an honest mind'. Proust quoted both opinions in a footnote to 'Of Kings' Treasuries' and in a further note referred again to *The Queen of the Air* where Ruskin described how the artist, whether painter or writer, revealed his weaknesses and affectations in everything he produced – the writer, especially, laid bare his soul in his choice of words and the hidden rhythm which lay beneath them.[1]

In the same note Proust went on to cite Sainte-Beuve as a second-rate artist because of the way he used archaic expressions to show his erudition. Marcel had been reading a new biography of Sainte-Beuve in 1904–5 and referred to it in other notes for *Sésame*. He thought the most widely read and admired literary critic in France consistently misjudged the work of contemporary writers such as Stendhal, Balzac and Baudelaire, all of whom he had known personally. As a journalist the need to deliver a weekly article meant that he never had time to go deeply into ideas and feelings.

The volumes of the Library Edition of Ruskin which Mme Proust had given Marcel for Christmas had begun to appear in 1903; the first fourteen volumes included all the early works, four volumes of *Modern Painters*, three volumes of *The Stones of Venice*, *The Seven Lamps of Architecture*, *Lectures on Architecture and Painting* and *Notes on Turner's Harbours of England*. As Marcel pointed out to Marie, the reproduction of the illustrations was particularly fine and his keen eye appreciated them to the full. In the introduction to Volume VI, the editors noted that Ruskin had taken especial care with the illustrations for the chapter 'Of Turnerian Topography'. There was, for example, a drawing of Nottingham and its castle which Turner had done in 1795 when he was twenty, and the same view drawn from memory thirty years later.

When he described the nature of the imagination and Turner's genius, Ruskin showed how the artist selected and altered details of a remembered scene to make a better whole; he painted the impression it made on his mind, the far higher and deeper truth of his mental vision, and he did this involuntarily, 'an entirely imperative dream has taken possession of him, he can see and do no other than as the dream directs'.[2] Writing about memory and imagination in connection with some of the great artists he had studied – Dante, Scott, Tintoretto, Turner – Ruskin admitted that the mental chemistry by which the dream summons and associates its materials was utterly inexplicable, though he had done his best to explain it in Volume II of *Modern Painters*.

Now, in Volume IV, he tried again. 'The imagination consists, not in a voluntary perception of new images, but an involuntary remembrance, exactly at the right moment, of something actually seen . . . The more I investigate it, the more this tenderness of perception and grasp of memory seems to me to be the root of Turner's genius.' Ruskin thought the imagination, far from being a deceptive faculty, was the most accurate and truth-telling faculty which the human mind possesses, all the more so because in its work the vanity and individualism of the man himself is crushed, its work is instinctive, it is 'used by a higher power for the reflection to others of a truth which no effort of his could ever have ascertained'.[3] For Ruskin, and for Turner, the revelations of 'involuntary memory' took the form of images, for Proust they took the form of sensations – bending down to unbutton a boot, stepping on an uneven paving-stone or tasting a biscuit dipped into a cup of tea. Many people, not only painters and writers, have had this experience; Proust had already made use of it in his early novel and hinted at its importance for his own aesthetic credo.

Reynaldo was busier than ever. He was rehearsing the choral music he had composed for Mme Bernhardt's forthcoming production of Racine's *Esther* which was to have a short run at the Théâtre Sarah-Bernhardt. Esther was played by Mme Ventura and Assuéras, King of Persia, by Mme Sarah as though she were a schoolgirl awkwardly and endearingly doing her best to be a bearded Eastern potentate. There was a specially written prologue declaimed by an old friend of Mme Sarah's, the actor de Max.

At the end of April Reynaldo began rehearsals for his concerts at the Théâtre de l'Athénée. The first, on 17

May, consisted of works by Lully not often performed at this time. The second concert presented music by the eighteenth-century composer Rameau. On 3 June he conducted another work by Lully at the Opéra-Comique, and five days later there was a big charity concert at the home of the Comtesse de Béarn when he again conducted the choruses from *Esther* with choir, orchestra and two soloists.

Extracts from Proust's translation of Ruskin's first Manchester lecture, 'Of Kings' Treasuries', appeared in three numbers of the monthly magazine *Les Arts de la vie* in March, April and May 1905, with a generous tribute to the help given by Marie, 'the eminent English metalworker, who more than once abandoned the masterpiece on which she was working, the funerary urn or the Dish with the Apple . . . Since her modesty has refused the title of collaborator in this translation, I should like at least to place it under her gracious patronage.'

Marie arrived in Paris with Mr Freer just as Marcel was correcting his proofs, 'too late for the chestnut blossom,' she wrote, 'but in time for Reynaldo's concerts'. She found Marcel much changed, ill and wan, his emaciated cheeks surrounded by a thick black beard. 'Only his voice smiled. "Kiss me for once, Mary," he said. "I think of you always so much. Have you seen many beautiful things in America?" *Sésame* was waiting and we had to make haste.' In one of his nocturnal notes to his mother, Marcel commented on the evening: 'Nordlinger's arrival put me on the right track . . . we've done a good job.'

Mr Freer was anxious to supervise the hanging of his pictures at the Whistler Exhibition at the Ecole des

Beaux Arts on 13 May; he and Marie then went to visit Marcel Bing, now installed in fine new premises in the rue St Georges because the Art Nouveau building in the rue de Provence was being demolished for road-widening purposes. The Gothic and oriental Art business had been transferred to the management of his son when illness forced M. Bing Senior to retire. 'I visited M. Siegfried Bing several times to report on my experiences,' Marie's memoir continued. 'It was doubly gratifying now to find that my efforts had resulted in financial success. I had, so I was told, made ten times my expenses, which caused a male member of the firm to say that I had spoilt the job for any man!'

After Reynaldo's concert on 17 May, Mr Freer and Mr Morse, who was also in Paris, took Marie and her Aunt Caro to dinner at Voisin's, a farewell party before Mrs Hinrichsen left for Hamburg. Under Marie's guidance the two gentlemen did some extensive sight-seeing, Notre-Dame, the Louvre (especially the oriental collection), the Sorbonne, the Cluny Museum and several private collections which, as Mr Freer told Colonel Hecker, 'are everywhere thrown open to us and we, accompanied by Miss Nordlinger as interpreter, counsellor and friend, are seeing practically everything oriental'. At the end of May, Marie and Mr Freer went to London for more sight-seeing – Richmond, Chiswick and Kew – and made a nostalgic tour of Whistler's old haunts in Chelsea. Before he returned to America, plans were made for her to go to Detroit the following year to help him sort out and catalogue his collections. Meanwhile he commissioned two translations from her, one a biography of Whistler by Théodore Duret, published in 1904 in Paris, the second a pamphlet, *Une Contribution à l'étude de la céramique orientale*, by Daniel-Marie Fouquet. An agent was also placing articles by her in French art magazines.

Soon after her return to Manchester both Marcel and Reynaldo sent her reports of their visits to the Whistler Exhibition. Marcel wrote: 'Chère amie, You arrived in Paris like the Messiah but you left like a demon . . . What an idea not to warn me you were leaving so soon! I would have tried to see you rather than face the *fait accompli* of the hateful "Manchester, Victoria Park, etc."' He noted that all the most beautiful paintings belonged to Mr Freer, and that there was a reaction of opinion against Whistler among the French artistic élite, an opinion expressed by J.E. Blanche in the same issue of *La Renaissance latine* in which Marcel's preface 'On Reading' had been published. 'If the man who painted the Venices in turquoise, the Amsterdams in topaz, the Brittanies in opal, if the portraitist of Miss Alexander was not a great painter, you might as well believe there never was one.' He sent his copy of *Sésame* to Manchester for her to solve some last problems, ending with a memory of 'the charming, fervent and meticulous Venetian aunt, the friend of art, of goodness and comfort, so well disposed towards the writer of this letter' if she happened to be staying 'in mysterious Victoria Park, which I can never picture'.

Reynaldo shared Blanche's opinion of the pictures as a triumphant example of good taste, but sometimes he found there was a clumsiness and poverty mingled with the refinement; however, he admired the etchings. He was resting at Versailles after his concerts, he told Marie, and finishing off some small jobs: 'Marcel, whom I saw at the big party given by Mme Standish at which I conducted *Esther*, has been in a bad way recently. But I am convinced that this state of health is necessary for him and that he would be unhappy the day he got better. All the same, I wish this day would come for the sake of his mother and friends.'

The publication of the preface to *Sésame et les lys* in the June number of *La Renaissance latine* was an important stage in Proust's development as a writer. It was not really a study of Ruskin, more a purely personal essay, as his editor noted. Ruskin spoke of reading as a conversation with friends wiser and more interesting than the people one usually meets. Proust disagreed. For him, what he called 'the miracle of reading' was a pleasure to be enjoyed in solitude. He remembered the books that had so absorbed him as a boy spending Easter holidays in the country, books which were calendars of a time that had vanished, of places that no longer existed, and the atmosphere of simplicity and contentment of those days; the dining-room where Félicie, the old cook, interrupted the child's reading with her questions as she laid the table for lunch; the gardening uncle who got up early on a chilly morning to work in his vegetable patch; and the other garden above the village, with its stream, pond, asparagus and strawberry beds; beyond the hedge where the boy sat hidden with his book, there were fields of poppies and cornflowers, and lanes bordered with briar roses and hawthorns (Marcel had described the same parks and gardens at Etreuilles in *Jean Santeuil*). He made gentle fun of his grandfather and great-aunt, of family meals and the expertise of the cook, and gave a humorous description of his bedroom with all its ornaments, curtains and layers of bedspreads, which hardly conformed to the ideas of William Morris and the London catalogues of Messrs Maple, and which seemed to lead a secret life of its own, like those other bedrooms he had known in other provincial towns.

He thought Ruskin did not go deeply enough into the importance of reading as a stimulus; books, he wrote, are an incitement to probe deeper into impressions and those regions of the self where the true life of the mind begins. Conversation with friends dissipates the intellectual and spiritually active powers we enjoy when we are alone with a book. Marcel, of course, was speaking for himself; other people, more robust in health and lacking his single-mindedness, might well be stimulated by contacts with other points of view. Minds tired of seeking the truth for themselves would look for it in books 'like honey ready-made by others' and in a long footnote he quoted Sainte-Beuve writing his great work on Port-Royal in the library of a convent in Dordrecht – a description to some extent imaginary, based on a selection of his own impressions when he visited Holland in 1902. An artist must create the truth for himself by his own efforts and dedicate his life to the search for truth as he and no one else sees it.

The preface ends with a memory of Venice. When he read books by great writers of the past, Saint-Simon, Racine, Dante or Shakespeare, Marcel had a feeling of time past inserted into the present time – as he did when he walked through an old town like Beaune, or when he remembered the two twelfth-century columns on the Piazzetta still towering above the crowds of tourists, understanding no word of the languages spoken around them but preserving 'the inviolate place of the past familiarly risen in the midst of the present like a ghost from bygone times, yet there in our midst, to be approached, pressed against, touched, motionless in the sun'.

Marcel sent a set of the galley proofs of 'On Reading' to Reynaldo for comment. He, in a hurry to catch the late train back to Versailles after an evening at the Lemaires', scribbled a hasty note at the top of the first page: 'You said to put observations in the margin, so I have – here they are . . . Binuls.' He thought the whole essay was admirably written, but, he asked, was this the whole of it – surely not? 'It seems to me that if your appreciation of reading as a stimulus to the mind is complete, your criticism of it as a paralysing agent is not.'

His comments, at once appreciative and teasing, show how well he knew his friend's mind. It was really too bad of Marcel to inflict sentences of twenty-one, or even fifty-five, lines in length on his reader (in the printed book, fifty-five lines became seventy-four!). Certain phrases were both funny and typical (*drolch et buncht*), and one was given the highest praise: 'This sentence, written with an unconscious and balanced perfection, is worthy of Voltaire and Mozart.' The passage on the convent at Dordrecht was, he thought, exquisite, poetic and profoundly artistic, but it was too bad of Marcel to assume that everyone knew the name of Ruskin's favourite painter ('but I suppose it's Turner?'), and with the idea that truths obtained from books in libraries by scholars and historians are the most dangerous of all, Reynaldo thought he was being provocative: 'They are not dangerous at all, you are getting involved with metaphysics!' A page on the merits of Théophile Gautier's *Travels in Spain*, and how an author unconsciously reveals his character in everything he writes, drew the comment: 'This is very true, but [Gautier] made a cult of outward appearances just as Bininuls does of sensations.' Reynaldo's suggestions were too late for inclusion in the magazine article, but several of them were added to the page proofs before publication of the book in 1906.

Metaphysical, humorous, ironic and sensual (in the

widest interpretation of the word), the basic elements of the Proustian style are to be found in 'On Reading', as are a number of the themes he would develop in his novel. He knew that he had found his own voice at last, though he told Robert Dreyfus that he wished he could write as succinctly and elegantly as Mme Straus.

The manuscript of *Sésame et les lys* had now gone to the printer, to Marcel's relief. He sent his copy of *Sésame* to Marie for some last corrections – 'I was much moved to see the word Rusholme printed on your postcard,' he wrote. 'You know it was there that Ruskin gave the "Lilies" and "Treasuries" lectures . . .' In July a further five volumes of the Library Edition were published. They included *Sesame and Lilies*, *The Two Paths*, *The Queen of the Air* and *Lectures on Art and Literature*. Some of the explanations from the new volumes were incorporated into Marcel's notes but, as he pointed out in the first of them, the English editors refrained from comment on Ruskin's ideas and were mainly concerned with textual variants, unpublished fragments and so on, and were of no use to someone like himself who wanted to discover the essence of Ruskin's thought.

In a long footnote on the first page of 'Of Kings' Treasuries' he noted that besides its literal meaning of 'sesame seed', Ruskin gave 'sesame' several symbolic meanings – it was the magic word to open the robbers' cave and find the treasure; it was an allegory for reading as a key to wisdom; it was 'bread for the mind' and books in libraries were 'kings' treasures'. These various meanings were only made clear at the end of the lecture. So Proust in *The Search* made subtle use of the word 'time' and his purpose was only revealed at the end of *Time Regained* when he, as author, set himself the task of writing the work which his reader was just finishing. In the same footnote Proust continued his analysis of the way Ruskin's mind worked which he had begun in the first part of the preface to *La Bible d'Amiens*, exploring 'the hidden links' between ideas expressed in other works by Ruskin. There was a notable lack of logical composition in Ruskin's writing, he thought; yet his works had a unity, not of composition but of his multiple preoccupations, so that finally he seemed to have obeyed a secret plan which gave, retrospectively, a kind of order to the whole conception. Commentators have read into this analysis of Ruskin's psychological processes a blueprint for Proust's novel, a secret plan based not on linear progression but on unconscious memories and preoccupations. Many of the ideas in the footnotes to *Sésame et les lys* found a place, often in similar phrasing, in the second part of *Time Regained*, thoughts expanded and deepened over the intervening years, so that he could write: 'What we have not had to decipher, to elucidate by our own efforts, what was clear before we looked at it, is not ours.'[4]

Marcel acknowledged receipt of Marie's amendments to *Sésame* with a cheerful letter. She had made him laugh with an outburst against the *Bulletin de l'union pour l'action morale*. The *Bulletin* had evidently published an article on William Morris and his ideas of interior decoration. Marie must have disagreed with something in the article as she did not care for the work of the English Arts and Crafts movement. In the last page of Marie's draft memoirs, written over fifty years later, there is another 'explosion' which would have amused Marcel. It concerned the second lecture, 'Of Queens' Gardens', in which Ruskin maintained that the education of girls should be taken just as seriously as that of boys, and that a girl's choice of literature should be not more but less frivolous than that of her brother, whether novels, poetry or history. 'Looking back today,' Marie wrote, 'I find it difficult to explain my enthusiasm for *Sesame and Lilies*, except for the fact that it was very much the thing to admire a lecture dealing so lengthily with the "weaker sex" by so great a writer.'

On 6 September Siegfried Bing died at his home in Vaucresson. Marie's column-length obituary was published in the *Manchester Guardian* on 5 October. Reynaldo was on a working holiday at Réveillon and wrote to condole with her; Marcel's letter followed a few days later. He and his mother had gone to Evian, Marcel still in poor health, Mme Proust suffering from a kidney complaint; she was so ill that Robert had to take her back to Paris. In a short note Marcel told Marie that he was anxiously waiting for news: 'I hope all this will vanish like a bad dream, but while it lasts I am most unhappy . . . I thought about you a great deal when I heard of the death of your friend M. Bing.'

Jeanne Proust died on Tuesday 26 September, at the age of fifty-six. Reynaldo wrote at once to Marie in Manchester. Mme Proust had never renounced her Jewish faith out of deference to her parents so there was no church service, nor even prayers at home, before the long drive to the cemetery at Père Lachaise led by Marcel and Robert. Numb with shock and grief, Marcel set himself to reply to all the letters of condolence he had received. Later Marie wrote: 'I had known Marcel now for nearly ten years but I could not have foreseen the extent to which his entire being was overwhelmed by this calamity. Two or three letters from him at this time are the only ones I ever destroyed, fearing they might some day fall into the wrong hands. By the time that

Proust's nature and life's work were better understood, I might have felt the reproaches I have met with were justified, but I have no regrets.' Other correspondents kept their letters. Mme de Noailles knew that suffering is an essential part of an artist's life and was not surprised to recognize in M's account of his grandmother's death (in *The Guermantes Way*)[5] phrases similar to those used by Marcel in his letters to her in the autumn of 1905. Eighteen months later he told her that when he went through his mother's papers he found an exercise book in which she had set down, hour by hour, the last illnesses of her father and mother and of her husband – heart-rending accounts which he could hardly bear to read. His mother's life, he felt, had been a continual sacrifice, and his had lost its only purpose and consolation.

Marie was on holiday at Baslow in Derbyshire. Reynaldo's next letter reached her there, with a newspaper obituary of M. Bing and news of Marcel: 'Marcel, still very downcast, is bearing his grief with touching simplicity and courage. Fortunately, his health isn't too bad, and I am hoping that the solitude of his life will now compel him to do all he can to get his health back so that he is able to be more active and keep busy.'

Marcel was at last thinking of going into a nursing home for a cure; after booking himself into one clinic he suddenly changed his mind and allowed Mme Straus to make an appointment for him with Dr Sollier, who arranged for him to take a shorter course at a nursing home in Boulogne-sur-Seine. Here he dictated a short note to Marie on 6 December: 'Monsieur Proust is having treatment in a nursing home where he is not allowed to write letters, but he is anxious that Mlle Mary should know that he has never ceased to think of her with tenderness, respect and gratitude.'

15
A Change of Direction

For Marie, 1906 was a year of transatlantic travel. Reynaldo was busy conducting concerts in Paris and Salzburg, giving lectures in Turkey, as well as visiting in London, Brittany and Venice. And for Marcel it was a year of recuperation and readjustment, of 'regrets and reveries'. Early in January Marie sailed for a six-week trip to Jamaica as companion to an elderly Manchester friend of the family. Reynaldo's concert performances of three Mozart operas with Mme Lehmann were held at the end of March and were a great success, as he reported to Marie on her return to Manchester – 'Not a single empty seat and all the best people there . . . We missed you, and Lilli did not have her "lady's maid" this time.' Mme Hahn sent a longer account, full of maternal pride.

'The theatre was packed full, everyone very smart – the entire aristocracy of France – supreme elegance, pearls, diamonds, flowers, cheers, encores, etc., and finances satisfactory – Reynaldo didn't make anything, but didn't lose anything either . . . [He] is acclaimed by everyone as a splendid organizer and a superb conductor.' Mme Hahn was very fond of Marie. According to Reynaldo's sister, Maria, writing to Marie in Manchester after her brother's death, Mme Hahn would have welcomed her as a daughter-in-law, but she once remarked to Clara Nordlinger, after the two cousins had left the room arm in arm, 'It's a pity he's too young for her'; to his mother Reynaldo was 'l'enfant gâté des dames' (a child spoilt by the ladies) and 'notre cher pigeon voyageur' (our beloved carrier pigeon)!

One of the artists who made her début as Cherubino in *The Marriage of Figaro* in March 1906, and kept happy memories of the concerts, was Dame Maggie Teyte. She had come to Paris straight from her convent school to study with Jean de Rezské, through whom she met Reynaldo. She admired him as both man and musician, describing him as tall and handsome. As a singer he had a very long breath, and marvellous timing. She found him great fun to work with, his performances of Mozart had charm and precision, and he was always ready to see a *double entendre*. Miss Teyte considered that she owed her subsequent success in Mozart operas to three men: Jean de Rezské who, as a teacher, insisted on technique rather than temperament; Sir Thomas Beecham; and Reynaldo.[1]

In April Reynaldo went to Turkey for a month, part lecture tour, part holiday. By the time he got back to Paris at the end of May, after a fortnight in London, Marie had already left for America. She arrived in Detroit on Sunday 29 April. The arrangement she had come to with Mr Freer was that she should stay two or three months to help him sort out his collections and catalogue them. She did not stay at Ferry Avenue because the house was undergoing extensive alterations to provide new exhibition and storage rooms; but she was there every day, including Sundays, with only an occasional day off. Mr Freer enjoyed her company as well as appreciating her capacity for hard work. Their relationship was based on a congenial working partnership. By mid-July they were busy installing the collections in the new rooms and completing the catalogue. At the end of the month Marie went to stay with the Morses in Evanston for a rest. When she returned to Ferry Avenue, Mr Freer thought she looked a hundred years younger than when she left. He too felt the need for rest and change and was planning an extensive tour of the Near and Far East for the coming winter and spring.

Meanwhile he was keen to show off the new rooms and their contents to friends and art experts. Marie was left in charge while he went to New York to see Professor Fennolosa and to welcome the Louvre's expert on oriental art, M. Migeon. Both gentlemen visited Detroit for a long weekend, where they had some interesting discussions. There were numerous visitors to Ferry Avenue during September, among them Mr and Mrs Henry O. Havemeyer who had a superb collection of Japanese objets d'art as well as paintings which Mrs Havemeyer had begun to buy in the 1870s when she was a student in Paris. She died in 1929, bequeathing paintings, Persian and oriental ceramics, prints and glass to the Metropolitan Museum in New York.

Marie must have found the company of such stimulating visitors both an education and a relaxation from her duties in Ferry Avenue – as well as providing a network of useful connections for the time when, after her marriage, she and her husband opened their showroom in the rue du Faubourg Saint-Honoré for the sale of pictures and objets d'art. Her departure for Hamburg and home was fixed for 4 October. 'The two months she came for have more than doubled themselves,' Mr Freer told Charles Morse, 'and during all this time she has rendered great service to my collection, as well as to have added to the pleasure of life in many ways.' He went to New York to see her off, and early in November set sail himself for Egypt, China and Japan.

During her five months' absence Marie received one long letter from Reynaldo which followed her to Detroit from Manchester. He had just arrived in Belle-Ile to stay with Mme Sarah and her family. 'Ma chère amie,' he wrote at the end of June, 'I have been wanting to write to you for some time . . . Marcel has asked me more than once for your address so as to send you his book . . . For some months now I have suffered from a bitter melancholy and, though I try not to let it show, it is eating away inside me . . . If I knew how to direct my own life as well as I can advise other people my character and destiny would be quite different! Mille affections et bons souvenirs, Reynaldo.' There is no trace of depression in the lively account he wrote for his journal about the two weeks spent in Belle-Ile in 1906.[2] He loved and admired Mme Sarah for her courage as much as for her vivacity and elegance. She was limping badly after a fall at the end of *Tosca* during her South American tour the previous year, an injury which led to the amputation of her leg during the wartime winter of 1915 when Reynaldo in the trenches was informed by telegram: 'Ami chéri, they are going to cut my leg off tomorrow morning. Think of me. Sarah.'

The house was full of guests: Maurice Bernhardt, his wife and two young daughters; Clairin, who had a studio in the garden; and other old friends. Reynaldo loved to hear Sarah and Clairin talk about the early days of her career. After dinner on his last evening he watched Sarah sleeping, her head drooping on her arm, and remembered some of her most moving roles: her feline movements in *Théodora*; the way she watched Scarpia in *Tosca*; the play scene in *Hamlet*; the exultation in her voice, dominating the shouts of the crowd, in *La Samaritaine*. It was time to leave: 'Come back next year, Reynaldo. We'll forgive you for leaving us now if you promise to come to America with us this winter . . .'

From Belle-Ile he went on to Munich and Salzburg, where a distinguished cast was rehearsing. He was flattered to be asked to conduct at the festival – but he could never forget how much Mozart hated Salzburg and found it ironic that a Mozart Festival should be established there rather than in Vienna or Prague, where the greater part of *Don Giovanni* had been written.

Mme Lehmann had difficulty in casting the role of the Don and finally engaged François d'Andrade from Berlin; he, though elegant and experienced, was past his prime. However, he gave a polished performance. Herman Brag sang Leporello; Geraldine Farrer, Zerlina; Joanna Gadski-Tauscher, Elvira; and Lilli Lehmann, Donna Anna. The orchestra was the Vienna Philharmonic. The performance received a rapturous reception and Reynaldo was offered a conducting tour in the United States. Mme Hahn, with Maria, Elisa, Tante Caro, some of the Hamburg friends and Saint-Saëns were in the audience. A card from Reynaldo to Marie after the second concert performance reported another triumph, while to Risler he wrote: 'The main thing is that I think we served Mozart well . . . you know how severely I judge myself. Well, yes, I think I can say it – I was quite pleased!'

The secret of his success as a conductor of Mozart lay perhaps in a journal note he made when he first began, with the encouragement of Saint-Saëns, to study the opera scores in 1897: 'It is a mistake to conduct Mozart as though he were a German; he is an Italian composer.' This was an unusual point of view at the time, when Mozart's music was neglected as much in Germany as in France, a neglect which the Salzburg festivals inaugurated by the Archduke Eugene and Mme Lehmann did much to redress (they did not become an annual event until 1920); so too did Reynaldo's performances in Paris and other French opera houses in the years before and after the First World War.[3]

After the excitement of Salzburg, Reynaldo went to Venice where he enjoyed success of a different kind. Many of his Paris friends were there, chief among them the Princesse de Polignac, the Comtesse de Guerne, Mme de Béarn, the Chevignés, the Grand Duke Paul, and the Fortunys. There were lunch and dinner parties; he sang his Venetian songs on the lagoon, on the Grand Canal and, at the request of Mme de Béarn, for a few friends in gondolas on one of the small canals, with just a piano and two oarsmen in the boat. The place they chose, at the junction of three small canals, with three bridges across them, was quiet and intimate, and the audience an appreciative one. Slowly, the bridges filled with strollers; the bigger, uninvited audience were over-joyed to hear him sing the songs he had written in their dialect – 'Ancora! Ancora!' they cried. It was an evening he remembered always with pleasure. On a postcard of the Rialto which reached Marie in Detroit some time in September, he wrote: 'Here I am again in Venice and last night I sang my songs on the canal before a huge audience; the gondoliers especially made it a great success!'

One evening after a party on Mme de Béarn's yacht he returned alone to his hotel with Antonio, the gondolier he always employed, thinking of Shakespeare and remembering that he had the idea in Salzburg of writing an opera on *The Merchant of Venice* which should be treated as Mozart had treated the story of Don Juan with contrasted serious and light-hearted scenes. The idea lay fallow until, during the First World War, he began to compose the music while in the Argonne under heavy shellfire. There was the usual difficulty in finding a suitable libretto, and it was not produced at the Paris Opéra until 1935.

Although he was not supposed to send letters from Dr Sollier's clinic during the six weeks he spent there, Marcel managed to write to a few selected friends and even receive visits from them. Reynaldo was deputed to keep Robert de Montesquiou informed about the invalid's progress. However, the psychotherapeutic treatment he received did not cure his nervous disorder, but at least he had kept the promise made to his mother – that he would try a cure. The New Year resurrected such painful memories of her that he could hardly bring himself to thank Mme de Noailles for her telegram and present: 'For me, who never believed in anniversaries, New Year's Day had a terrible evocative power,' he wrote. He stayed at home and corrected the proofs of *Sésame et les lys*, which was published in June, receiving excellent notices from the literary reviewers. André Beaunier wrote a short pen-portrait of the author for *Le Figaro* and a week later praised the translation as 'a masterpiece of intelligent flexibility, a marvellous success'. Marcel sent a copy of the book to Marie, with his name crossed out on the yellow paper cover and hers inserted in its place, but it never reached her; in accordance with her wishes, he modified his tribute to her help and just mentioned her name with that of Charles Newton-Scott, who had helped with some of the translation problems.

He was now considered an expert on Ruskin and his works. Early in May he wrote a review for *La Chronique des arts et de la curiosité* of a translation of Ruskin's *The*

Stones of Venice (abridged Traveller's Edition) by Mme Peigné-Crémieux and praised her interpretation of Ruskin's prose. It was six years since he, Marie and Reynaldo had been in Venice with Mme Hahn and Tante Caro, and he was haunted by dreams of Italy. His mother's great friend, Mme Catusse, sent him a postcard of Florence, where she was spending a holiday; he would love to go to Florence, he told her, someday, perhaps – Venice was 'too much a graveyard of happiness' and he did not feel strong enough to revisit it, but he had recently received a further five volumes of the Library Edition of Ruskin which included *Mornings in Florence, Val d'Arno,* the lecture on 'Michelangelo and Tintoret', *Giotto and his Works in Padua, The Guide to the Academy, Venice* and *St Mark's Rest,* all again with numerous admirable illustrations. Volume XXIII, containing the last three works, had reproductions of all Giotto's *Vices and Virtues* in the Arena Chapel at Padua, and of fourteen paintings by Carpaccio, the St Ursula cycle, in the Accademia.[4]

Proust seems to have written fewer letters than usual in 1906 except for those he sent to Reynaldo. Since the early days of their friendship, Reynaldo had been a constant solace and support; now, during his recurrent bouts of melancholy, Marcel wrote to cheer him up – pages of high-spirited nonsense, absurd verses, wordplay, illustrated by pen sketches with explanatory captions, and showing an extensive scholarship and knowledge, lightly worn, of books, history, art. They included parodies of letters (supposedly from Comtesse Greffuhle, president of a Concerts Society). There was a long ballad in the style of Villon on the pleasure of making investments – all this in the special language they used, with the habitual nicknames and misspellings. He repeatedly asked Reynaldo to burn the letters after reading them, warnings that Reynaldo ignored.

Their minds were so much in tune that, as Marcel said: 'I feel, when I write to you, that I am writing to myself,' and, on another occasion, 'I can't say I think of you often, because you are always present in my mind as though you were one of its essential elements.' The gaiety and affectionate intimacy of these letters reveal an unsuspected side of Marcel's complicated personality yet it was one his close friends knew well. Marie wrote, in the introduction to her English translation of *Lettres à une amie*: 'You could not fail, whether in society or in the seclusion of the sickroom, to succumb to the charm and originality, the delicacy, the compelling strength of his grace'; and Sydney Schiff noted that he was like a glorious spoilt child in the eagerness and curiosity with which he asked endless questions, and the charm, of which he himself was well aware.

Some commentators have thought, and Marie agreed with them, that many of the letters were too trivial and childish to be worth publishing. When she brought the Proust–Hahn correspondence back to Manchester after her cousin's death, she chose sixty-eight of the 162 letters then available as being of general interest. The rest often need copious explanations and even then are not easy to understand (and are impossible to translate).

Mme Straus continued to be a sympathetic correspondent. When Marcel thanked her for her appreciation of his essay 'On Reading' he praised her talent for writing with such simplicity and wit. The Dreyfus case was in the news again. At last, after seven years of effort by his family and supporters, Captain Alfred Dreyfus had been completely vindicated; on 20 July he was reinstated in the army with the rank of major and made an officer of the Légion d'Honneur. 'What you say about the Dreyfus affair,' Marcel told Mme Straus, 'is naturally the funniest, most profound and best-written thing that could be said on the subject.'

He was thinking of taking a holiday, perhaps at Trouville. At the last minute he decided to go to the Hôtel des Reservoirs at Versailles so as to be near Paris and able to visit his ailing uncle, Georges Weil, who had been so good to him after Mme Proust's death. Apart from one visit to his uncle's sickbed which made him so ill he could not attend the funeral, he never left his room for the first six weeks and never went out of the hotel during his five months' stay there. He was consoled by frequent visits from Reynaldo and other friends and passed the time reading, chatting with the servants and watching the world go by from his window, like Tante Léonie in *Swann's Way*.

On her return to Europe from Detroit, Marie spent the month of November with her grandmother in Hamburg where a hasty letter from Reynaldo told her that he hoped to have a few days in London before embarking on his American tour at the end of December. He asked her to translate some of his lectures into 'the language of Shakespeare and Longfellow' for his American audience. When he wrote again, on 29 December, he had decided not to cross the Atlantic after all – the agent who had booked the tour had no funds, Mme Hahn was not well and he had not been looking forward to the journey.

Marcel sent a copy of *Sésame* to Manchester which reached her on 10 December. He explained that so far no royalties had been paid on the sale of the book, but he would gladly send her an advance if she needed it as he no longer had to account to anyone about how he spent his money. He was leaving the flat in the rue de Courcelles because the lease had expired at the end of September; and in any case it was now too big for him, and too full of memories. As a temporary measure, he had decided to rent a flat at 102, Boulevard Haussmann, formerly owned by his great-uncle, Louis Weil, which his mother and her brother had inherited.

His letter began: 'Chère, chère, chère, chère Mary . . . how close you are to my heart and how little absence has separated you from me! I think of you constantly with so much affection and with an indestructible longing for the past. In a shattered life, in a heart destroyed, you keep a fond place . . . Are you working? I no longer am. I have closed for ever the era of translations which Maman encouraged – and as for translations of my own, I no longer have the courage. Did you see beautiful things in America? How is your aunt, to whom please remember me? And whom I recollect as one of the most remarkable Stones of Venice. Nothing could move, nothing could affect the rigidity of her principles. But how I liked her and how fond she seemed to be of you! And she represented so perfectly for me the *Mornings in Venice* which I never saw . . . the early riser who doesn't know what it is to stay in bed.'

'As for translations of my own, I no longer have the courage' – the same phrase again – what was stopping him from beginning the long-planned original work? Was it writer's block, a lack of confidence? In *The Search* Proust exaggerated M's propensity for self-depreciation, making it one of the reasons, together with his 'nerves', for delay in getting down to work.[5]

Reynaldo acknowledged Marie's translation of his lecture on Gounod – it was absolutely perfect, even flattering: 'I had no idea I had expressed myself so aptly nor with such elegance!' In a footnote he added: 'Marcel wonders if it was you who sent him a Ruskin calendar and Gainsborough's *Blue Boy*?'[6] And he sent her his new collection of songs, *Les Feuilles blessées*. Marcel was delighted that Reynaldo had not gone to America. He relied on him for all sorts of errands; when Reynaldo visited art exhibitions, antique and book shops, or the sale rooms, he would find a small water-colour by Madeleine Lemaire to be given to Louisa de Mornand or twelve volumes of Walter Scott (in English, preferably illustrated) for Marcel's cousin, Adèle Weil.

Mme Hahn and Reynaldo spent the New Year in bed with coughs and colds. Marcel too was bedridden but he thanked Marie for the calendar with a quotation from Ruskin for each day of the year. 'I cannot let you leave without thanking you with all my heart for the calendar of days which become delights, each one bringing with it a "thing of beauty, a joy for ever" [in English].' He wrote 'I cannot let you leave' because Mr Freer had invited her to join him in the Far East – she never in fact visited China or Japan.

16
Cabourg

Although the flat in the Boulevard Haussmann was not really ready for occupation (in spite of the best efforts of Robert Proust, Mme Catusse and Félicie), Marcel suddenly decided to leave Versailles at the end of December and move into his new home. For the next three months he complained continually about the hammering going on in adjacent flats, his consequent insomnia and the damage to his health. Knowing that Marie was interested in everything he wrote, he sent her a brief letter to Manchester with copies of two articles he had written for *Le Figaro* in February and March, the first sparked off by an item in the same newspaper, the second by a book of memoirs he was reading.

The news item was about a man he knew slightly and with whom he had recently exchanged letters, Henri van Blarenberghe, who, in a fit of dementia, had stabbed his mother to death and then killed himself. Marcel's article, 'Sentiments filiaux d'un parricide', made of this domestic tragedy a Greek drama – the unhappy murderer was not a brutish criminal 'but a noble example of humanity, a tender and pious son, driven by an inexorable fate'. Some of his readers found the article in poor taste, others admired it as an attempt to give a mythical dimension to a contemporary news story.

In the second article Marcel found another way of giving depth to contemporary portraits by setting them in a historical perspective. Confined to his room by illness and bad weather, he read everything available, the daily papers, literary reviews, the most recent novels sent to him by friends and acquaintances, historical novels by Dumas *père,* and the first of five volumes of the memoirs, recently published, of the Comtesse de Boigne, a lady whose life-span covered five reigns, for she was born in 1791 and died, aged eighty-six, in 1867.

The article appeared in *Le Figaro* with the title 'Days of Reading', but the reminiscences simply provided a pretext for airing some of the ideas which preoccupied Marcel. His thoughts progressed in a sort of spiral, from books to the marvels of the telephone and its unseen operators, the Vigilant Virgins,[1] and then back to books, the memoirs, and so to the medieval-sounding names of eighteenth-century aristocrats – Odon, Ghislain, Josselin, Adhéaume – names borne by some of his own friends, descendants of the original holders; but he found his contemporaries far less glamorous than their ancestors because the latter inhabited the dream world of his imagination. He realized that actual places and people never fulfilled the hopes invested in their names by his fantasies. It would be wiser, he added wryly, to replace all social relationships and journeys to distant places by a reading of the *Almanac de Gotha* or the railway timetable. The other alternative, the one he put into practice, would be to create a world for himself of fictional people and places based on those he had known – and again he used the Homeric comparison of the ghosts which Ulysses dispersed with his sword when they begged him to give them life or burial. The title of the article had originally been 'Snobbery and Posterity' but, Marcel explained, this would have to wait until a later date because his wandering thoughts had been constantly interrupted by the pleading ghosts, the varied characters for a novel which haunted him, half submerged in his mind. The editor of *Le Figaro* cut his article by two whole columns.

These two columns, he told Reynaldo, were the only pages which really pleased him; here was a 'translation of himself' which needed little alteration to become part of his novel – the society drawing-rooms he described became the drawing-room of Mme de Villeparisis; her relationship with the Guermantes and her liaison with the retired diplomat, M. de Norpois, reappeared in *The Guermantes Way*.[2] The ladies who wrote memoirs like the one he had been reading were nearly always on the fringe of fashionable society, the famous guests they entertained were few but were enough to fill the pages of their diaries. Really fashionable hostesses had no time to write because they were always visiting or receiving visitors.

In his letter to Marie of 13 April Marcel asked her to return the two articles in case he should want to collect his work in book form. The winter had been such a miserable one for him that he could not remember if he had thanked her for the Ruskin calendar she sent him for Christmas. The letter ended: 'I am so tired I haven't the strength to write any more. Will you allow me, from so far away, to embrace you?' He was evidently too exhausted to mention an event, an important one for Reynaldo, which took place the same evening, in the music room of the Princesse de Polignac, when he conducted the first performance of his orchestral suite, *Le Bal de Béatrice d'Este*, scored for wind instruments, two harps and piano, evoking court ballets in sixteenth-century Milan in a tuneful and slightly ironic way. The programme included music by Vincent d'Indy, songs by Fauré and another piece by Reynaldo, a choral work based on an ode by Horace, *La Fontaine de Bandusie*.

This was the first big party Marcel had attended since

his mother's death. As soon as he got home he sent Reynaldo a letter to thank him for making him go to it. He thought Reynaldo had conducted superbly, but some of his facial expressions and gestures were rather exaggerated, and his strenuous piano playing had nearly caused the candles to fall over and set fire to the paper roses which decorated the platform. 'I did admire the way you succeeded in making so many society people listen in silence,' Marcel wrote. He had observed the audience closely and noted one lady's rather tipsy laughter and another's foolish running commentary on Fauré's *Les Roses d'Isphahan*. Most of all, he noticed how much older everyone looked since he had last seen them (with the exception of their hostess who, now aged forty-two, managed to combine the charm of maturity with an air of youth). In *Time Regained*, at the last big party given by the Princesse de Guermantes (formerly Mme Verdurin), Proust heightened these impressions so that the guests, with their white hair and wrinkled faces, seemed to have assumed disguises for some grotesque fancy-dress ball.[3]

It had been a busy few months for Reynaldo. In February he was invited to lunch at the British Embassy to sing after the meal for King Edward and Queen Alexandra, who were in Paris on a private visit. He was writing incidental music for a play by Maurice Maeterlinck, to be performed in Russia and New York; and he was collaborating with Jules Lemaître on another play. He had at last, and thankfully, finished *Promethée*. During the spring Chaliapin made his debut at the Paris Opéra in a series of concerts of Russian music promoted by Diaghilev. The success of these concerts encouraged the

Russian impresario to bring Mussorgsky's *Boris Godunov* to Paris with Chaliapin in the title role, and then the following year, 1909, the Russian Ballet, with which Reynaldo was to become involved.

Mme Sarah and her company were on tour in provincial France; Reynaldo joined them in Angers where he remembered his visit with Massenet in the cold winter of 1892. At the end of June he was back in London, dividing his time between the Meyer cousins in Hill Street and the Mond cousins in Stratton Street. Marie was there too, staying with friends in Kensington (she did not much care for the ambience of Reynaldo's smart relations). Notes reached her every day: 'Come to lunch tomorrow'; 'Come and have tea at the Ritz with one or two special people – I count on you!' While she was in London, Marie received a second proposal of marriage. She refused the offer because her suitor was an orthodox Jew and she had no wish to leave Europe to live in South Africa.

She went, of course, to the two lecture recitals which Reynaldo gave at Lady Sassoon's house in Park Lane. The first, on 25 June, was entitled 'L'Evocation par la musique'. He sang his own compositions and old French songs to an audience in which there were many of his admirers, as *The Times* reviewer noted. The same reviewer expressed surprise that no mention was made of Debussy, 'the great modern master of evocation in music, whose chief, if not only merit, is the creation of musical atmosphere'. The second recital on Friday afternoon, 27 June, was devoted to Gounod, whose *mélodies* Reynaldo considered to be undeservedly neglected.

The other noteworthy event was the party given by Consuelo, Dowager Duchess of Manchester, for the King and Queen, the Landgrave of Hesse and his wife, members of the Court, the diplomatic corps and assorted society people. Reynaldo wrote a racy account of the occasion in his journal. He had brought from Paris the same musicians who had performed *Le Bal de Béatrice d'Este* for the Princesse de Polignac in April, but there were no music stands for them, he as conductor was expected to wear court dress – knee breeches, silk stockings, buckled shoes, which he had to borrow from somewhere – and his hostess insisted on playing and singing with him Spanish songs which she remembered from her girlhood! The orchestral suite was to be the main item in the concert to entertain the guests before dinner. The Queen, whose deafness made conversation difficult, was placed by Reynaldo as close to the musicians as possible. She was delighted by the suite and wanted to hear it played over again. Afterwards Reynaldo sang songs by Offenbach to amuse the King. It was at Coombe, the country home of Lord and Lady de Grey, that Reynaldo met Queen Alexandra on subsequent occasions; he always greatly admired her simplicity and natural charm and she loved to hear his *mélodies*.

Owing to his London engagements, Reynaldo was not able to get back to Paris in time to sing for Marcel's guests at a big dinner party he gave at the Ritz Hotel on 1 July, in honour of M. Calmette, director of *Le Figaro*, and M. Beaunier, its editor. Marcel had engaged Gabriel Fauré to play after dinner but he was taken ill at the last moment and Edouard Risler agreed to take his place (for the vast fee of 1,000 francs). Risler's programme of music by Beethoven, Schumann, Chopin, Wagner, Couperin and Fauré was so long that there was no time for him to play any of the pieces by Reynaldo that Marcel had hoped to hear. It was all a great success, but expensive, as he told Reynaldo: 'For the same money, I could have had the Society of Wind Instruments in *Béatrice* if they had been in Paris.'

As soon as Reynaldo returned to Paris, he sent Marie a copy of Mme de Noailles' new book of poems, *Les Eblouissements*. Marcel's review had appeared in *Le Figaro littéraire* on 15 June, but, as Reynaldo pointed out when Marcel read the draft to him, it was much too long for the front page of the paper and would certainly have to be cut – there was always so much that Marcel wanted to say. He thought he would like to write a book on 'The Six Gardens of Paradise', beginning with the 'poet's garden' of Mme de Noailles, then Ruskin's garden at Brantwood, Maeterlinck's with its beehives and Monet's water garden at Giverny.[4]

Marie's copy of *Les Eblouissements* reached her with a letter from Reynaldo dated 26 July, in which he asked her to translate into English yet another of his lectures: 'It is fiendishly hot, and although I am a little apprehensive about the journey to Belle-Ile, I am looking forward impatiently to rest and fresh air on Sarah's rock. My ballet is called *La Fête chez Thérèse* and is based on the lovely poem in *Les Contemplations* which you probably know. I am very happy with the project, which gives me a lot of scope . . .' Of course, Marie knew the poem – Marcel quoted a favourite line when he wrote to her in Auteuil.

By the time Reynaldo got back to Paris from Belle-Ile, Marcel had already left. He was feeling better. After some hesitation, he suddenly made up his mind and went off to the Grand Hotel at Cabourg, where he had spent childhood holidays with his mother and grandmother. The train journey from the Gare Saint Lazare and arrival

at the hotel brought back memories of Marcel's last holiday with his mother two years before. The bedroom, with
its square mirror, reminded him of the room he had
occupied at Evian, and the sea-view from the window
made him think of Venice. 'Maman retrouvée en voyage,'
he wrote in a new notebook. Perhaps it was on this holiday that he experienced an involuntary memory similar
to the one he described on M's second visit to Balbec,
one of the most poignant episodes in the whole of *The
Search*, when M realizes, stooping to unbutton his boots,
a year after his grandmother's death, that she has gone
for ever, and that the heart has its intermittences. As
time ticks away, imperceptibly but surely, feelings and
perceptions change. It was not just the loss of his grandmother that M experienced, it was also that of the young
man he had once been.[5]

Although Marcel complained to one of his correspondents of feeling sterile and unhappy, the holiday in
Cabourg had the same vitalizing effect on him as the
weeks spent at Beg-Meil with Reynaldo. He was full of
plans for a book. His interest in churches and painters
revived, and he now discovered the pleasures and perils
of motoring. His former school friend Jacques Bizet
owned a taxi company which operated during the summer on the Normandy coast, and on the Riviera during
the winter. Bizet employed several young drivers, two of
whom, Odilon Albaret and Alfred Agostinelli, eventually
played important parts in Marcel's life.

During August and September 1907 they drove him
round the villages and churches of Normandy. He went
off, nearly every day, with one or other of the young
chauffeurs. He visited, by taxi, Georges de Lauris at
Houlgate, Mme Straus at Trouville, Louisa and Robert
Gagnat (Albu's successor) and other friends who were

staying in the neighbourhood. A new valet, Nicolas Cottin, had gone with Marcel. He, with his wife, Céline, had replaced the old family servant, Félicie Fitau, who retired at the beginning of July; he had worked for the family when Dr Proust was alive and stayed with Marcel until the outbreak of war in 1914.

One young guest at the Grand Hotel who met Marcel there was particularly impressed by the accuracy of his memory, his knowledge of church architecture and his humour. René Gimpel was the son of a Paris art dealer; he too was keenly interested in visiting the small villages and churches in the Normandy countryside. Marcel read *Les Eblouissements* aloud to René, and discussed plays and books, especially Balzac's novels, which repaid constant rereading. He told him, too, the general outline of the series of novels he was planning, one of which had 'an improper and controversial subject'.

Marcel sent two long and affectionate letters to Reynaldo while he was in Cabourg to keep him up to date with the seaside gossip and, in the first of them, to ask him to send his manservant, Léon, round to the Boulevard Haussmann flat and post urgently to Cabourg five volumes of the Library Edition of Ruskin. He needed Volumes VI, VII, XII, XIV and one on Turner, the number of which he could not remember (it was XIII). Volume VI contained *The Seven Lamps of Architecture*, illustrated by Ruskin's drawings of architectural detail. The long preface described all the places in northern France visited by John and Effie Ruskin on their honeymoon in 1848, an itinerary fairly closely followed by Marcel during his drives with Albaret and Agostinelli in 1907.

Volumes VI, XII and XIII were all concerned with Turner. In Volume VI there was the chapter from *Modern Painters*, Volume IV, 'Of Turnerian Topography', in which

Ruskin analysed Turner's genius and the nature of the imagination, involuntary memory and dreams. (Some of these volumes, probably VI and XIII, were intended for Mme de Clermont Tonnerre on loan, especially for the illustrations.) As well as the volumes of the Library Edition, Marcel asked for a little book on Carpaccio from his bookshelves and a second-hand copy, if one could be found, of Turner's *Rivers of France*. The 'Lectures on Art and Architecture' in Volume XII included a pamphlet written in support of the Pre-Raphaelite painters which, in spite of its title, dealt mainly with Turner's use of colour. Once again, Ruskin emphasized the tenacity of Turner's memory and his ability to 'forget himself and forget nothing else'. In Volume XIII he wrote a brilliant preface for *The Harbours of England*, describing Turner's marine paintings; this inspired Proust's own descriptions of the sea at Balbec and Elstir's pictures of 'Turner-esque seas'.

When M visited Elstir in Balbec, most of the pictures he saw in the studio were seascapes; he thought the charm of them lay in a sort of metamorphosis of the things represented in it, 'analogous to what in poetry we call metaphor'. Elstir tried to reproduce things not as he knew them to be but according to the optical illusions of which our first sight of them is composed. This is what Turner did too, as Marcel pointed out in the preface to *La Bible d'Amiens*.[6] Elstir's description of the church porch at Balbec is a pastiche of Ruskin; the sculptures round it form 'the finest illustrated Bible that the people have ever had'. His explanation to M about the carvings was most erudite, yet, wrote Proust, this exceptionally cultivated man, when he sat down to paint, made himself deliberately ignorant, he made an effort to strip himself, when faced with reality, of every intellectual concept. And he advised his young visitor not to ration his daydreams: 'If a little daydreaming is dangerous, the cure for it is not to dream less but to dream more, to dream all the time. One must have a thorough understanding of one's daydreams if one is not to be troubled by them.'[7]

Drafts for the beginning of a novel were soon to proliferate, with sections describing childhood holidays in the country and at the seaside, notes on M's family, his friends, the drawing rooms of people he knew, both bourgeois and aristocratic. Only the artists – painter, writer, actress – were not yet allotted the leading roles they were to play in *The Search*. One of the drafts related a touching childhood memory which may have been intended for publication as a short story. Maman and little brother Robert were going away on a visit, leaving a miserable M to follow with his father after a few days. They were staying with relatives near Chartres and the child, aged five and a half, had been dressed to have his photograph taken. Robert had been given a pet goat which he wanted to take with him. Maman said 'No!', so the child, resplendent in ribbons and lace, disappeared into the garden to bid the beloved animal a tearful farewell. He was found eventually by his mother and brother dishevelled and sobbing in frustrated fury, his toy cart in one hand, his other arm round the goat, looking not at all like 'those rural pictures by English artists which depict a child nursing an animal'.

Marcel's desire to find just such a genre picture as illustration for his story might account for his request to Reynaldo for Volume XIV of the Library Edition, which contains Ruskin's *Academy Notes* for 1855–9. As well as reproductions of sketches by Prout of Abbeville, Amiens, Lisieux and Evreux, it contained some of W.H. Hunt's fruit and flower paintings; Hunt also painted pictures of peasant children. In January 1908 Marcel wrote to a sub-editor at *La Gazette des beaux arts* asking him to find a suitable English engraving, presumably to illustrate his story. In the final version of the scene in *Swann's Way* Proust reduced his draft from seven pages to twenty-five lines. Instead of little Robert, it was M as a child at Combray who bid a tearful farewell not to a goat but to his favourite hawthorn blossoms in words originally attributed to his brother: 'Oh, my poor little hawthorns, it is not you who want to make me unhappy to force me to go away. You, you have never done me any harm, so I shall always love you!'[8]

After Cabourg, Marcel spent four days in Evreux to see the cathedral and several churches; with Agostinelli as chauffeur, he visited Caen and Lisieux where they arrived after dark and the young man shone the car headlights on the façade of the cathedral so that his passenger could see and touch the leafy branches in stone on either side of the porch which Ruskin had described. Only a quick call was made to the Clermont-Tonnerres at Glisolles and the promised volumes of Ruskin were sent to Mme Elizabeth by parcel post.

Marcel recounted his motoring adventures in an article, 'Impressions de route en automobile', published by *Le Figaro* on 19 November. He described how, as the car sped along the winding road to Caen, with each change of direction the two towers of Sainte-Etienne and the spire of Saint-Pierre, far away in the distance, danced round the horizon. When the car drew nearer to the town, other steeples and the vertical layers of rooftops below them joined in the complicated fugue. He wrote of their arrival at Lisieux at night and compared his young companion, as he touched the instruments on the dashboard of the car, to St Cecilia improvising a tune on the clavichord.

When he eventually revised his newspaper articles for publication in *Pastiches et mélanges* in 1919, Proust admitted that his interest in churches in 1907 had been to provide material for a novel and that he had 'translated' the dancing spires of Caen into those of Martinville-le-Sec which M in *Swann's Way* had seen on a ride in Dr Percepied's carriage. The two long paragraphs which M scribbled in pencil as they drove back to Combray made him so happy because he had managed to describe his impressions that he began to sing at the top of his voice like a hen that has laid an egg! These paragraphs, slightly revised, formed the one piece of writing in the whole novel which indicated the 'invisible vocation of which this book is the history'. They were eventually sent to *Le Figaro* (in *The Guermantes Way*) and their publication was anxiously awaited by M and his mother until they appeared at last, an indeterminate number of years later, in the penultimate section, *The Fugitive*.[9]

By the end of 1907 the long apprenticeship was over. Work in progress can be roughly charted from the notebook Proust used during the next two years, from the exercise books in which he wrote his innumerable drafts, from a number of surviving loose pages and letters to his friends. It is possible, but unlikely, that he might have started work on a novel in 1905, after his mother died and *Sésame et les lys* had been published. This novel would have been as different from that of 1908–9 –

which he called 'my Sainte-Beuve' – as that of 1909 differed from *Swann's Way* in 1913, and the projected three-volume novel of 1913 from the unfinished masterpiece of 1922.

17
Notes and Drafts

In New Year 1908 Reynaldo insisted on keeping to his concert schedule despite a temperature and sore throat. Marcel reproached him for sacrificing his gift for composition to a meretricious social success, even though this had come about 'in such a flattering as well as elegant and remunerative way', referring to the many invitations Reynaldo received for lecture recitals in centres other than London and Paris. Marcel could not understand that Reynaldo, with expensive tastes and an inability to deal with money matters, needed to earn a good living.

As a New Year present Mme Straus sent Marcel five small notebooks. For the next two years he used the largest of them to jot down thoughts as they occurred to him and to make notes on what he was reading. In his letter of thanks he told her that he hoped soon to begin a rather lengthy piece of work. On the first two pages of the notebook (the *carnet*) there are references to Vautrin and Rubempré in Balzac's novels, dreams about his mother and father, the difficulties of falling in love, and whether his mother would understand his novel – the answer was 'No'!

In a more cheerful vein, he was amusing himself by writing pastiches on the subject of a recent court case, the Lemoine affair. This concerned an engineer who claimed to have discovered a method of making diamonds. Lemoine persuaded the banker Sir Julius Werner to invest a large sum of money in the process, but when he refused to reveal his formula Sir Julius took him to court. The prosecution was able to prove that Mme

Lemoine had bought the diamonds at a jeweller's shop; the swindler, released on bail, promptly escaped to Turkey. Marcel's pastiches were published on the front page of the literary supplement of *Le Figaro* in February and March. He presented the case as Balzac might have done in one of his novels, or as essays by the historian, Michelet, the drama critic Emile Faguet, or the Goncourt Brothers in their published diaries; the pastiche of an extract from a novel by Flaubert was printed with Sainte-Beuve's review of the novel. He particularly enjoyed writing a long essay in the style of the religious historian Ernest Renan, whom he had so much admired in his schooldays – he could have written ten volumes in Renan's style, Marcel told one friend, because he had adjusted his inner metronome to Renan's rhythm.

Proust had been writing pastiches of the writers he admired since he was a student. The light-hearted essays in *Le Figaro* of 1908 reveal his uncanny ability to capture a tone of voice – both he and Reynaldo were well known to their friends as excellent mimics. This gift for comedy is apparent in his novel in the way his characters express themselves; Swann's prevarications, Bloch's pedantic references to Homer, Dr Cottard's dreadful puns, Oriane's wit, the special vocabulary used by the Verdurins. In *Time Regained* he wrote an account of a dinner party given by Mme Verdurin for her friends as the Goncourt Brothers might have written about it in their diaries. When M read it, he concluded in despair that he had no gift for observation and no hope of achieving success as a writer.[1]

Ruskin was the subject of a pastiche (unpublished) entitled 'The Blessing of the Stag' which purported to be a study of frescoes by Giotto depicting the Lemoine swindle. The elaborately overwritten introduction included a description, not of the approach to Venice by gondola as in *The Stones of Venice*, but of Paris seen from an aeroplane 'in these Ibsenesque, sceptical and neurotic times'! Far from being stifled by Ibsenesque gloom, Marcel's mind was seething with ideas and plans. In May he sent Louis d'Albuféra a list of projects he wanted to write: a novel about Paris, an essay on Sainte-Beuve and Flaubert, another about women, and one on pederasty which he thought would be difficult to get published.

He consulted Robert Dreyfus about a long short story on the subject of a lawsuit which had been in the news since the autumn of 1907. It concerned a friend of the Kaiser's, Prince Philip von Eulenberg, who was arrested in May 1908 on a charge of homosexuality. Marcel dropped the idea of such a story because he felt that, however entertaining an anecdotal novel might be, a true work of art did not draw directly on actual events – art was too important, too superior to life, to be satisfied with straight reportage.[2]

Thanks to the help Marie was able to give to Marcel Bing with her extensive knowledge of oriental ceramics and prints, her work for Mr Freer, and her writing (journalism and translation, doubtless helped by Reynaldo's contacts), she could now afford a small flat in Paris at 60, rue Legendre, within easy walking distance of Aunt Elena and Reynaldo in the rue Alfred de Vigny and Bing's premises in the rue Saint Georges. Reynaldo helped her to furnish her new home with furniture he had inherited from Méry Laurent. She was used to living frugally, but he and Marcel worried about her circumstances – Marcel wrote to Reynaldo from Cabourg in August enquiring about her 'present and future material situation' and her

plans for the summer. Mr Freer had been, briefly, with
the Nordlingers in Manchester during the autumn of
1907 and then in London. After an extended tour to
Egypt, Palestine, Turkey, Greece and Vienna, he reached
Paris in August 1908 for a week at the Hôtel Meurice
before going on to London.

London was full of French visitors during the summer.
On Wednesday 8 July Reynaldo gave a recital at 25, Park
Lane, Lady Sassoon's home, performing his own *mélodies*
and accompanying Mme Bathori, from La Scala, Milan, and
her husband, from the Paris Opéra, in a programme of
songs by Fauré, Chabrier and, this time, also Debussy.

Early in July, Marcel told Robert de Montesquiou that
'on days when I'm not too ill, I struggle, without making
much progress, at work on a novel which may perhaps
give you a better opinion of me if you have the patience
to read it'. As soon as he was settled at the Grand Hotel
in Cabourg with his valet Nicolas Cottin, he wrote to
Reynaldo. He was exhausted, unable to write, convinced
he had paralysis of hand and brain as a result of all the
work he had done on his novel since January. He had
drafted a number of episodes and listed them in his
notebook, beginning with 'Robert and his pet goat'; then
the 'Two Ways to Villebon and Méséglise' – Villebon was
a country house near Illiers and Méséglise an actual village in the same area; items three and five both
concerned love and inversion; item four described the
disruption of the child's evening ritual by a visitor: 'I go
upstairs, Maman's face then and afterwards in my
dreams, I cannot get to sleep, concessions, etc.' Item
five referred cryptically to the magic of aristocratic
names and the castles belonging to them (in particular
one called Fantasie which had a sad history) and how the
maternal features are revealed in the face of a

debauched son or grandson. The last item in the list was what the narrator had learnt from the 'Two Ways'.

Marcel was haunted by thoughts of girls, of love and its deceptions, of trees seen from a train which no longer meant anything to him – his heart was too cold to enjoy the beauty of the countryside.

So, during the first six months of 1908, he sketched, quickly, without revision, *au galop*, as he had begun *Jean Santeuil* in 1895, episodes which belong to different parts of *The Search*. And he was planning ahead; a note on page three of the *carnet* refers to the second part of his work when the narrator takes a young girl to live with him without possessing her 'because happiness in love is not possible for me'. This note was followed by two lines on old age and the names of people Marcel knew in society – he was thinking about the last big party in *Time Regained*. Further on in the *carnet* he reminded himself to add to his conception of art in the last part of his novel that he must probe more deeply into those memories from the subconscious which brought him such happiness; as for the 'impressions' which seemed to conceal new truths and ideas, he must convert them into their spiritual equivalent, that is, he must create a work of art.[3]

At the end of the season, late in September, Agostinelli drove Marcel from Cabourg straight to the Hôtel des Reservoirs at Versailles. Reynaldo was already there, working on the music for his ballet. Marcel's asthma started again soon after his arrival and he was confined to his room where Reynaldo wrote while Agostinelli and Nicolas played dominoes with Marcel. On the few occasions when he felt better he began to write again. He noted a particular staircase at the hotel, its carpet, wallpaper and the vases of blue cinerarias which would eventually be described in *Cities of the Plain*. On the same page of the *carnet* he wrote about a different kind of memory: 'We believe the past to be mediocre because we think it, but that is not the past, it is the uneven paving stones in the baptistery of St Mark's – photograph of St Mark's baptistery to which we have given no further thought and which brings back for us the blinding sunlight on the canal.' This is the crucial 'involuntary' memory which Proust used in *Time Regained* to introduce his ideas on life, love and art. There is no mention in the *carnet* of tea, toast or biscuit.[4]

The exercise books (the *cahiers*) Proust used during the years 1907 and 1908 were filled with sketches describing the discussions he had with his mother, the jokes they shared with Félicie, Mme Proust's sense of humour and her habit of apt quotation from Racine, Molière and Mme de Sévigné, a habit she retained in her last illness; some of this material was used in the final version of *The Search*, though not directly – M's grandmother has many of Mme Proust's characteristics. Besides the notebook and the *cahiers* there were seventy-five sheets of loose paper with additional material for a novel, including a description of Venice, another episode at the seaside in Brittany or Normandy, and a meeting of the narrator with two girls. There are also notes outlining the development of the plot, and two 'introductions', a short one of half a page and a much longer one, a sort of preamble which begins 'Every day I attach less value to the intelligence . . .' In addition to these seventy-five sheets, there are twenty similar sheets on which, in the same hasty handwriting, Marcel drafted a critical essay on Sainte-Beuve.[5]

He had read a life of Sainte-Beuve in 1904 and referred to him several times in the notes to *Sésame et les lys*, especially a note in the preface, maintaining that the famous critic misjudged all the great writers of his time. An obituary notice of one of Sainte-Beuve's pupils published in *Le Figaro* in July 1907, in which the critic's scrupulous research was lavishly praised, goaded Marcel to quote and comment on his judgements and his theory of literary criticism. If Reynaldo enjoyed reading Sainte-Beuve for the clarity of his style and the encyclopaedic knowledge which combined entertainment with education, Marcel acknowledged his erudition and his excellence as a journalist but thought him superficial in his judgements and doubted his merits as a stylist or as a critic of literature, especially of books by his contemporaries. He wrote under pressure to meet his weekly deadlines and had no time to think deeply about his work.

Sainte-Beuve believed that in order to understand an author's work it was necessary to study in detail his background, family, friends, attitude to religion and women, and the turning points in his career, but Proust insisted that a book 'is the product of a different self to the self we show in our habits, our social life, our vices . . . and this deeper self can only be discovered and recreated by an effort of will coming from the heart, not the intelligence'. In a brief paragraph at the beginning of his essay Marcel explained that he would give his own ideas on how literary work should be valued, ideas which he had already broached in the prefaces to his two translations of Ruskin; he would then go on to consider art in general terms and end with his personal view of 'what art might have meant to me if . . .' – the sentence is unfinished, and the article was never published.

He drafted essays on three writers whom Sainte-Beuve had not appreciated: Nerval, a poet who also wrote novels; Baudelaire, a poet who wrote poems in prose and had been a journalist; and Balzac, the greatest novelist of the century – this essay, like the one on Baudelaire, took the form of a discussion with Mme Proust. In these essays Proust was testing and developing his own ideas on how the creative mind works, just as he had done in the prefaces and notes to his Ruskin translations, his articles for *Le Figaro* in 1907 and his essay on Sainte-Beuve. He used the title 'Contre Sainte-Beuve' twice, once in a draft when he remembered that he had a drawerful of notes on the subject[6] and again in a letter of August 1909 to the editor of *Le Mercure de France* where it is used as the title of 'a sort of novel'.

The longest essay, thirty pages at the back of *cahier* 1, was about Balzac. Sainte-Beuve's attitude towards his great contemporary had been a disparaging one. Balzac's stroke of genius, which Sainte-Beuve had failed entirely to understand, was the idea which came to him in 1842 when he had already published several novels – he thought of linking them by bringing in the same characters at different stages of their lives, so that his readers came to know and recognize them and accepted them as real people rather than imaginary ones.[7] They all became part of *La Comédie humaine*.

The draft continued with the thought that a writer should dedicate himself entirely to his work because dilettantism never created anything, and then, with no perceptible change of gear, just as at the end of his 1907 article on the memoirs of Mme de Boigne, the ghosts that were begging him to give them life suddenly took shape and emerged from the shadows. Without preamble Proust introduced his readers into the library of the Comte de Guermantes which contained early editions of all Balzac's novels. The Comte and his brother (Guercy, later Charlus) could talk for hours about the novels. Their enthusiasm was not shared by an impoverished cousin of the family, a Mme de Villeparisis. So the ideas about Balzac which Marcel discussed with his mother were transferred in *The Search* to the drawing-room conversations of his fictional characters.[8]

He wrote and rewrote the pages in his *cahiers*, shifting the focus from semi-autobiography to general ideas about creativity to show the difference between good journalism, like Sainte-Beuve's, and great writing as in the work of Balzac, Chateaubriand or Ruskin. Sometimes using the third person, more often writing as 'I', he gave people and places their real names – Robert, Marcel, Maman, Félicie, Harrison, against a background of Auteuil, Chartres, Dieppe, Evian, Jumièges and Réveillon. In *cahiers* 6 and 7 Marcel was trying out at least eight possible openings for his novel. Half asleep – 'for already I had the habit of working during the night and sleeping in the daytime' – the different rooms in which he had slept since childhood floated through his half-conscious mind so that when he woke up without knowing where he was, everything whirled round in the semi-darkness – objects, countries, years. As in the overture to *Swann's Way*, his ideas were worked out, not in accordance with the accepted canons of logical thought, but as they occurred to him, linked by memories and preoccupations from the subconscious, the hidden links he had traced in the preface to *La Bible d'Amiens*.

On 3 October *Le Figaro* reported the sudden death of Sarah Bernhardt during a dress rehearsal at Nîmes; her light-hearted denial, 'I haven't the time to be ill,' was published next day. Marcel wrote at once to Reynaldo, back at home in Paris: 'I thank the good Lord for preserving this admirable friend for you, someone who loves you and understands you and knows how to charm your difficult, melancholy heart.' Reynaldo was spared a loss he would have felt deeply.

It was Marie who had to face tragedy. Early in October her youngest brother, Harry, just twenty-one, was on holiday at Port Erin in the Isle of Man with their sister, Connie, and a party of friends. As on many other occasions, he went for a night's fishing with one of the local fishermen. They never returned. Marie went back to Manchester at once to be with the family. Letters from Mme Hahn and Reynaldo followed her there. By 17 October Marie wrote to say that the family had to accept their loss. Reynaldo sent her a brief telegram, followed by a letter, and Marcel wrote to her soon afterwards:

'Ma chère, chère Mary, Reynaldo whom I am too ill to see but who writes to me, has taken me through every stage of anxiety and sorrow, as if my own kith and kin were concerned . . . All I can say is, that I weep bitter tears for this young man whom I never knew. You, for whom I so much wanted joyful things (as though you were not worthy of much more than that), how can I bear the thought of you suffering such dreadful distress? And your parents, and all of you. I bear your desolation like a cross that is too heavy, and can only think of you and mourn. Votre Marcel.'

The sudden death of someone as young as Harry Nordlinger must have brought home to Marcel his own vulnerability. It was not only his precarious state of health, the frightening attacks of asthma, the fear of draughts, dust and fatigue, but a constant awareness of man's mortality – an accident in a car, a runaway horse, a germ of disease, any of these could be fatal. 'I feel that something quite insignificant could destroy me,' he wrote in the *carnet*, an idea elaborated in the preamble to his novel: 'At a time when my days are numbered (but is this not true for every one of us?), it might be thought rather frivolous of me to write an intellectual piece of work.' To Mme Straus he commented about his work that it was so annoying to think so many things and to 'feel that the mind in which they are stirring will soon perish without anyone knowing them'.

His extensive reading continued. He bought a number of books by Sainte-Beuve; Lauris lent him *Port-Royal* (seven volumes). He was also reading the memoirs of Chateaubriand and Saint-Simon, who wrote about life at the court of Louis XIV and the Regency. Pages of the *carnet* were filled with notes pointing out errors of style, judgement and character in Saint-Beuve's work. But he was still unable to decide what form his own work should take. When he returned to Paris from Versailles at the beginning of November, he expressed his doubts to Mme de Noailles and Lauris; should he write a classical essay on Sainte-Beuve 'in the manner of Taine', or should he put what he had to say in the form of a conversation with his mother?

In the *carnet* he wrote after the note on Venice and the baptistery of St Mark's: 'Perhaps I should bless my bad health which has taught me, by the burden of fatigue, immobility, silence, how to work. Warnings of death. Soon you won't be able to say all that. Laziness, or doubt, or lack of strength, take refuge in uncertainty as to the form art should take. Should it be a novel, a philosophical study, am I a novelist?' This was rhetorical – he had always intended to write a novel, but it was to be an entirely original one. 'This essential, only true book . . . does not have to be invented by a great writer since it exists already in each one of us . . . it has to be translated by him. The duty and task of a writer are those of a translator.'[9]

It is clear now, from his notebook and the exercise

books in which he wrote his drafts, that he was laying the foundation for another far more mature version of the novel he had begun at Beg-Meil in 1895. It would reveal how an artist is formed not by events or activities but by dreams and illusions, by the ebb and flow of feelings, the intermittences of the heart. His novel would be a justification of all those apparently wasted years, the history of a vocation, a quest for identity, a translation of memories, the creative fruit of 'a lucid and authentic search.'

Caricature by S.E.M. of Reynaldo Hahn at the piano with Montesquiou,
Madeleine Lemaire at the back and Coco de Madrazo on the right,
c. 1900

a il g avoit Bri, guich, ...
U poloit j'ai mis R, tehe (Refrain de chanson
de vieux temps)

Petit projet de quatl detail
E related au beaucoup travail
a gauche on voit Marie et Félicie
Qui font le mires et disant qu'elle die.

a droite Bminds ne pet ouvie podre legres
El Binchdicub viet par s'amuser
Bminds s'ide ou genou et de bras
Binchdicub ... par colona qu'il que at
en deux guvil

Tout ceci pour montrer à Binchdicub q alge
jour z'il fan

G il ne apomto pas ... que lui
envoie petit des rudicas

Sketches from Proust's letters to Reynaldo, with text in their special language

Opposite: Stained glass window showing the servants, Marie and Félicie, doing the washing (left window); Reynaldo behind a Gothic column tries to open Marcel's anti-asthma powder which he has lit

Top: 'Karlilch par Wisthlerch' (Carlyle by Whistler), sketch in a letter to Reynaldo Hahn, 1908

Above: Statue of the prophets at Chartres Cathedral, all labelled 'RH' with the comment 'Horribly difficult to do, some of them reasonably like'

Overleaf: 'Abziens (Kasthedealch)', Amiens Cathedral, west front

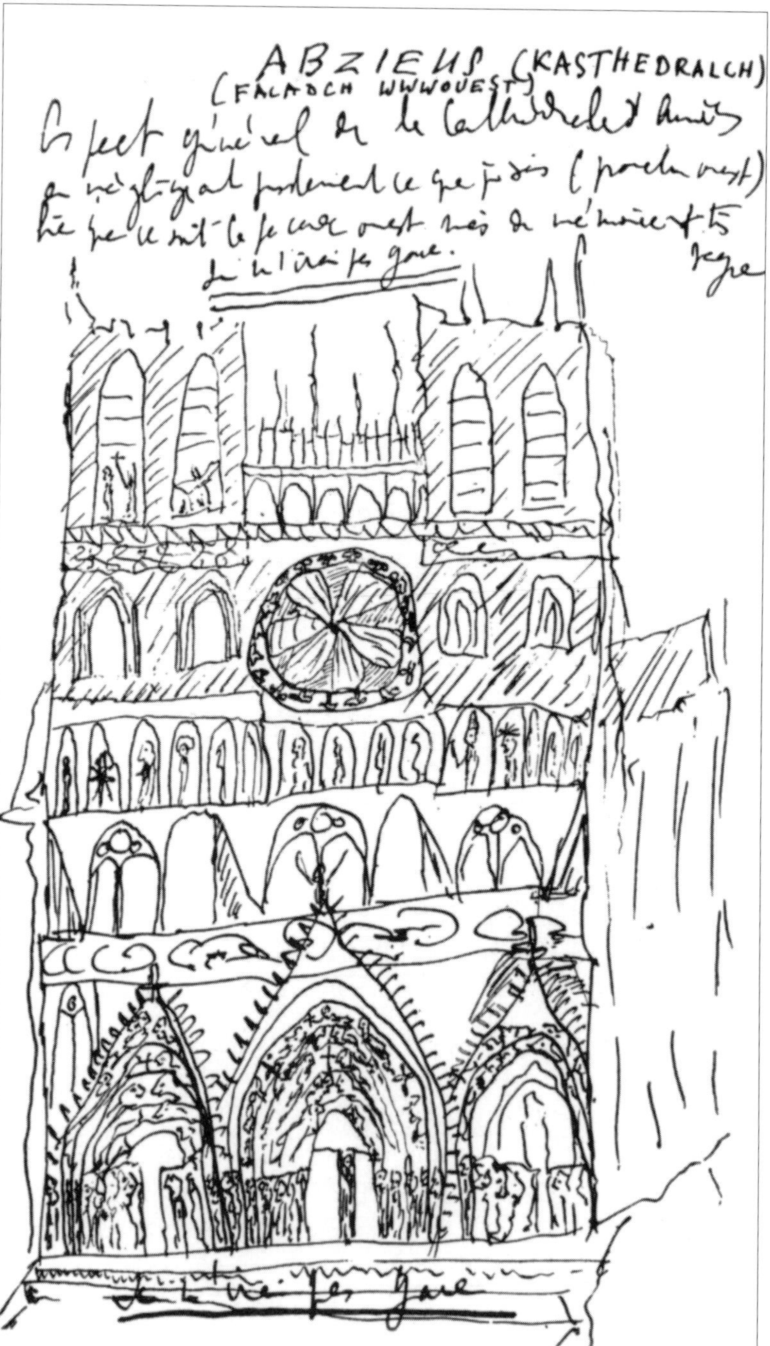
ABZIEUS (KASTHEDRALCH)
(FALAOCH WWWOUEST)

18
The Ways Decided

There is no record of the date on which Marie returned to Paris from Manchester after her brother's death; it was probably late in 1908 or early 1909. She was certainly there when Mr Freer wrote to her on 22 March asking her to trace and return to New York some photographic slides belonging to his old friend Professor Fennelosa, who had died in London the previous autumn. Marie was occupied with her work for Marcel Bing, her translations and occasional journalism. She spent the summer in Paris, welcoming Mr Freer for two weeks in May and June before he continued on his way to China and Japan by way of Berlin, Rome and Cairo.

In August Marcel went as usual to Cabourg and Reynaldo to Belle-Ile, but Marie stayed in the rue Legendre; earlier in the year she had become friendly, probably through their mutual involvement in Marcel Bing's business, with the man she married two years later. Rudolf Meyer-Riefstahl was a lecturer at the Sorbonne and an expert on art of the Near East. Although resident in France for several years, and with no intention of returning to live in Germany, he did not take French nationality, as this would have been against his father's wishes, so that when the war broke out in 1914 he and Marie were treated by the French authorities as enemy aliens.

There is no documentation of any kind for this period of Marie's life and she never spoke of it, but it would seem that personal as well as business interests kept her in Paris, a supposition borne out by the slightly sardonic reference to her in a letter from Marcel to Reynaldo in July. They do not seem to have approved of Marie's new friend – although he was cultured and charming he was perhaps not quite the man they would have wished for her, and he was five years younger.

To mark the centenary of Haydn's death in March 1809, a number of leading French musicians were asked to contribute to a set of piano pieces, musical transcriptions of his name. Six of them complied – Debussy, Dukas, Hahn, d'Indy, Ravel and Widor. During the year Reynaldo began to record for the gramophone some of the songs he performed most frequently; besides his own compositions, there were songs by Chabrier and Gounod's setting of Byron's poem *The Maid of Athens* (sung in impeccable English), also arias from Bizet's *The Pearl Fishers*, Rousseau's *Le Devin du village*, his own musical comedies, and from Offenbach. He continued to record as singer, accompanist and conductor until the 1930s. In June he became music critic of *Le Journal* after the death of Catulle Mendès, and stayed there until July 1914. Marcel read and commented on his weekly articles, praising his stylish writing and teasing him about his erudition.

Marcel reported on the state of his health to Reynaldo just as he used to do to Mme Proust; it was Reynaldo (and occasionally Mme Straus or Mme Catusse) who did errands for the invalid, buying presents for his friends, consulting bankers about his investments or dealing with the authorities about Nicolas Cottin's military service. Such requests to Reynaldo were interspersed with absurd and affectionate verses, gossip about and sketches of their acquaintances. In a letter from Versailles he sent a sketch of 'Karlilch par Wisthlerch', writing briefly about his desire to get on with his work and to discuss a great many things with Reynaldo because he could say about the two of them, as Ruskin said of Carlyle, that he was the only person with whom he could agree, whether to praise or blame![1]

He worked hard throughout the year. He already had a large cast of characters for his novel: the narrator's family in Combray and Paris with their friends and servants; Swann with his wife and daughter; the bourgeois Verdurins and their circle; the aristocrats and their relations; doctors and a diplomat; the artists – author, painter, actress. The book had no plot in the conventional sense. It had to be very long to 'isolate the invisible substance of time', he explained later, it was a series of novels of the unconscious, not a work of reasoning, because 'all its elements have been furnished by my sensibility, perceived without understanding . . . and put into intelligible form with as much difficulty as if they were alien to the intelligence, like a musical theme'.[2] M as narrator is a shadowy figure compared with the major characters drawn from all the people Proust had studied so closely since his adolescence seen, like the spires of Martinville, from different perspectives, in all their individuality.

The opening pages were written: early morning in the bedroom, his article published in *Le Figaro* and discussed with his mother. And the last chapter was drafted – another discussion with his mother in which he would explain his ideas on Sainte-Beuve and what he thought the task of an artist should be.

'Begin with mistrust of the intelligence,' he noted in the *carnet* and, several pages further on: 'To go deeply into ideas is less important than to go deeply into memories because the intelligence is not creative . . . reality is within oneself.' On the next page he reminded himself to add to his conception of art in the last part of his novel 'how to put into words impressions which are gone in a flash but which are more valuable for an artist than a theory of the universe'.

At a very early stage Proust thought of making Swann the main character. There are drafts in which it is Swann who goes to the seaside and falls in love with the girls there. Swann was an extension of Jean Santeuil, he was the narrator's alter ego – when Proust was writing *Un Amour de Swann* in 1911 he copied word for word the scene of jealous inquisition between Jean and Françoise and then rewrote it for Swann and Odette.

In *Time Regained*[3] Proust explained that the raw material of his book came from Swann, he was the catalyst of primary importance who was responsible for M's decision to write a book; he was the father of M's first love, Gilberte; he introduced M to the author Bergotte, and at his suggestion M and his grandmother went to a seaside resort, Querqueville (which became Balbec), where they met Mme de Villeparisis and her young relative, Montargis (later Robert de Saint-Loup), and through him the aristocratic family of Guermantes, the Duchess, Oriane, the Duke and his brother, the Baron de Charlus.

Swann's history is given in several of the drafts in *cahier* 4. He has replaced M. de Bretteville as the visitor who deprives the child of his mother's good-

night kiss. In the early pages of the *cahier* the narrator and his family had moved their home in Paris
to a building which they shared with an unnamed
count and countess, a lady with whom the young
man fell in love – it took ten pages to describe the
disillusion which follows when acquaintance with
someone ripens into familiarity. At close quarters
the magic is lost – for M everything is in the imagination.

There was one occasion at least when Marcel's
imagination led him to the deeper truth for which he
was searching. In *cahiers* 6 and 7 he gave an account
of a visit he made to the ancient abbey church of
Jumièges, not far from Rouen, with its two great
towers, its mixture of romanesque and Gothic architecture, and the eighteenth-century palace above it
on the hill. Why, his mother asked him, when everything she hoped would give him pleasure had proved
a disappointment, had he enjoyed 'Guermantes' so
much?

The metamorphosis of Jumièges into the château
of Guermantes is an example of how Proust's imagination worked, how a legend could be created out of
an actual place, how facts could be translated into
art. Here, in Jumièges/Guermantes, time assumed
the dimension of space and so could easily be recognized. Jumièges was undergoing that chemical
process by which Ruskin described the creative act –
past and present were fused. The magic of names
and places lay in the imagination.[4]

Proust was still secretive about his work. He
thought his friends might try to dissuade him from
his dispassionate enquiry into the homosexual fraternity, the breed of 'men-women' whose representa-

tive he had briefly sketched in *Jean Santeuil* as the Vicomte de Lomperolles and which he expanded in *cahiers* 6 and 7 into a 'portrait' of the Comte de Guercy (later Charlus) and of the solitary childhood and unhappiness of other frail individuals belonging to the same 'accursed race'. These accounts were repeated almost word for word in *Cities of the Plain*.[5] After *cahier* 7 there are several *cahiers* of 'outlines' written quickly to get the main episodes down on paper, episodes which find their place in very different parts of the work.

In *Jean Santeuil* the names of places and characters were never firmly established either in the way they were spelt or in their attribution. In the same way the names Querqueville, Montargis, Carmen/Wanda in these early drafts were changed when Proust corrected the proof sheets of Volume One. Some characters disappeared altogether, or played a less important part in the narrative. One, the composer of the little phrase which became the 'national anthem' of Swann's love for Odette, was not given a name until 1913, when he appeared on the proofs of *Swann's Way* as Vinteuil, replacing an elderly naturalist called Vington who had given the boy M a collection of minerals.

In June Proust told Georges de Lauris that he was exhausted with beginning his *Sainte-Beuve*, which he found quite detestable. Early in July he complained to Robert Dreyfus that he had had a frightful day – the electric light had been burning for sixty hours.

He was much more cheerful when he wrote to Reynaldo from his bed later in the month to tell him about a present he had received from Madame Greffuhle, a magnificent potted vine hung with grapes, which he immediately sent on to Marie, 'la Nordlinka', though he thought she would probably have preferred a postcard. He would have liked to send her some roses as well so that he could bring in Nerval's line about 'the trellis where mingle the vine and the rose' (which he had quoted in the draft of his essay on Nerval), but then Mallarmé's 'When I have sucked the clarity from grapes' might be more economical as roses were not mentioned and he already had the grapes! He added a couplet of his own: 'I'm afraid that my novel on old Sainte-Veuve [*sic*] may not, you'll agree, appeal much to La Beuve.' It couldn't be helped if 'La Veuve' (Madame Lemaire) recognized some of her own idiosyncrasies in those of Proust's fictional hostess. The letter ended with a plea for discretion: 'Please keep quiet about all this. I chatter on to you as I used to do with Maman, but she never repeated *anything!*'

Lauris wanted to know if *Sainte-Beuve* was finished. 'Indeed not!' Marcel replied. He did not know where to find a publisher; Calmann-Lévy, who were about to publish a new novel by Lauris, would certainly refuse such an 'obscene' book as his. In mid-August Marcel sent an urgent and confidential letter to Alfred Vallette, editor-in-chief of *Le Mercure de France*, to ask whether he would publish, in fortnightly instalments and at the author's expense if necessary, a book 'which despite its provisional title, *Against Sainte-Beuve: Recollection of a Morning*, is a genuine novel and an extremely indecent one in certain sections. One of the characters is a homosexual.' Sainte-Beuve's name was not mentioned by chance, Marcel explained. The book ended with a long conversation on Sainte-Beuve and aesthetics . . . . The whole novel was simply the implementation of the artistic principles expressed in the final part which was a sort of preface placed at the end. And he assured M. Vallette that there was no hint of pornography – in any case, the text was not definitive.

M. Vallette was not prepared to accept the book, but M. Calmette, director of *Le Figaro*, who was at Cabourg when Marcel arrived at the Grand Hotel, offered to print extracts in his paper. The novel was already far too long to appear in instalments, as M. Calmette suggested.

Writing to Mme Straus at the end of August, Marcel complained that his work had been interrupted when he left Paris and he was only just getting down to it again, but he hoped she might soon be able to read what he had written because he had just begun, and finished, a whole long book. In October the opening section was sent to be typed and in November Marcel read the first 200 pages to Reynaldo, who enthusiastically approved of them, as did Georges de Lauris and the Bibescos when they were shown the typescript.

In 1909 the ballet company brought from Russia by Diaghilev took Paris by storm. After producing *Boris Godunov* at the Opéra the previous year, the Russian impresario took over and completely transformed the Théâtre du Châtelet, where Pavlova, Karsarvina and Nijinsky danced in Fokine's *Les Sylphides*, Ida Rubenstein in *Cléopatra*, with costumes and sets by Bakst, and the whole brilliant company in the barbaric Polovtsian Dances from Borodin's *Prince Igor*.

The success of Reynaldo's new ballet, *La Fête chez Thérèse*, at the Opéra in February 1910 encouraged Diaghilev to commission another work from him.[6]

Marcel went to the dress rehearsal, but not to the first night nor the party afterwards. The weather in February was atrocious, torrential rain caused the river Seine to rise to unprecedented heights and the cellars at 102, Boulevard Haussmann were flooded. Marcel was now and for the remaining twelve years of his life totally engrossed in his work except for the yearly visits to Cabourg and the social occasions when he refreshed his observations on people and collected new ideas for his fictional characters.

The manuscript which Reynaldo had approved in November had now doubled in length. First there was Combray with the two ways; at the end there were the uneven paving stones and a gathering of the major characters in their old age. In between there was a vast amount of material to be sorted out and fitted into the different stages of the work because Proust had learnt to select from his memories – there is no account of M's schooldays (except for Bloch as school friend), nor of studies at the university, no military service; there are only casual references to Ruskin and a bare mention of Sainte-Beuve when M's article on the spires of Martinville was published at last in *Le Figaro*; finally, and most important, there is no reference to his three published books, the book reviews and dozens of newspaper articles, the thousands of pages drafted for a novel from 1895 to 1909.

There was no sudden revelation in Proust's life like the *coup de théâtre* of the madeleine and the cup of tea in *Swann's Way*. *The Search* was a slow growth, from the short story about Violante and 'the novel going on perpetually in her head' (1893) to the uneven paving stones of *Time Regained* and 'the idea of my work, in my head, forever in the process of becoming'.[7]

19
A Lasting Friendship

The Search has been called a musical work, composed with Wagnerian leitmotifs in counterpoint, reacting with each other. Music and literature were the firm base of the friendship between Reynaldo and Marcel. Together they read everything, from Plato and Nietzsche to modern novels, Sainte-Beuve, Chateaubriand and Dumas *père*. They both, in their different ways, wrote about music, Reynaldo as a professional critic, Marcel as a keen listener. In his first book there are short pieces on listening to music, including one on the charm of popular songs and tunes, and the pastiche of Flaubert. In the drafts for a novel begun at Beg-Meil in 1895 there is a hasty sketch on the consoling power of music, a sonata for violin and piano by Saint-Saëns and a very early involuntary memory scribbled on a piece of torn paper.[1] The little tune from the sonata became the 'national anthem' of the love affair between Jean and Françoise in *Jean Santeuil*.

In 1911–12 Reynaldo was often away from Paris. Marcel, hard at work on *Swann's Way*, found consolation and relaxation in music. In February 1911 Diaghilev invited Reynaldo to visit St Petersburg to play the score of his ballet music for *Le Dieu bleu* to the Director of the Conservatoire, M. Glazounov. Before he left, Marcel sent Reynaldo an enthusiastic account of a new invention to which he had recently taken out a subscription. The theatrophone relayed live performances from theatres and music halls in Paris and elsewhere to listeners at home via their telephones. Marcel had heard the third

act of *Die Meistersinger* from the Opéra and, the following evening, the whole of Debussy's *Pelléas et Mélisande*
from the Opéra-Comique. He teased Reynaldo: 'I am
going to irritate you horribly by talking about music,'
and went on to criticize Wagner's libretto in Act III,
Scene 1, but then, he added, 'musical heresies which
irritate you pass unnoticed by me'. Reynaldo's review of
Die Meistersinger on 20 February was published the following day – he thought it well sung, but he was sceptical about the enthusiasm shown by the fashionable audience who thought they understood Wagner because they
were able to recognize several favourite tunes.

Marie sent Marcel a telegram to tell him that
Reynaldo had arrived safely in Russia. He enjoyed his
three weeks in St Petersburg, his hosts entertained him
handsomely, the ballet music was much appreciated and
he became friendly with Fokine, the choreographer, and
Nijinsky, with whom he had several amusing adventures.
Another long letter from Marcel continued the discussion on Wagner and Debussy.[2]

This year Marcel went to Cabourg rather earlier than
usual in July. His work was making progress. There was
a resident typist at the Grand Hotel, an English woman,
a Miss Hayward, who typed the next part of his manuscript to send on to Reynaldo who was in Belle-Ile with
Mme Sarah after his yearly visit to London. Marie and
Rudolf Meyer-Riefstahl were married quietly in Paris on
17 July. Marcel wrote to her a few days later, apologizing
for his long silence and wishing her and her husband
much happiness.[3] He remembered how he and his
mother used to wonder when she would find a man
worthy of her 'marvellous qualities and exquisite gifts'
and praised the skill with which she had carried out the
commission for Dr Proust's memorial plaque (though

the family seemed now to find it a not particularly good likeness).

After the birth of their son, Albert, in 1912, Marie and Rudolf moved from 72, rue du Faubourg Saint-Honoré to a house with a garden in Sèvres where they continued to deal in textiles and ceramics from the Near and Far East in which they specialized, as well as books, modern prints and objets d'art. They kept in touch with Charles Freer, keeping him informed of acquisitions and sales, sending him books, articles and catalogues. In October 1913 Rudolf organized an exhibition in a Paris gallery of Chinese rugs, textiles and paintings; early in 1914 he wrote to Mr Freer asking him to lend, from his Near East collection, Persian miniatures, book illustrations and bindings for an exhibition which he was hoping to organize in New York. Mr Freer declined; he was already in poor health.[4]

Reynaldo had taken French nationality in 1909 and was now obliged to do three weeks' military service with the 31st Infantry Brigade at their headquarters in Melun, between Paris and Fontainebleau. He served as a private, because he had not the required educational grades to be an officer, never having gone to school in France; he enjoyed the experience and stayed on, as Proust had done at Orléans in 1889, to dine and wine in the mess – the commanding officer happened to have a sister who was an opera singer. Afterwards, at the end of August, he went on to Versailles to finish orchestrating his ballet score.

Reynaldo teased Marcel about his metaphysical ideas. While they disagreed about the merits of certain composers and writers – Saint-Saëns, Debussy, Wagner, Beethoven, Ruskin and Sainte-Beuve – they did agree on the fundamental things. Through his relationship with

Reynaldo Marcel was able to develop his own ideas on music in the same way that his reading of Balzac's novels, Bergson, Sainte-Beuve, and especially his study of Ruskin, inspired him to think long and deeply about how an original work of art is created. Music was always a consolation. Asthma and weather permitting, he went to the opera and ballet with Mme Straus or Mme Greffuhle and to chamber music concerts – he especially enjoyed a performance of Beethoven's late quartets by the newly formed Capet Quartet.

The death of Mme Hahn on 25 March 1912, after several years of ill health, was as devastating for Reynaldo as the death of Mme Proust had been for Marcel in 1905. Work was the best remedy. He spent three weeks in Hamburg with his sister Isabel and then went back to Paris to conduct Mozart's *Don Giovanni* at the Opéra-Comique at the end of April and on 13 May his ballet *Le Dieu bleu* at the Châtelet. Though the dancers included Nijinsky, Karsarvina and Nijinsky, it was not a success. Reynaldo's version of 'oriental' music could not compete with the colourful 'barbarism' of Borodin or Stravinsky.

After his usual holiday in Cabourg Marcel was anxious to find a publisher for what was already a long novel of 700 pages, with a second volume in typescript almost as long, and a third drafted. Thanks to M. Calmette four short extracts from Volume One were published in *Le Figaro* between March 1912 and March 1913. The help of other friends was enlisted – Mme Straus, Lucien Daudet, the Bibescos, René Blum (an old friend on the staff of the newspaper *Gil Blas*) and another friend from the days of the Dreyfus trial, Louis de Robert, a writer

and invalid like Proust himself. In six months three publishers rejected the book, Fasquelle, Ollendorff and,
greatly to Proust's disappointment, *La Nouvelle Revue
Française* (the NRF), whose directors, André Gide and
Jacques Copeau, did not consider him a suitable author
for their list on the grounds that he was a wealthy ama-
teur, not a professional writer.

The work needed an overall title – Marcel thought
The Intermittences of the Heart might do. As for chapter headings, Reynaldo accused Marcel of laziness.
Surely he could find something less banal than 'Mme
Swann at Home' or 'Death of My Grandmother'? Marcel
replied with a two-page list of suggestions, not all of
them meant seriously. He asked Reynaldo to offer
another extract from Volume One, which he had just
written, to the literary editor of *Le Temps* (who refused
it). The extract was from his book *Time Lost*, a new
title, and consisted of the dinner parties at the
Verdurins which Reynaldo had found amusing, and a
shortened version of two episodes where Swann heard
the music which became 'the national anthem' of his
affair with Odette, and then again, after the affair had
ended, at Mme de Saint-Euverte's musical evening,
when the little tune spoke to him of 'the forgotten
refrains of happiness'.

'Recoiling from the horrible banality of calling this
"the little phrase from the sonata",' Marcel told
Reynaldo light-heartedly, 'I shall call it *Time Lost* and if
it gives the impression that this volume is time wasted,
it can't be helped. It really isn't a cliché, is it? . . . No,
no, of course it isn't!' Swann first heard the sonata some
time before he met Odette. One particular phrase in it
seemed to offer him a possibility of rejuvenation, a
chance to change his life and live a more meaningful

existence. No one could tell him the name of the composer, and he forgot the experience. When Odette took him to meet the Verdurins he learnt that the music which had so enthralled him was from the andante of a work by Vinteuil, whom he remembered as an elderly piano teacher at Combray, a sad, timid man, heartbroken by the death of his wife and the behaviour of his only daughter with a lesbian friend. Odette played the little phrase for Swann again and again so that it became their theme song and lost the deeper meaning it once had for him. When he heard the andante again at Mme de Saint-Euverte's, he was filled with pity and admiration for the composer who had drawn such strength from his suffering that he seemed to have an unlimited power of creation.

In the second volume of *The Search*, which begins with the section 'Mme Swann at Home', Swann and Odette are married and the adolescent M, in love with their daughter, Gilberte, is a frequent visitor to their home. Odette plays the tune from Vinteuil's sonata for him. Now it reminds Swann not of the woman he loved but only of the places where he had heard it – Jean Santeuil had a similar reaction.[5] For M the sonata grew more significant in the course of the novel.

Marcel knew that Reynaldo would enjoy the description of the guests at Mme de Saint-Euverte's soirée – such people who showed their appreciation of the music by nodding their heads, tapping their fingers or their feet (usually out of time with the piece being played) had often been the target of the friends' displeasure. The deliberately unobtrusive entrance of Oriane, Princesse de Laumes (before she became Duchess of Guermantes), who was well aware that she was the awaited star of the evening, is splendid comic writing. Even the performance of Vinteuil's great work, the septet, in *The Fugitive*, has its moment of comedy when M heard a snore and suspected their hostess of nodding off, only to realize that her small dog was asleep beneath her chair.

Affectionate letters followed Reynaldo on his travels. After an exhausting but lucrative tour of Romania he went to recuperate in Hamburg with his sister Isabel. When he got back to Paris at the end of February 1912 Reynaldo undertook to negotiate with a fourth publisher, a friend of René Blum. Bernard Grasset was a kindly, energetic young man who had just gone into business. He agreed, without even reading the book, to publish it at the author's expense. The contract was signed on 11 March 1913, and within a month Marcel received the first page proofs for corrections and additions.

On 19 April Marcel went to a recital given by the Romanian virtuoso violinist Georges Enesco and the French pianist Paul Goldschmidt to hear the sonata in A major by César Franck. It made a deep impression on him. Reynaldo knew and admired Franck at the Conservatoire where he had been professor of organ. A modest, retiring man, he was acclaimed as a teacher and organist rather than as a composer, but he enjoyed success with a string quartet performed for the first time a year before his death in 1891. Franck's otherworldliness appealed to Marcel. Vinteuil's name was added to the page proofs of *The Search* and the necessary amendments were made to the text. Both Reynaldo and Marcel agreed, in the different accounts they gave of the composers who inspired Vinteuil's sonata and septet, that Saint-Saëns and Franck were the most important, followed by Wagner and Fauré.[6]

By the time Albertine was installed in M's home during his parents' absence, he was quite familiar with

Vinteuil's sonata. While his mistress was out shopping, he sat at the piano to play it, comparing it with the emotional impact of the themes which Wagner introduced in *Tristan*. Music, he realized, enabled him to descend into himself to discover new ideas. He remembered his walks at Combray along the path to Guermantes when he dreamt about a career as an artist. Was art more 'real' than life, he wondered. The performance of Vinteuil's septet at Mme Verdurin's soirée was a further revelation. M was overwhelmed by the old composer's creative profundity, revealing new worlds to the listener – his work was 'a summons to a super-terrestrial joy', 'a bold approximation to the bliss of the Beyond', but would he, M, ever be able to produce a similar, really original work? How strange, he thought, that one of the century's great masterpieces should be written by an insignificant old man whom he used to meet on holiday at Combray during the month of May, and that it should be saved for posterity by the reformed friend of Mlle Vinteuil.

Other friends besides Reynaldo were given the proofs of *Swann's Way* to read. Lucien Daudet was especially appreciative and understanding, and Louis de Robert made some helpful suggestions, but he thought readers would find the scene at Montjouvain in which Mlle Vinteuil and her friend desecrated her father's photograph distasteful and that it should be omitted. Proust explained that in his projected third volume the recognition of Vinteuil as one of the century's greatest composers was due to the work done on transcribing his manuscripts by his daughter's friend who had learnt to venerate the old man.[7]

The year 1913 should have been a peaceful and

triumphant one for Marcel with the completion and publication of his first volume, yet he complained to his friends that he had never been so miserable nor had so many worries. It was not simply that he had invested unwisely and lost money on the Stock Exchange. Sometime in January he had a visit from the young man who had been his chauffeur at Cabourg in the memorable summers of 1907–8. Alfred Agostinelli was now twenty-four, charming and intelligent. He had lost his job in the south of France and came to Paris in the hope that Proust would employ him. He was accompanied by Anna, a young woman who passed as his wife. Proust already had a regular taxi driver in Paris, Odilon Albaret, who had also driven him in Cabourg, so he took Agostinelli on as secretary to type his manuscripts and gave the couple a room in the flat. He paid them generously, but he and Anna disliked each other; she was difficult, suspicious and jealous. To make matters worse Marcel was hopelessly in love with Alfred. It was a disastrous situation for all concerned. Inevitably there were quarrels, probably because Alfred felt the need to escape, to be free from his employer's incessant questioning, just as Reynaldo had done in 1896. In November he and Anna packed their bags and went back to Monaco. Like many young men of the time, Agostinelli was mad about machines; he persuaded Marcel to let him take flying lessons at an aerodrome near Paris, lessons he continued in Monaco under the name 'Marcel Swann'.

Swann's Way was published on 18 November. The reviews were favourable thanks to energetic lobbying by the author's many friends. Marcel was particularly pleased by a letter from André Gide who, after rejecting the work for the NRF, now declared himself enraptured by it and hoped that Proust would let Gallimard, printers to the NRF, publish the next two volumes.[8]

Reynaldo was also having a success. He was giving a series of nine lecture-recitals on the art of singing for the young people who attended the courses at the Université des Annales. The first was given on 22 November, and repeated two days later, the last in July 1914, when he also lectured on Fauré. Marcel read the text of the first lecture in manuscript and gave it the highest praise, comparing it, for sound knowledge and presentation, with the best of Ruskin's most esoteric lectures – Reynaldo should reread the opening pages of *Sesame and Lilies*! In the eighth lecture Reynaldo spoke about the appeal which music makes to the emotions, and its mysterious ability to create images and evoke forgotten memories; he was referring to instrumental music which, more than books or pictures, had a transcendental quality, beyond space and time, especially for an imaginative mind. Proust described Vinteuil's septet in very similar terms – it was 'truer than all known books', it aroused in M the same feelings of joy as the sight of the spires of Martinville or the trees at Balbec, or the taste of the madeleine dipped into a cup of tea, impressions which he must try and convert into their spiritual equivalent.[9] Reynaldo's lectures were published in *Conferencia*, the monthly journal of the Université des Annales, and later as a book, *Du Chant* (1920).[10]

On 30 May 1914 Alfred Agostinelli made his second solo flight after getting his flying licence. Disobeying instructions, he flew out to sea, took a turn too sharply, stalled the engine and plunged into the sea. He drowned within sight of the shore. The very day of his death Marcel received a grateful and apologetic letter from him, which ended with a reference to their last drive together: 'I shall never forget that doubly crepuscular drive since night was falling and we were about to part . . .', a phrase used by Proust in Albertine's last letter to M after she left him.[11] Proust in 1913 bought a fashionable pianola, as M did for Albertine, so that Agostinelli, who was no pianist, could play new pieces of music to him – unfortunately the pianola company could not supply Beethoven's late quartets, for which, they said, they had never been asked.[12]

The Germans declared war on Sunday 3 August, the German Army invaded Belgium and by the beginning of September advanced as far as Senlis, twenty-five miles from Paris. The French counter-attacked and drove them back. Marcel's brother, Robert, was operating under fire at Verdun, Reynaldo was in Melun with his regiment, all able men were mobilized, including Odilon Albaret and Nicolas Cottin.

In September Marcel decided to go to Cabourg for the last time, accompanied by his new housekeeper, Albaret's young wife, Céleste. Reynaldo wrote to him at the end of October from Albi. He was afraid that the visit to Cabourg might revive painful memories of Agostinelli. No, Marcel replied, it had not been as bad as he expected, there had been moments, even hours, when he forgot Alfred. 'Dear Boy,' he continued, 'don't condemn me as fickle but blame the person who didn't deserve fidelity! I really loved Alfred but in the last analysis in feelings of grief there is an element of the involuntary and an element of duty which sustains the involuntary part and ensures its durability. This sense of duty doesn't exist in the case of Alfred who behaved very badly towards me and I don't feel bound to him by a duty of the sort which binds me to you. It isn't because others have died that grief diminishes but because one dies oneself. If I ever attempt to formulate such things it will be under the pseudonym of Swann. When you read the third volume, called in part "Within a Budding Grove", you will recognize the anticipation and unerring prophecy of what I've experienced since.'

It was not through Swann that he was to embody these thoughts on grief, forgetfulness, the changing self, the intermittences of the heart.[13] Swann appears for the last time halfway through the expanded novel at the end of *The Guermantes Way* during a party given by the Princesse de Guermantes when he tells the Duchess Oriane that he is ill with cancer and has only a few months to live.[14] It is now M. de Charlus who takes the centre of the stage, as Proust always intended, with Morel, the Verdurins, Jupien, and especially Albertine, the girl whom M met as an adolescent at Balbec and later kept closely supervised in his flat, spoiling and tormenting her, alternatively an adoring suitor and a sadistic tyrant. This affair was anticipated in an early note in the *carnet* of 1908[15] about the second part of the novel where a girl is kept as companion but without pleasure because he does not love her. The unfortunate Agostinelli seemed to fit into Proust's imagined scenario – life imitated art.

Marie, Rudolf and their son, as enemy aliens, left house, friends and business and went back to Manchester where they rented a small house in Victoria Park not far from Gladville. Their daughter, Polly, was born here on 1 September. In view of her British birth Marie was allowed to stay in England with her children while her husband sailed to New York where he hoped to set up as a dealer with the help of introductions from Mr Freer, who was not hopeful about the prospects. When

Marie followed him to New York in 1919, she found that he had a 'wife' and young family there; she divorced him in 1923 and lived with her children and brother Albert in Manchester. Rudolf studied for a PhD and became a professor at Columbia University, New York.

At the end of this miserable year, 1914, Marcel told Lucien Daudet how worried he was about his brother Robert, operating on casualties in the front line, and about Reynaldo, who insisted on sharing all the dangers of war with his regiment. 'I can't tell you how many proofs of moral courage he has shown since the beginning of the war . . . he really is a rock of virtue on which one can build and live.'

In January 1915 Reynaldo moved with his regiment from Albi to the Argonne, a sparsely populated region of forest and farms east of Paris, where he spent the next two years in considerable danger and discomfort. He was a clerk in the adjutant's office. He tried to write a little each day, in the lull between shelling and bombardment – a march for the regiment, a choral piece, *To the Dead of Vauquois*, where his regiment had fought a fierce battle. He wrote light revues, he sang for officers and men whenever there was a piano to be found, and composed a set of twelve waltzes for two pianos, *Le Ruban denoué*, which he played to Marcel when he got to Paris on leave in November. Marcel praised them extravagantly – they were sublime!

Mme Lemaire and Suzette had been at Réveillon under German occupation since the beginning of the war when Prussian officers were billeted on them. As the war progressed they were not far from the front line, in the middle of the heavy artillery, as Mme Lemaire reported to Maria de Madrazo. She had frequent news of Reynaldo – he never complained, but she thought it so sad for him that his talents were not made full use of just at the peak of his career. He began an opera in two acts based on the story of Nausicaa from Homer's *Odyssey*, drafted the first act of his opera *Le Marchand de Venise*, and set to music five of Robert Louis Stevenson's verses for children. In 1917 he was promoted corporal-despatch rider and the following year moved to Paris to the cipher office in the Ministry of War.

The tragic waste of the 1914–18 war darkened Proust's outlook and increased his obsessions. He led a life of total dedication to his work with courage and strength of will. He knew the magnitude of his achievement in interpreting the enclosed world of his imagination, portraying the basic truths of human nature, the pleasures and pains of growing up and growing old, the frailties of body and spirit, the joys of art; it was the chronicle of an epoch, of the changes in society between 1890 and 1920. In 1919 the second volume of *The Search*, *Within a Budding Grove*, won the major literary award, the Prix Goncourt, thanks largely to Léon Daudet's active support.

This success brought Marcel new friends and admirers. In the copy of *Within a Budding Grove* that he gave to Reynaldo he wrote a light-hearted dedication: 'To Funibels, the best beloved, the kindest, the cleverest. From his old pony, now an old nag but still faithful.' *The Guermantes Way* appeared in 1920, *Cities of the Plain* in 1922.[16] In January 1919 his landlady at 102, Boulevard Haussmann announced that she had sold the building, which was to be altered and made into a bank, so that he and Céleste had to move to another apartment. At the last minute, in May, they found one on the fourth floor at 8 bis, rue Laurent-Pichat, home of the actress Réjane and her son, Jacques Porel, where they stayed four months and then moved to a dreary furnished flat on the fifth floor at 44, rue Hamelin; most of the family furniture and carpets had already been sold or given away. He was awarded the Légion d'Honneur in September 1920.[17]

To the end of his life Proust kept his admiration for Ruskin, as he told Sydney Schiff, the future translator of *Time Regained*, not long before he died. 'Between what a person says, and what he extracts by meditation from the depths where the bare spirit lies hidden and veiled, there is a world of difference . . . Ruskin has expressed at least a part of this fairly well. I no longer remember where, but if you wish I will find it for you.' The passage is to be found in one of the first books by Ruskin which Marcel possessed, in Marie's annotated copy of *The Queen of the Air*: 'Great art is the expression of mind of a great man, and mean art, that of the want of mind of a weak man . . . you may read characters of men, and of nations, in their art as in a mirror . . . for a man may hide himself from you, or misrepresent himself to you every other way, but he cannot in his work; there, to be sure, you have him to the inmost.'[18]

In November 1922 Marcel caught a chill which turned into pneumonia – he refused all medical treatment and would not take proper nourishment. Reynaldo called each day to ask how he was; at Robert Proust's request he wrote a last note: 'Mon cher petit . . . I'm sorry that nothing I can say will influence you and you won't even try to eat a little purée as you promised me – you, my dearest friend, one of those whom I have loved most in my life.'

Marcel died on Saturday afternoon, 18 November, and was buried with his parents in the cemetery of Père Lachaise. Reynaldo's other beloved friend, Sarah Bernhardt, died on 26 March the following year.

Postscript

Reynaldo's greatest successes came in 1923 and in 1925, too late for him to share with Marcel their difficulties and triumphs. In 1921 he was asked to compose an operetta in the style of Lecocq's *La Fille de Madame Angot*, with a similar heroine, a country girl who brings her produce to the Paris market in what used to be les Halles. She is called *Ciboulette* (Chives). The light-hearted, well-written libretto contains good dialogue, some delightful duets and a lively waltz in the third act. Ciboulette, with the help of an older friend, Duparquet, becomes a famous singer and wins the heart of a young nobleman. The operetta was tried out in Monte Carlo at the end of 1922 and opened in Paris to great acclaim, at the Théâtre des Variétés, in April 1923, with Edmée Favart in the title role and Jean Périer, who had sung Pelléas in 1902, as Duparquet.

Two years later Sacha Guitry, actor, dramatist and producer, invited Reynaldo to collaborate with him on a musical comedy specially written for his wife, the star of the Paris stage, Yvonne Printemps, *en travesti* as the young Mozart on his first visit to Paris. Reynaldo, with his great knowledge of, and love for, Mozart, could not fail to produce a tuneful score, which included references to *Figaro*, *Don Giovanni*, the Paris symphony, a violin concerto and the ballet music *Les Petits Riens*. *Mozart* was as big a success in London as in Paris. Guitry and Hahn worked together several years later on another music comedy, *O Mon Bel Inconnu*, starring Arletty, with Simone Simon and Guy Ferrant. He continued to write musical comedies – *Les Temps d'aimer* (1926), *Brummell* (1930), *Malvina* (1935) – as well as a great deal of incidental music for plays and films, but he did not neglect more serious work, chamber music, a violin concerto (1928), oratorios, ballet music, and his grand opera, *Le Marchand de Venise* (1935) – in this work, he said, he had put the best of himself.[1]

During the 1920s he was director of music at the casino at Cannes for a four-month winter season of opera and concerts, linked with a short summer season at Deauville, where the casino was run by the same syndicate. Angus Morrison, a young pianist from London, often met Reynaldo at Deauville where his uncle, René Lambert, was in charge of the singers. He had fond memories of Reynaldo's breadth of musicianship, his charm, wit and simplicity of manner – and his love of good food.

Reynaldo became deeply disillusioned by the parochialism and backbiting of the theatrical and musical world, but he had his circle of firm friends, Henri Bardac, René Schrameck, Yvonne Sarcey (Mme Brisson, the director of the Université des Annales), his sisters, Isabel, Maria, Clarita, and Clarita's daughter, also Clarita, Comtesse de Forceville. And then there were the young musicians he encouraged – the tenor Guy Ferrant, Magda Tagliaferro, who gave the first performance of his piano concerto (1930), his charming *Sonatine* (1935), and the lovely soprano Ninon Vallin; with them he gave recitals and concerts in Paris and toured the regions. In 1933 he became music critic of *Le Figaro* using the pen name 'Clarendon', and published his early journal, Notes (*Journal d'un musicien*). Some of his music articles in *Le Journal* and other papers were published in 1935 with the title *L'Oreille au guet (The Listening Ear)* and a second collection of his *Figaro* articles in 1946, *Thèmes variés*. His field was wide; it included cinema, radio and gramophone records, his opinions always expressed with elegance and honesty. He defended the Conservatoire against its detractors, remembering the 'minutes profondes' he had enjoyed in its concert hall; he wrote trenchantly about the pre-1914 salons where music was taken seriously; the *lieder* of Schumann, Schubert, the *mélodies* of Gounod, Saint-Saëns, Duparc, Fauré, Chausson and Lalo, all echoes of what he called 'the interior voice', were truly chamber music, written for a special audience who could appreciate them.

Marie continued to live at her old home, Gladville, with her children, her mother, sister Connie and brother Albert. She took over the housekeeping and reconciled herself to the fact that henceforward Manchester, from which she had been so eager to escape, was to be her permanent home. In 1930 she and her brother Albert, who never married, moved with her son, and daughter Polly, to Ladybarn Road, Fallowfield, where she spent the rest of her life.[2]

Polly wrote about her mother: 'She never complained or even commented on the enormous change in her way of living. I recall only her pride in, and appreciation of, Manchester. Early in the 1920s we went to Switzerland via Paris where we collected the necessary currency provided by a small legacy from the estate of Marcel Bing, a windfall enjoyed by all Bing's employees. In Paris we were introduced to Cousin Reynaldo, a glamorous figure whose visiting card admitted us to any theatre, including the Opéra for a performance of Massenet's *Thaïs*. I remember Mother saying to Reynaldo: "Now, tell me something about Marcel." This was, of course, only two or three years after Marcel's death. The answer was: "No, no – he changed completely, he was quite, quite different." Once in France, my mother changed too – she seemed to take on an added vitality – she was completely at home and confident.

'Another summer we explored Brittany, but did not manage to go to Belle-Ile. By 1932 when the money from the legacy was almost gone we went to Provence. During one of these holidays, she spent hours with a packet of old letters written in spidery French handwriting, transcribing them laboriously in longhand, "in case anyone else ever wanted to read them".

'She was an unconventional mother with high standards and wide interests. She kept up her interest in arts and crafts. She was a decisive committee member of the Red Rose Guild of Craftworkers initiated by Margaret Pilkington, honorary director of the Whitworth Art Gallery, and took an active part in its exhibitions. She invigilated exhibitions by local artists and was asked to manage, very successfully, the first lending library of original contemporary pictures which was opened in Lewis's big department store in Market Street.'

On the outbreak of war in 1939 Marie continued to receive cards from Reynaldo. He left Paris with his housekeeper, Marie Martel, Guy Ferrant and his mother, in May 1940 when the Germans occupied Paris and stayed first in Toulon, then in Cannes where he directed another winter season of concerts and opera with revivals of both *Ciboulette* and *L'Ile du rêve*. In spring 1942 *Ciboulette* was enjoying another successful revival in Paris at the Théâtre Marigny when it was proscribed by the German authorities because its composer was half-Jewish. His bank account was sealed, no royalties were paid and he was forced to ask René Schrameck to sell what valuables he still possessed. In December 1942 he and Marie Martel moved to Monte Carlo, where he still refused to conduct or play for the Germans. His niece, Clarita, sent him weekly food parcels to keep him alive and he spent the time composing chamber music and a new musical comedy, *Le Oui des jeunes filles*. His hotel room overlooked the harbour where a stray shell from a British submarine aimed at a German minesweeper moored beneath his window exploded, causing much damage and casualties; he was unhurt but badly shaken. He, Ferrant and Marie Martel returned to Paris in February 1945 where, in March, he was elected to the Institut de France's Academy of Fine Arts and appointed director of the Opéra.

The following year *Thèmes variés* was published and he, with Ninon Vallin and Magda Tagliaferro, gave concerts in London, Geneva, Brussels, Marseilles and Toulon. He had an operation for a tumour on the brain during the autumn. Marie Riefstahl visited him twice, flying from Croydon to Paris; they arranged to meet in Provence to make a final choice of his letters from Proust for publication. Reynaldo died on 28 January 1947.

Until the appearance of *Swann's Way* few of Marcel's friends gave him credit for a serious concern with literature. Perhaps only Reynaldo, Marie and one or two others appreciated, without fully understanding, his unusual genius. As Marie wrote in the preface to *Lettres à une amie*: 'Whether or not he repudiated friendship, ours endured . . . As his books reached me, I found, and continue to find, hidden between the lines, our *Remembrance of Things Past*, with messages none but I can decipher.'

Marie Nordlinger Riefstahl died in October 1961 at her daughter's home in Altrincham, Cheshire. Polly died in 1986, so this memoir, while celebrating the friendship between Marie, Reynaldo and Marcel, commemorates a loving collaboration between two friends from the next generation of Proust's admirers. Polly revised her mother's English version of Marcel's letters, while I translated her letters from Reynaldo and read a great deal of Ruskin as well as some of the many books and articles written about Proust before and since 1961. Together and with our families, we visited Venice, Rome and Florence; Dieppe, Rouen, Chartres and Illiers; New York, Boston and, especially, Washington, to study Mr Freer's papers in the library of the gallery named after him at the Smithsonian; lastly, and most frequently, Paris, for exhibitions commemorating Proust, and for performances of Reynaldo's music.

My thanks are due to family and friends for their support, above all to Polly for twenty-five years of lively comradeship both abroad and here at home in the Manchester suburbs where Marie spent the last forty-seven years of her long life.

Bibliography

In the notes that follow, references to Proust's works are abbreviated as shown in the left-hand column below.

KI, II, III   References to *The Search* come from the translation in three volumes entitled *Remembrance of Things Past* by C.K. Scott Moncrieff and Terence Kilmartin (Chatto & Windus, 1982; also published by Penguin, 1983). This translation is based on the definitive edition of *A la recherche du temps perdu* edited by Pierre Clarac and André Ferré in three volumes (Bibliothèque de la Pléiade, Gallimard, Paris, 1954).

JS   *Jean Santeuil*, ed. Bernard de Fallois, 3 vols (Gallimard, Paris, 1952).

Plé JS   *Jean Santeuil* (with *Les Plaisirs et les jours*), ed. Pierre Clarac with the collaboration of Yves Sandre (Gallimard, Paris, 1971).

Hop JS   *Jean Santeuil*, translation of the 1952 edition by Gerard Hopkins (Weidenfeld & Nicolson, 1955; Penguin, 1985).

CSB   *Contre Sainte-Beuve*, ed. Bernard de Fallois (Gallimard, Paris, 1954).

Plé CSB   *Contre Sainte-Beuve* (with *Pastiches et mélanges,* essays and articles), ed. Pierre Clarac with the collaboration of Yves Sandre (Gallimard, Paris, 1971).

BA   *La Bible d'Amiens* (Mercure de France, Paris, 1904).

SL   *Sésame et les lys* (Mercure de France, Paris, 1906).

Carnet   *Le Carnet de 1908,* ed. Philip Kolb (Gallimard, Paris, 1976).

Cor   La *Correspondance de Marcel Proust*, ed. Philip Kolb, 21 vols (Plon, Paris, 1970–92).
Marcel Proust: Selected Letters, ed. Philip Kolb, notes and translation by Terence Kilmartin, 3 vols (Collins, 1989).
Lettres de Marcel Proust à Reynaldo Hahn, ed. Philip Kolb (Gallimard, Paris, 1956).
Lettres à une amie: 41 lettres de Marcel Proust à Marie Nordlinger (Editions du Calame, Manchester, 1942).

Autret, Jean, *L'Influence de Ruskin sur la vie, les idées et l'œuvre de Marcel Proust* (Droz, Geneva, 1955).

Autret, Jean et al., *Marcel Proust on Reading Ruskin, prefaces to La Bible d'Amiens and Sésame et les lys*, translated and edited by Jean Autret, William Burford and Phillip J. Wolfe (Yale University Press, New Haven, CT, 1987).

Bardèche, Maurice, *Marcel Proust, romancier*, 2 vols (Les Sept Couleurs, Paris, 1970). Interesting for his interpretation of the *cahiers.*

Curtiss, Mina, *Letters of Marcel Proust*, translated by Mina Curtiss (Chatto & Windus, 1950).

Gavoty, Bernard, *Reynaldo Hahn, le musicien de la Belle Epoque* (Buchet/Chastel, Paris, 1976).

Hahn, Reynaldo, *Du chant* (Pierre Lafitte, Paris, 1920).

Hahn, Reynaldo, *La Grande Sarah* (Hachette, Paris, 1930).

Hahn, Reynaldo, *Notes, journal d'un musicien* (Plon, Paris, 1946).

Hahn, Reynaldo, *L'Oreille au guet* (Gallimard, Paris, 1937).

Hahn, Reynaldo, *Thèmes variés* (J.B. Janin, Paris, 1946).

Hahn, Reynaldo, various articles and reviews in *Candide*, *Le Figaro*, etc.

La Sizeranne, Comte Robert de, *Ruskin et la religion de la beauté* (Hachette, Paris, 1897).

Nordlinger-Riefstahl, Marie, articles in *Adam*, *The London Magazine*, *X Magazine*, *Le Bulletin de la Société des amis de Marcel Proust et de Combray*, Nos III and VIII (1953 and 1958), *Le Figaro*, *The Listener*.

Notes

Introduction
1. *La Correspondance de Marcel Proust*, ed. Philip Kolb, 21 vols (Plon, Paris, 21 volumes, 1970–92).

Chapter 1: A Youthful Prodigy
1. Reynaldo's brothers were all much older than he was. The five Hahn sisters were: Elisa, Mme de la Plaza (known as Mme la Générale in the family); Elena, Mme Ferdinand Kugelman, who lived in Hamburg; so did Isabel, married to her cousin Emil Seligmann; Clarita, Mme Seminario, who lived in Paris; and Maria, who married Raimundo de Madrazo in 1899 and also lived in Paris.
2. A *chanson* is a popular or traditional song, a *mélodie* more of an art form.
3. Carl Meyer (1851–1922) was knighted in 1910. There is a charming portrait by John Singer Sargent of Adèle Meyer and her two children.
4. The seven poems were: 'Chanson d'autumne', 'En sourdine', 'Tous deux', 'L'Heure exquise', 'La Dure Epreuve va finir', 'L'Allée est sans fin' and 'Paysage'.

Chapter 2: Patrons and Friends
1. Marcel gave this sketch to Reynaldo. After his death in 1947 it came to Marie in Manchester, and her daughter gave it to the Bibliothèque Nationale in 1965.
2. Plé JS, p. 675.
3. Letter to Robert Dreyfus, September 1888.
4. When she read *The Guermantes Way* and *Cities of the Plain* in 1921, she told Marcel that his books brought back many memories of twenty or twenty-five years before and that she was not at all shocked by the subject of homosexuality; he and she had often discussed it during his visits.
5. Letter to Dr Proust, autumn 1893.
6. *Hommage à Marcel Proust*, 1923.
7. Article in *Candide*, 29 August 1935.
8. Published in *La Revue blanche* in 1893.
9. 'O lovely youth, asleep amid the trees, awakened by Reynaldo, May he be praised, smile upon the enchanter Reynaldo, cytherean, poet and singer.'

Chapter 3: Dieppe and Beg-Meil
1. *Notes, journal d'un musicien*, p. 25.

Chapter 4: Pleasures and Days
1. 'When I read a particular author, I soon discovered beneath the words the tune of the song, which in each author is different from every other, and as I read, unintentionally I hummed it softly to myself, making the notes go faster or slower, or interrupting them, to mark the bars, as one does when singing . . .' (CSB, p. 301).
2. 'Que peu de temps suffit à changer toute chose! Nature au front serein, comme vous oubliez! Et comme vous brisez, dans vos métamorphoses, Les fils mystérieux où nos cœurs sont liés!' (Victor Hugo, *La Tristesse d'Olympio*, tenth verse).
3. Hachette, 1930.
4. *La Grande Sarah*, p. 163.
5. *L'Oreille au guet*, p. 182; *Thèmes variés*, p. 181.

The Translation of Memories

Chapter 5: The Young English Cousin

1. Gladville, much altered and enlarged, still stands in Anson Road, now part of the A34, the old main road south. With the adjoining house, it is part of the Manchester Foot Hospital and the Chiropody Department of Salford University, and there is a large car park and extra offices in the garden. Most of the big old houses in Victoria Park have gone, replaced by blocks of flats and university residences, but there are still plenty of trees.

2. In *Swann's Way* the shapeless characters of Odette's outsize calligraphy show the incoherence of her mind, her lack of education, sincerity and decision, and in *The Fugitive*, when M and his mother are in Venice after Albertine's death, there is confusion about the signature on a telegram which actually came from Gilberte, not Albertine (Hop JS, p. 636; KI, p. 242; KIII, pp. 656, 671).

3. *Notes, journal d'un musicien*, pp. 45 and 62.

4. *La Grande Sarah*, p. 80ff. In *Within a Budding Grove* M, seeing the famous actress La Berma as Phèdre for the second time, noted the same sacerdotal gesture in Act III described by Reynaldo, and realized the reason why he had been so disappointed the first time he was taken to the theatre to see her was because he had a preconceived idea of what great acting should be. On the second occasion he was able to appreciate her genius for losing herself completely inside the character she was portraying – she became transparent, simply 'a window opening on a great work of art', just as the composer Vinteuil did when he was immersed in the music he was playing (KI, p. 473ff; KII, pp. 39–54).

Chapter 6: A Celebrated Affair

1. Léon Daudet was largely instrumental in obtaining the Prix Goncourt for *Within a Budding Grove* in 1919, and Proust dedicated the next volume of *The Search* to him.

2. During the 1914–18 war Marcel put a joking reference to *L'Ile du rêve* into *Time Regained*. Dr Cottard appeared at Mme Verdurin's parties 'in a colonel's uniform which might have come out of Loti's *L'Ile du rêve* (it bore a striking resemblance to that of a Haitian admiral and at the same time, with its broad sky-blue ribbon, recalled one of the "children of Mary!")'.

Chapter 7: Apprenticeships

1. In *Swann's Way* Marcel falls in love with the white hawthorn blossom decorating the church at Combray for the services in May, 'the month of Mary', and with the pink hawthorn along the path to Tansonville where Charles Swann and his family live (KI, pp. 121, 150–3, 158).

2. Hop JS, p. 466.

3. Even today, so many years later, the articles are perfectly preserved and legible.

4. In *The Search* Proust did not describe the Affair directly but filtered it through the attitudes and conversation of his characters. Bloch was the typical Dreyfus supporter; the retired diplomat, M. de Norpois, never actually stated a firm opinion; the Duke of Guermantes was a waverer; and Swann too had reservations about committing himself either as a Jew or as a former Army officer.

5. This is the version given in the Pléiade edition of Jean Santeuil, p. 397; in the 1952 edition of Bernard de Fallois, only Beg-Meil is mentioned (twice) and not Réveillon.

6. When Marie published her letters from Proust in 1942, it was assumed that this sentence referred to *Swann's Way*. *The Search* grew out of the drafts for *Jean Santeuil*, which was not published until 1952; there was never a time when Proust stopped making notes of ideas and characters.

7. Vol. II, Chapter II, para. 29.

Chapter 8: A Passion for Ruskin

1. Proust had studied Leibniz and knew his theories about the monad and pre-established harmony. Emerson used the phrase in his essay on self-reliance and Marcel made use of it on several occasions. Emerson wrote: 'To believe your own thought, to

254

believe what is true for you in your private heart is true for all men, – that is genius. This sculpture in the memory is not without pre-established harmony.'
2. The first edition of *The Two Paths* (1859) has 'Translation rights reserved' on the title page.
3. Marie's doggerel verse 'A Symphony in Yellow', which amused Marcel, was a creditable play on the word 'jaune' in its two meanings of 'yellow' and 'the yolk of an egg'.

> Le jaune de l'ajonc
> Est un jaune assez bon,
> Mais le jaune des soucis enflamme.
> Je n'aime pas la moutarde,
> Elle est tellement criarde . . .

> (The yellow of gorse is not at all coarse,
> But marigold yellow provokes me.
> Mustard is hateful, so crude and distasteful . . .)

In *Swann's Way* Proust described the buttercups on the riverside walk to Guermantes, yellow as the yolk of eggs, a gilded expanse at which he gazed lovingly, enjoying their unproductive beauty (KI, p. 183).
4. Preface to *The Spoils of Poynton*.
5. *Præterita*, Vol. III, Chapter I, para. 23.
6. After Reynaldo's death in 1947 the BBC broadcast a memorial concert of his work which included this chorale, dedicated to Marcel. It was conducted by Constant Lambert, a firm friend of Reynaldo's, who wrote to Marie to tell her that he thought the piece 'superbly written for the voices'.

Chapter 9: Venice
1. KIII, pp. 661–2.
2. Vol. II, Chapter 4.

Chapter 10: Work in Progress
1. *La Grande Sarah*, pp. 106–7.
2. BA, pp. 299–303.
3. The photograph was probably of the alms dish which Marie had completed in Hamburg, with a cockerel on a blue enamel ground as centrepiece and which she showed to Marcel when she returned to Paris in 1903.
4. Reynaldo's journal (published in 1933) was compiled from undated jottings which he made between 1894 and 1912. In its 300 pages Marcel is mentioned only eight times. His other friends, Mme Bernhardt, Coco de Madrazo, Liane de Pougy are occasionally referred to, his family never.
5. Proust's letters to Reynaldo Hahn were published in 1956, edited by Philip Kolb. They cover the period between 1894 and 1915, with a long gap from 1896 to 1906 when the letters were lost or destroyed, only a few turning up from time to time. The later ones, from 1906, written in their private language, are almost impossible to translate. Marie and Reynaldo were probably right in choosing a selection for publication.
6. There is some confusion about the dates of Marcel's excursions with his friends in 1902–3 as Fénelon was in Constantinople at Easter 1903.
7. Plé JS, p. 741; not in Hopkins.
8. Plé CSB, pp. 474–7.
9. Hop JS, pp. 198–205; Plé JS, pp. 447–55, and notes pp. 1031–2.
10. KII, p. 427.
11. KII, p. 580.
12. To Robert Brussel, quoted by Gavoty, pp. 278–9.

Chapter 11: The Art Nouveau

1. In her revised but unpublished edition of *Lettres à une amie* Marie added a note: 'Proust had visited the Art Nouveau and in due course sent Robert de Saint-Loup there to buy his "Carrières and furniture in the Modern Style". In 1947, M. Robert de Billy showed me on his writing-table a bronze Japanese sword guard inlaid with a silver alloy which Marcel had given him more than forty years previously – it also came from chez Bing.'

2. Reynaldo had just received a copy of Marie's edition of her letters from Marcel, *Lettres à une amie*, and immediately reviewed it for the front page of *Le Figaro*, 21 April 1945.

3. Plé CSB, pp. 463, 468.

4. The golden tiara of Saitapharnes (reputedly third century BC) had been bought by the Louvre on 1 April 1896, and for years had been suspected as a fraud. Following an official report published on 11 June 1903, the Louvre authorities admitted that they had been deceived and the tiara was removed from its showcase.

5. *The Stones of Venice*, Vol. II, Chapter IV, last para.

6. 'Mais du passé profond ne peut rien ressaisir' – this Alexandrine line is in quotation marks in the last paragraph of the preface; is it a quotation from a poem of his own, or someone else's?

7. BA, p. 95.

8. Proust had evidently forgotten that he already wrote to her as 'Dear Friend' in the letter she received in Venice, May 1900.

9. Robert Proust's only child, a girl, was born the previous day, 25 November, and named Suzette Adrienne.

Chapter 12: Japanese Water Flowers

1. Of the twenty-two letters which Marie received from Marcel this year, nine were written in the first two months; as he never put dates on any of them, their sequence is not easy to establish. Marie sometimes noted the date on which she received them or replied to him.

2. The quotations in this letter from Ruskin and Whistler show the extent of Marcel's background knowledge and reading. In November 1903 *La Chronique des arts et de la curiosité* published two articles by him on Dante Gabriel Rossetti and Elizabeth Siddal. On 2 January the same review printed his criticism of two books in German on Ruskin.

3. KIII, pp. 381–2, 899.

4. Marie commented: 'Technical details, like every kind of exact information, were grist to Proust's mill. In a footnote to *Sésame et les lys*, he made the process of enamelling into a symbol of the art of writing (p. 85). In *Swann's Way* we find "the crude, almost violet blue, suggesting the background of a Japanese cloisonné and the polychrome enamel of pansies", and in *The Guermantes Way* Proust proceeds to "embed, beneath an enamel of royal blue, the glorious images, the mysterious, illuminated, surviving relics of the Prince of Borodino's gaze". These images are fused in the verses he wrote for me.'

5. 'Les brebis affamées tournent les yeux vers eux et ne sont pas nourries, Mais enflées de vent et des brouillards pestilentiels u'elles respirent, Elles se corrompent intérieurement et répandent des émanations impures et contagieuses, Outre celles que l'horrible loup à patte sournoise, Chaque jour dévore avidement, sans qu'aucun compte en soit rendu.'

6. In 1945, when she was able to send copies of *Lettres à une amie* to her friends in France, Marie received a touching little letter of thanks from Suzette Lemaire who was then nearly eighty. She wrote from the Château de Réveillon on 2 October: 'I shan't tell you that your lovely book has woken my memories because they have never slept. I must tell you that I still possess, in Paris, the beautiful buttons you made for me when you worked at Bing's. Another confession – the things people have written about Marcel since his death have annoyed me, either because they treat him as the pontificating leader of a literary school, or they make too much of his affectations. The real Marcel was restored to me when Reynaldo sent me what he had written about your book and Marcel's gift of divination and the preface to your book brought him back even more successfully.'

7. 'In case of need I should know how to "make a springtime"' – the phrase comes from one of Mme de Sévigné's letters, which were the favourite reading of Mme Proust. *Lettres inédites de Mme de Sévigné*, Vol. II, p. 317, 16 April 1690.

8. *Cahier 2.*

9. In *La Correspondance de Marcel Proust*, Vol. IV, p. 238, Professor Kolb surmised that this letter was written at the end of August. Marie herself dated it mid-May. She had written to Marcel about their holiday in Venice four years earlier, remembering their happy excursions. By mid-August she had received the offer from M. Bing to visit America, and in September she was full of energy and enthusiasm. In the Introduction to Volume IV, Professor Kolb wrote: 'She had the romantic outlook of all young girls of that period' and was hoping for a marriage proposal – from Marcel! In 1904 she was no longer a young girl; she was twenty-eight.

10. KII, p. 676.

11. Harpocrates was the Greek god of silence and meditation. The reference to George Eliot's novel *Middlemarch* and the grey cloak worn by Dorothea Casaubon during her honeymoon in Rome may have been prompted by Marcel's feeling that he was working away at something (the translations of Ruskin) which was not what he really wanted to do – he was 'amassing ruins', like the elderly Mr Casaubon with whom he had already identified himself in an earlier letter to Marie, 'dreaming footnotes' for a great work 'of attractively labyrinthine extent'.

Chapter 13: A New Venture

1. Vaucresson was three miles west of Saint-Cloud, on the left bank of the Seine.

2. KI, pp. 771–3.

3. SL, Preface, p. 40.

4. SL, p. 35.

5. 'The Ten O'Clock' was a lecture given in London, Cambridge and Oxford by Whistler in 1885. Marie had evidently not read her copy of *The Gentle Art of Making Enemies*! The lecture, published as a brochure in 1888, was reprinted in Whistler's book. She could admire the artist while disliking the man. Her preference for 'the dignity of reticence' was outraged by the way in which he lashed out at his critics and their total incompetence.

Chapter 14: On Reading

1. SL, pp. 78, 94; *The Queen of the Air*, paras 102, 106.

2. Modern Painters, Vol. IV, Chapter 2, paras 15–16.

3. Modern Painters, Vol. IV, Chapter 2, paras 17 and 21.

4. KIII, p. 914.

5. KII, pp. 343–57.

Chapter 15: A Change of Direction

1. BBC recording, broadcast in 1968.

2. *La Grande Sarah*, pp. 135–56.

3. In the course of his career as a journalist Reynaldo wrote many times about Mozart; both his books of collected articles begin with a lengthy section on the history and performance of the operas and on their audiences.

4. The frontispiece to Volume XXIII was a reproduction of a fresco by Botticelli in the Sistine Chapel, one of a series depicting the life of Moses, which Ruskin had copied over thirty years previously and which had never been published. It showed Jethro's daughter, Zipporah, a slim, melancholy, elegantly posed young woman, dressed in oriental trousers and a richly embroidered shawl, carrying a distaff. As Proust never went to Rome to see the original fresco, it was on Ruskin's version that he based his

description of Odette's appearance in *Swann's Way* (KI, pp. 243–5). Odette reminded Swann first of Zipporah and then, later, of other Botticelli paintings, the *Primavera*, the *Virgin of the Magnificat*, and Judith, on whose face, Ruskin had written in *Mornings in Florence*, there was 'a sweet solemnity of dreaming thought'.
5. Professor Shattuck, in his paperback on *Proust* (Fontana Modern Master, 1974), calls it a form of mental cramp and devotes a whole chapter to what he calls Proust's complaint.
6. In *La Chronique des arts et de la curiosité* (9 March 1907) Proust reviewed a book about Gainsborough by the art historian Gabriel Mourey, which, he noted, contained several references to Ruskin.

Chapter 16: Cabourg
1. Three of the paragraphs on this subject were repeated in *The Guermantes Way*, KII, p. 134.
2. KII, p. 187ff.
3. KIII, p. 960ff.
4. Instead he wrote the gardens into his novels: the garden at Combray where M's grandmother walked round and round in the rain and his parents entertained a visitor whose arrival upset the child's bedtime routine; Swann's garden at Tansonville, full of lilies, irises and nasturtiums; the gardens of the Champs-Elysées where M played with Gilberte Swann and where, when he was older, he walked with his ailing grandmother and overheard a discussion between the park-keeper and the woman in charge of the public lavatory, known as 'La Marquise', who selected her customers just as Mme Verdurin or the Duchesse de Guermantes made their choice of dinner guests. Each social class has its own form of élitism!
5. KII, p. 783.
6. KI, p. 894ff.
7. KI, pp. 899–902.
8. KI, p. 158.
9. KI, p. 196ff; KII, p. 412; LIII, pp. 4, 579ff.

Chapter 17: Notes and Drafts
1. KIII, p. 728ff.
2. He went on to quote a remark made by a character in Oscar Wilde's essay 'On the Decay of Lying' to the effect that the death of Lucien de Rubempré in Balzac's novel *Les Splendeurs et misères des courtisanes* was the greatest sorrow he had experienced. Wilde himself discovered afterwards, through his trial and imprisonment, that there were even greater sorrows. It was in 1908 that Wilde was reburied in the cemetery of Père Lachaise, with Epstein's huge sculpture above his grave.
3. Overture to *Swann's Way*, KI, p. 49 (Carnet, p. 41), and *Time Regained*, KIII, pp. 886–912.
4. If we assume that the episode of the tea and toast actually took place, in the first draft Proust wrote it was the old cook who brought the narrator a warm drink on a cold night. Félicie Fitau, the family cook, retired in July 1907, so it must have happened before this date, and only later, when he was rewriting the first part of his novel, did he substitute his mother for 'my old cook'.
5. There are more than sixty surviving *cahiers* at the Bibliothèque Nationale in Paris. These were numbered not by Proust but by the Keeper of Manuscripts in 1967, the early numbers 1–7 based on the research done by Bernard de Fallois for his *Contre Sainte-Beuve* (1954). Most of the seventy-five loose sheets have apparently disappeared, leaving only a version of 'Robert and his pet goat'.
6. Cahier 2, p. 21 verso; Plé CSB, pp. 217, 830.
7. Ever since the holiday at Beg-Meil when he and Reynaldo had been reading *Les Splendeurs et misères des courtisanes*, Marcel had been fascinated by the relationship between the criminal, Vautrin, and the young Lucien de Rubempré, one of the characters at the end of *Les Illusions perdues*. This episode reminded Marcel of Hugo's poem 'La

Tristesse d'Olympio', in which the poet revisited a place where he had been happy with his mistress. The meeting of the two men was 'La Tristesse d'Olympio de la pédérastie', a phrase used in the *Carnet*, p. 2 verso, in the draft of his essay on Balzac and again in *Cities of the Plain*, KII, p. 1084. There are more references to Balzac in these two volumes than in all the rest of *The Search*, KII, p. 1084. In *cahier* 6 he drafted some paragraphs about the third sex, 'les tantes' described by Balzac, the men-women whom Proust called 'la race maudite'; these paragraphs provided the opening pages of *Cities of the Plain* and described a character later named Palamède de Charlus.
8. Plé CSB, pp. 279–85; KI, p. 764; KII, pp. 510, 1084ff.
9. KIII, p. 926.

Chapter 18: The Ways Decided
1. 24 October 1908.
2. Interview for *Le Temps*, 12 November 1913.
3. KIII, pp. 953–5.
4. CSB, p. 284ff.
5. Plé CSB, pp. 262–6, and KIII, pp. 637–48.
6. This was to be an oriental ballet, *La Dieu bleu*, with Nijinsky as a Siamese god; the scenario was by Coco de Madrazo and the young Jean Cocteau, costumes and décor were by Bakst.
7. KIII, p. 1099.

Chapter 19: A Lasting Friendship
1. Plé JS, pp. 183 and 197.
2. There is a condensed version of what was an ongoing argument between the two of them in the conversation about the two composers, and Chopin, in *Cities of the Plain*, when M on holiday at Balbec received a visit from Mme de Cambremer and her daughter-in-law: KIII, pp. 842–4.
3. He wrote to 'Mme Riefstahl', which was the name they always used rather than 'Meyer', because in the house where Rudolf had his rooms there were other people called Meyer. Riefstahl was Rudolf's mother's maiden name.
4. Agnes B. Meyer, a young American woman married to a New York financier, wrote about her friendship with Mr Freer, whom she met in 1913. She and her husband were keen collectors of oriental art and students of Chinese and Japanese culture. In 1915 Freer decided to spend his winters in New York to be near to dealers and auction houses, and the Meyers got to know him better; he explained to them that the reason he had never married was that there was congenital syphilis in his family. By 1917 it was apparent that he had inherited the disease as his mental state became increasingly unstable. Mrs Meyer remained a devoted friend until his death in 1919. His gallery in Washington was opened on 2 May 1923. (*Charles Lang Freer and His Gallery* by Agnes B. Meyer, Washington, DC, 1970).
5. Proust rewrote two other incidents from *Jean Santeuil* for his novel when Swann's jealousy led him to spy on Odette (*Swann's Way*, KI, pp. 299, 307).
6. In November 1916, at Marcel's invitation, the Poulet Quartet came to his bedroom to play Franck's quartet in D major for him twice through. Earlier in the year he wrote to Maria de Madrazo with a request for information. He explained: 'On principle, in my sequel to Swann, I do not mention any specific artist . . . At the beginning of my second volume, a great artist under a fictitious name, who symbolizes the great painter in my book as Vinteuil symbolizes the great musician (such as Franck), says to Albertine that an artist is supposed to have discovered the secret of old Venetian textiles, etc. This is Fortuny.' M bought Fortuny dresses for Albertine.
7. *The Captive*, KIII, p. 263.
8. *Swann's Way* has three chapters: 'Combray'; 'Swann in Love'; 'Names of Places, the Name'. The first selection, 'Overture', begins with the narrator lying in bed in the half-world between waking and sleeping, remembering other bedrooms he has slept

in, especially the one at Combray; in the 1909 version of his novel, provisionally entitled *Against Sainte-Beuve*, he thought he might begin with his article published in *Le Figaro*. Titles for the two volumes he intended to follow *Swann's Way* were: Volume 2, *The Guermantes Way*, which began with 'Mme Swann at Home' and ended with 'The Salon of Mme de Villeparisis', and Volume 3, *Time Regained*, had 'Within a Budding Grove' as its first heading, and included 'Death of My Grandmother', 'The Intermittences of the Heart' and, finally, 'Perpetual Adoration'.

9. KIII, p. 381.

10. Proust wrote a 'portrait' of Reynaldo about this time, but it was not published in *Conferencia* until December 1923. He described Reynaldo's close friendship with the Daudets and Mallarmé, he praised the simplicity and spontaneity of his early *mélodies* and his first opera, written when he was twenty-three. He also praised the high quality of his writing in his weekly music articles and pointed out that great artists such as Ingres or Delacroix were misjudged by their contemporaries who found them old-fashioned in their efforts to embody 'the Muses of Suffering and Truth'.

11. *The Fugitive*, KIII, p. 477.

12. *The Captive*, KIII, p. 378.

13. 'Each one of us,' he wrote in *The Fugitive*, 'is a succession of different selves. But we are no more disturbed by the fact that, after a lapse of years, we have become another person . . . than we are disturbed at any given moment by the fact of our being, one after another, the contradictory person, ill-natured, sensitive, refined, caddish, disinterested, ambitious, which we are in turn every day' (KIII, p. 657).

14. KII, p. 617.

15. *Carnet*, p. 3 verso.

16. The last three volumes were edited by Robert Proust and Jacques Rivière who worked for the publishers, Gallimard. *Time Regained* was published in 1927.

17. Mme de Noailles and Colette received the award at the same time; Reynaldo got it in 1924, although Marcel had hoped he might be honoured in 1911 when he was already a household name in the drawing-rooms of Europe. Marie Nordlinger Riefstahl got the award in 1958 'for services to French literature'.

18. *The Queen of the Air*, para. 102.

Postscript

1. The opera was revived by the Portland Opera in Oregon, USA, in 1996 and included in the list of the top ten productions of the year by the music critic of the London *Observer*. Hahn, he wrote, is remembered as a *petit maître*, but his achievement was considerable, as composer, conductor, singer, accompanist, critic and director.

2. Marie's son Albert joined the RAF as a pilot on the outbreak of war and was killed flying over Scotland in 1941.

Index of Persons

Above: The Sarahtorium at Belle-Ile, Brittany. Sarah Bernhardt, Reynaldo Hahn, Clairin and other guests, c. 1904

Right: Drawing of Reynaldo
Hahn by Cocteau

Reynaldo
chante "l'île
Heureuse"

Right: Marcel Proust at
Cabourg, 1907/8